To Kerri Wheeler,

Twisted Secrets

With best regards!
Hope you enjoy
the read!
Third novel in
production!

Susan M. Hacken

ALSO BY THE AUTHOR

Fiction
Twisted Lights

Spiritual/Inspirational
Dancing with Angels

Twisted Secrets

Susan M. Hoskins

Integrity Press, Ltd.

Published by
Integrity Press, Ltd.
P.O. Box 8277
Prairie Village, KS 66208

Library of Congress Cataloging-in-Publication Data

Hoskins, Susan M.
        Twisted Secrets
1. Fiction
Catalog card number 98-071167
ISBN 0-9656581-1-2

Cover design by Smart Graphics

Printed in the United States of America

10 9 8 7 6 5 4 3 2 1

First Edition

To Our Readers:

We honor the sacred place within each of us that is the true source of inspiration. With gratitude and purpose, we present *Twisted Secrets*.

Integrity Press, Ltd.

D e d i c a t i o n

Twisted Secrets is a novel about a mother
and daughter's love.
It matters little if the bond is created by birth or by choice.
For those who are fortunate enough to
experience this kind of love,
the mother-daughter bond enriches the soul
and nurtures the heart.
It is a bond that cannot be broken.
It is a love that lasts forever.

With great love and appreciation,
I dedicate *Twisted Secrets* to
my mother, Mary Elizabeth Hoskins,
and to my daughter, Danaria Marie Farris.
Two of the greatest women I am blessed to know and love.
My life is enriched beyond measure by you both.

Acknowledgments

I would like to acknowledge and thank Rayna Horner, my faithful friend and spiritual mentor. Without your wisdom and guidance, the creation of this book would not have been possible. You are truly an angel walking on the earth plane.

I would like to thank my dear friend and associate, Jan Snyder. You hold the highest vision for my work. You know your stuff, lady . . . both as a writer and as a marketer. I am honored to know you and to benefit from your expertise.

Integrity Press, Ltd. is blessed with a wonderful team of creative people. I have worked with two fabulous editors, Roderick Townley and Deborah Hirsch. Roderick, you continually challenge me to reach deeper within myself and set a higher standard for my work. Deborah, you are the "queen of the comma." Your attention to detail is unequaled. Chris Smart, you have once again created the book cover I envisioned. Thank you for tolerating my neurotic phone calls.

To my dear friends, thank you for viewing me with eyes that did not waver. Thank you for helping me hold the vision of *Twisted Secrets.* That which was conceived in spirit has now, with your help, become reality. I am most grateful.

To Bill Hoskins, my dear cousin, thank you for your contribution to this book when it was an early work in progress. Your love of Ireland was of great inspiration. And a special thank you to my dear Irish friend, Ann Sullivan. Your wit and zest for life inspire me daily. You make me proud to be Irish.

Susan M. Hoskins

And finally, I would like to thank my family for supporting and loving me through both the good times and the bad, especially my sister, Carroll Hoskins Michaels. Danaria and I love you, John, and the boys tremendously.

Susan M. Hoskins

Kansas City, MO
Friday, February 14, 1992

Darkness fell early on Kansas City. Winter had been unseasonably mild in the City of Fountains, leaving people unprepared for the true wrath of its furious nature. Everyone seemed edgy, frazzled and not quite themselves with the first big snowstorm of the year. It was Valentine's Day night, yet the restaurants and shops were virtually deserted.

Ward Parkway, the prettiest tree-lined boulevard in the city, was almost devoid of cars as Sam Ellis negotiated his Jeep Wagoneer through the thickly falling snow. It was late, just before eight o'clock. Sam had hoped to break away from the hospital much earlier, but a last-minute complication with a surgical patient had forced him to remain at St. Vincent's long past his usual quitting time.

Secretly Sam hoped that he would be missed at home. But he feared his tardiness would barely be noticed. Shaking off the beginnings of a bitter mood, Ellis allowed his vision to stray from the road to the bouquet of red roses and bottle of chilled champagne nestled on the seat beside him. With their busy schedules, he'd not talked with Sydney since earlier that morning, but with any luck he would find her at home. After all, it was Valentine's Day. Perhaps for once they could spend an evening alone in front of a roaring fire with no thoughts of work to distract them. Perhaps they could put aside their differences and find their way into each other's arms to celebrate this special night reserved just for lovers. Perhaps . . . but more likely not.

Turning west off Ward Parkway at 55th, Sam slowly made his way to Mission Hills, the elite suburb of Kansas City located just southwest of the Country Club Plaza. It was there just off Tomahawk Road on a quiet cul-de-sac called Verona Circle that he lived with his wife, Sydney, and their adopted Iranian daughter, Lydia.

At forty-four, Samuel Carlson Ellis was a tall, broad-shouldered, lumbering giant of a man with thick, curly brown hair and eyes the color of coffee laced with cream. He had the physique of a football player. But despite his size, he was a gentle man and a skilled surgeon.

He and Sydney had been married for three years. Their marriage for the most part was a good one. Quite simply, Sam loved Sydney with his heart and his soul. He enjoyed his work as the Chief of Staff at St. Vincent's Hospital, but he valued his marriage more than his career—something Sydney chose not to do. Sydney Lawrence was the anchor newswoman for KMKC-TV and thrived on the challenge of her job. But more important, she loved the status of being who and what she was. In truth, her marriage to Sam Ellis was not enough. Sam knew it and so did Sydney. And deep inside it broke Sam's heart. It was hard to share only a piece of her world when she was the essence of his.

But Sydney was not doing the news this evening. The substitute weekend anchor was filling in for an extra night. It was not because of Valentine's Day or any special celebration planned with Sam. It was rather because of the nature of the story she was working on. The story that consumed her. The story, the damned story, that threatened to destroy her. Despite her promotion to anchor, Sydney still pursued the investigative stories nobody else had the guts to pursue.

Gliding down the quiet cul-de-sac toward home, Sam felt a familiar chill as he passed the deserted mansion that had once belonged to Ali Hassan, Lydia's biological father. The lavish estate stood empty now, seized by the United States government along with every other asset that Hassan left behind. Everything, that is, but the most important—a lovely child by the name of Lydia, a daughter who was the light shining bright in Sam's eyes. Every time he passed the mansion on the way to his own smaller colonial home, Sam Ellis was reminded just how precarious life could be. One moment life seemed in order and well managed. Suddenly, in the course of a day and the passion of a moment, everything that once seemed so important is altered forever.

Signaling a turn into his drive, Sam sensed that something was wrong. To the rear of the house stood the two-car garage. The door was open. Sam's side was, of course, empty. Sydney's new metallic blue Lexus filled the other. Parking his Jeep Wagoneer, Sam peered closer. Sydney's Lexus was dry. She had been home at least for a few hours. But why had she left the garage door open?

Security was important, particularly since Ali Hassan had never been found. At night or when they were gone, the alarm system was always activated. And when they returned home, the garage door was lowered. Had Sydney been preoccupied or merely careless? With the threats they'd been receiving, such a breach of security was unthinkable.

Closing the garage door Sam muttered, "It's the story! Always the damned story!"

Sam's nightmare had begun shortly before Thanksgiving with a phone call for Sydney. The hushed voice on the other end was raspy. The man called seemingly just to pay her a compliment. Said he admired her guts for reporting the stories she chose to explore. Said nobody else had the courage to touch them. Sydney accepted the compliment graciously. Besieged with another hectic deadline, she had started to terminate the conversation. But the caller had a different agenda. He told her that he had a matter of importance to discuss. Revelations that if properly handled could make her other stories this past year pale in significance. And even though Sydney was a seasoned journalist, well schooled in the quirks of humanity, she found herself intrigued. With permission of the station manager, Jake Kahn, she met with the mysterious informant in a public place and listened to his remarkable tale. From that point forward she'd been hooked.

Sam knew few of the details. Sydney had said it was a matter of confidentiality, but he knew better. Kept in the dark he couldn't react, only speculate, about the drama and the potential danger.

All he knew was that beginning in the summer of 1991, there had been a series of arson fires in the City Market—a renovated area filled with bars, restaurants and shops located just blocks north of downtown. One man had been killed, the owner of a popular bar and restaurant. Several other businesses had been destroyed. People in the area were scared. Customers, so plentiful in years past, were afraid to venture downtown. Many buildings were boarded shut. The area had been declared unsafe. There were no suspects and few clues.

Sydney's informant told her the fires had been carefully planned to send a clear message. There was a power struggle for control of the City Market. It all had to do with the conviction of John Gotti, the undisputed head of the Costra Nostra. The *Family* in Kansas City was in chaos. Most of the bosses of local families had been convicted of federal crimes along with John Gotti, leaving the leadership of the Kansas City crime syndicate up for grabs.

There was a war beginning with a new generation of men vying for power. One guy, a seeming nobody, a grunt in the organization, found himself with an ax to grind. His brother was the man killed in the first fire. Loyal to one particular family in Kansas City, he was an old-timer in the Costra Nostra who paid his dues and played by the rules. He told Sydney that the young had no respect for the old-timers. They were going about this all wrong. And, in his opinion, they had to be stopped if the *Family* was to survive. He had searched for the right person to help him break the story and prevent an all-out war. Sydney Lawrence, with credentials and courage, was just that person.

The informant knew who'd been setting the fires and why. Slowly, as he began to trust Sydney, he gave her tips to check out. Now, having followed his leads, she was nearly ready to break the story but she needed more proof. She hadn't divulged much to her boss. She wanted all her facts in order before she sought his approval to air the exposé. She knew that the story would have regional appeal. What she didn't realize was that what was happening here in Kansas City had serious implications with the Costra Nostra throughout the country.

The informant had gone into hiding, but his involvement with Sydney became known to the wrong people. That's when the threats began. The threats . . . she refused to take seriously.

"It's just a part of the job," she assured Sam. "We get them all the time. If you give thugs power, they win. It's only a scare tactic, Sam. Somebody wants me to back off, that's all. The sooner I go public, the safer I'll be."

It started with typewritten, anonymous letters to the station, followed by phone calls at work and at home. The message was always the same. "Walk away, Sydney Lawrence. Let it be." The police had nothing to go on; the FBI would take none of it seriously. It was then that Sam Ellis knew his wife was in real danger.

Grabbing the roses and champagne, Sam gingerly made his way from the garage to the back door of the house. It was dark; Sydney had failed to leave the light on. That's why he didn't see the set of footprints leading from the yard to the garage and back again.

Muttering under his breath, he shifted the flowers and the champagne to one hand while he fumbled for his keys with the other. Sam turned the key in the lock and threw open the back door, half expecting the sweet smells of a home-cooked meal to engulf him. But the kitchen was empty.

He called out, "Sydney?" No one answered. Switching on the lights, he continued his search through the dining room, down the hall to the living room, then just beyond to the library. It was there that he found her. With the phone in her ear, she had eyes only for her computer. She neither heard Sam nor saw him enter her study. She didn't see his look of disappointment.

"Sydney," he repeated. "I'm home."

This time she slowly pivoted in her chair to face him. Dressed only in a heavy robe of navy blue terry cloth, with her hair askew and no makeup, it was plain to see that her thoughts were not of him. Seeing the champagne and the roses, she appeared at first confused. Then slowly she paled as her mind registered that this was no ordinary day.

"Let me call you back, Tommy," she said softly. Replacing the receiver, she rose quickly, a sheepish look crossing her face. "I'm sorry, honey. I forgot. I got too involved . . ."

"With the story," he finished for her. Rather angrily he shot back, "It doesn't matter."

"Oh yes, Sam, it does," she countered, hurrying to him. Embracing him in a warm loving hug, she said, "It does matter. Very much. You matter. I'm so sorry . . ."

Resigned, Sam handed Sydney the roses and the bottle of chilled Dom Perignon.

Feigning excitement, she chirped, "Give me just a minute to wrap this up and get off the computer. Then we'll light a fire and crack the champagne."

"Sure, whatever," he muttered. "By the way, why did you leave the garage door open?"

"I didn't," she answered absently. "I shut it when I came in. Why?"

"Nothing," Sam countered, realizing she probably just forgot. "Where's Lydia?"

"Upstairs with her friend, Mary Beth. It seems there's a big basketball game at school in the morning, so she's spending the night. Is it still snowing outside?"

"Yes," Sam answered, his voice mellowing just a bit. "Maybe we could take a walk later."

Genuinely smiling, Sydney replied, "I'd like that very much."

At thirty-six, Sydney Lawrence Ellis stood tall and lean, with hair the color of autumn fire and inquisitive hazel eyes. She had a keen mind coupled with a sharp tongue that made people either like her or hate her.

His mood warming, Sam took a few tentative steps toward her.

"Did you call Joe Morrison like I asked?"

"Oh honey, don't start," Sydney chided. "As a matter of fact, I called him this morning. He promised to look into the threats. He said he'd have the local boys put a tracer on my phone at work and here at home. He said it's probably nothing, but to be careful. He'll call us next week with details. Okay? Are you satisfied?"

"No!" Sam shot back. Tired of games, he decided it was time to speak the truth. Besides, he was hurt and he didn't give a damn if she knew it.

"I won't be satisfied until you give up your ridiculous obsession with this Godforsaken story before it gets you killed . . . before it gets us all killed! Let it go, Sydney. No damn career is worth this!"

Wheeling around sharply, Sydney's hazel eyes were searing. "How dare you speak to me about careers! I'm married to a doctor, remember? Your patients always come first!"

"Now that's unfair! It's different with me."

"It's no different! You've always put medicine ahead of us. You're a doctor, for godsake! You have to! Well I have an important career, too. I have the exclusive on an important story with national appeal. I got great exposure with the networks when we broke the exposé on the black marketing of organs. Now I have the opportunity to go national with another story. I've gone about as far as I can in Kansas City. How can you deny me the chance to be noticed again by CNN and the other major networks? This is a hell of a competitive business! Most reporters never get a chance like this. Why are you standing in my way?"

"Be reasonable, Sydney. No so-called ticket to the top is worth our marriage. It's very lonely at the top without someone to share your life. Think about it, Sydney, before it's too late!"

Enraged, Sydney started to argue, but a pale, drawn figure standing in the doorway stopped her.

"Oh God, Lydia . . ."

Sam turned. At fourteen, Lydia was a beautiful girl on the brink of becoming a truly magnificent woman. She had a lovely olive complexion, raven hair and huge, ebony eyes. Her finely chiseled lips quivered as she came upon Sam and Sydney arguing.

"It's okay, sweetheart. We were having a little disagreement, that's all."

"It's the hospital," Lydia stammered, "for you."

Sam accepted the cordless phone and moved to the far end of

the library, away from Sydney and from Lydia. He was disturbed by the scene with Sydney, but now he was even more disquieted by the news he was hearing.

"How bad is it?" he asked. "Life flight can't be dispatched. All aircraft have been grounded by the storm. What's the status on ambulances?"

He paused as the doctor in charge of triage gave him the facts.

"Okay, alert OR to stand by. We'll be needing all three rooms most of the night. Have them postpone all elective surgeries for tomorrow. And call in another surgical team. This sounds like a bad one."

Sam switched the phone off. Taking a deep breath, he turned back to the two women he'd come to love most in the world.

"There's been a bad accident. The snowstorm caused a ten-car pileup on the interstate. We've got multiple injuries. We're the closest facility, so the victims are being transported to St. Vincent's now. I'm afraid I'll be gone most of the night."

Sam handed the phone back to Lydia. Kissing her on both cheeks, he wrapped his girl in his strong but gentle embrace.

"I'll see you tomorrow," he promised.

"Good night, Daddy."

He waited until Lydia had disappeared up the staircase to rejoin her friend. Then slowly he turned to Sydney.

"Let's not fight," he pleaded. "In a way, I know you're right. You deserve the chance to become whatever you want, and I support you."

"Oh Sam . . ."

"Let me finish. You've proved your point. It's Valentine's Day, and I'm leaving you now because of my job. But it's different. My job doesn't put us in danger."

Sam took his wife in his arms a final time and held her tightly. She seemed not to respond, but a slow, sad tear rolled down her cheek.

"I love you, baby," he whispered softly. "And no matter what . . . I always will."

It was Sam finally who had to pull away. He started for the

door, but something drew him back. There was more he wanted to say . . . but he couldn't find the words. The roses and the champagne lay ignored on the table in front of the empty fireplace.

"I'll see you in the morning," he promised.

With a heavy heart, Sam walked away. He didn't see the tears running down Sydney's cheeks. He didn't hear the words she yearned to say. "I love you, Sam. More than anyone or anything else in the world, I love *you*." These were the words her heart screamed, but something inside held her silent.

The short walk from the back door to the garage was a treacherous one. Slipping on the ice, Sam struggled to remain on his feet. With the ice and snow now covering the ground, he could imagine how bad the accident must be. He was tired, but somehow he'd have to call on reserves. He'd be in surgery most of the night. Dialing in their secret code, Sam hit the control pad just outside the garage. His mind reeling, he waited for the garage door to open.

Two vehicles beckoned. Automatically he started for his Jeep Wagoneer, but then remembered something Sydney had said. Something about Lydia and a basketball game in the morning. Glancing over his shoulder to the eerie western sky, all he could see was a thick blanket of snow coming down. No end in sight. It was then he put his wife and daughter's needs above his own. His Jeep was unbeatable in the snow. And so he decided to take Sydney's car to the hospital in order to leave his Wagoneer behind.

Rotating his key ring, he thrust the spare key to the Lexus into the ignition. He turned the key smartly to the right. It was then that the bomb exploded, shattering windows up and down the block. In the passionate flash of a moment, everything that had seemed so important was no more.

Susan M. Hoskins

2

Tuesday, February 18
11:00 a.m.

The February cold snap had broken, turning the snow to muddy slush, splattering limousines, as the funeral procession followed the hearse into the private cemetery.

Sydney accepted the driver's hand and emerged from the rear of the first car. Shivering against the cold, she cast her veiled glance to the sun, yearning for a measure of warmth, or at the very least a hint of comfort. But unfortunately for Sydney Lawrence Ellis, there was neither. And even though she was dressed correctly for the weather in a smart black Chanel suit, Sydney felt only a numbing chill, as if her very blood had been drained along with Sam's.

The breeze was biting as the intimate group of mourners climbed the gently sloping hill to the grave site Sydney had chosen in the cemetery overlooking the city. Determined to maintain her composure, Sydney crested the hill and paused, waiting for the pallbearers and Sam to arrive. Glancing beyond the site, she savored the view she had chosen. Straight ahead she found St. Vincent's and, just beyond, the Plaza, where the holiday lights had delighted them and where they often dined and loved to shop. To the left was Mission Hills, and the quiet street, Verona Circle, where they had lived for the past two years. Yes, she decided, as the pallbearers arrived, if nothing else she had chosen Sam's resting-place well.

Taking her seat under the canopy beside the grave, she waited for the minister to begin. The past few days had been a blur. Between the police, the media and friends, Sydney had found no time to mourn. The unthinkable had happened; her correct, well-ordered world had crumbled. Soon enough there would be nothing left but grief, but for now . . . she felt nothing but emptiness and loss.

Many of Sam's colleagues had come by to pay their respects; so many that Sydney remembered neither their faces nor their names. Today she had insisted that the services be private, for, despite Sam and Sydney's public allure, it had been their privacy that they had treasured most.

With practiced formality, the minister took his place in front of the casket and, intoning a familiar prayer for the dead, invited the group to bow their heads. Determined to let no one see inside, Sydney secured her netted veil as she sat erect with her hands folded in her lap. Her mind was numb from the pain but, refusing all medication, not dull. She was angry at the assassin, at God, even at Sam for making the choice that would kill him. But most of all Sydney hated herself for putting her success, her celebrity status, her career, above everything else she held dear. Sam had been right. If only she had chosen to listen.

His prayer concluded, the minister cleared his throat. Sydney allowed her eyes to roam just slightly to the right, where Lydia was seated in a pale, trembling heap beside her. Her huge dark eyes stared vacantly past the minister into the distance, her cheeks streaked by the tears she cried. At least she can cry, Sydney thought, wondering if the flood of tears would ever come for her.

As the minister's voice rose and fell in a steady, practiced rhythm, Sydney felt his pitiful glance upon her. In disgust she turned away, wanting no man's pity, nor a stranger's meaningless words of hope.

Fixing her eyes upon the closed casket, Sydney struggled to see beyond the gleaming ornate wood. Inside, Sam lay peacefully upon a white satin pillow, or so Sydney imagined, for the reality of what remained of Sam Ellis was too ugly for his widow to bear.

His eyes, of course, would be closed, but it was his eyes that Sydney would remember always. His alert, intelligent, light brown eyes. When he laughed, it was as if diamonds in his eyes sparkled. But when he was angry, they were searing flames. It was his eyes that haunted her now as she recalled their final moments together . . . moments of anger, moments of pain. Gazing at her one last time, his eyes had been filled with disappointment and hurt. It was a memory she would carry with her always.

Sydney glanced up, the drone of the minister's resonant voice piercing her thoughts, intruding upon her own haunting reverie.

"He was a brilliant doctor and a compassionate human being, and we who loved him will miss him so . . ."

In a minute, perhaps two, the service would be over. The first dirt would be thrown. Shortly, the coffin would be lowered and the earth would swallow him up.

No, she cried inwardly, she couldn't let that happen. Not without burning every detail of him into her heart, before it was too late, before he was no more.

From the feel of his bare skin next to hers as he held her in the morning . . .

To the curly brown hair she brushed from his forehead as he lay naked and drenched in sweat after lovemaking . . .

To his mouth—he had such a strong, decisive yet gentle mouth, a mouth that could crush hers at will or tease her playfully for hours . . .

And his laugh—high atop the cemetery hill she heard Sam's laugh echoing in the distance. It was a contagious laugh that shook a room, causing strangers to grin.

He was a gentle soul, slow to anger. Easy to love.

Feeling her heart wrenching in two, she cried, "Oh God, Sam, why did you have to die?"

And in that moment she knew the truth. She had taken their love for granted. Sam Ellis had been a simple, uncomplicated man with few needs and sparse wants. He had dedicated his life to serving. He had loved Sydney with all his heart.

Secure in the knowledge that Sam Ellis was forever hers, she held the power and the control, so she had never loved Sam with total abandon. She never had to because he had loved enough for both. Clutching her breast, she realized she had always held a piece of her heart in reserve where it could remain aloof, untouched and free. Now Sam was dead, and perhaps with him, her own limited capacity to love.

The minister asked the mourners to bow their heads one last time. Then Sydney felt a tug upon her sleeve as her boss, Jake Kahn, gently helped her to her feet. Like a robot, Sydney allowed Kahn to guide her to the casket.

Laying a single red rose upon his casket, Sydney said good-bye. Sam Ellis was dead and so was the naive, self-centered, invincible woman known as Sydney Lawrence.

With great effort, Joe Morrison came to his feet and stood. Letting the others pass before him, he trudged slowly to Sam's grave and paused. There, he remembered the man who even he— tough and macho though he was—had come to love and respect.

At forty-five, Joe Morrison was not a tall man, nor would he ever be viewed as handsome. He had cobalt blue, cynical eyes and brown, unruly hair. He was a man of singular passion—his career with the FBI. Beyond work, there was little to call his own, and only a fistful of friends he held dear.

The man about to be interred had been one of those few. Yet he had not known Sam all that long or well. Joe Morrison felt terribly guilty. He had never told Sam just how important his friendship really was. But while Morrison believed he had not done Sam justice in life, he had, at least, flown to Kansas City from Washington immediately upon hearing about Sam's death. No, he could do nothing more for Sam Ellis, but he could be present in case Sydney needed him.

He whispered, "Good-bye, Sam, I'll miss you. Don't worry about Sydney. I promise you that if she ever needs me, I'll be right there."

Abruptly, Joe Morrison turned his back on the casket and started down the hill. He fumbled for a cigarette. Cupping his hands against the brisk north wind, he lit up. At the bottom of the hill, Morrison held back as the small group of intimates gathered around Sydney. Watching her in such pain, his own impenetrable heart ached. He, above anyone else, comprehended her robotic movements. He had lived by the motto himself. Let no man see what's really inside your heart and then no one can hurt you.

Morrison watched as Sydney, together with Lydia, entered the first car. He wondered aloud, "What in the hell will happen to her now?"

A decisive tap on his shoulder jolted him back to the present.

"Ride with me to the house, Joe," said KMKC station manager, Jake Kahn. "Sydney wants a word with both of us."

Taking the last car, the two men settled into the rear seat of the limousine, not knowing what to say to each other as they began the short drive to Verona Circle.

"It was good of you to come, Joe. It means a lot to Sydney that you're here."

Morrison shrugged.

"It's a goddamn shame," Kahn muttered. "Sam Ellis was a decent man."

Gnawing at a hangnail, Joe remained mute.

With a sigh, Kahn gently removed the glasses teetering precariously on the tip of his nose and methodically wiped them on his tie. Nearing sixty, he was a short, balding fellow with a paunchy gut and a dictatorial hand, particularly when it came to governing his station. He was a reporter from the old school who never shied away from a story. That's why—despite the danger— he had allowed Sydney to pursue her exposé, and why only minutes after Sam's burial, he refused to leave Joe Morrison alone to grieve.

"How could the local guys have screwed up so badly, Joe? I called the FBI myself, right after the threats began. Why weren't agents assigned to protect Sydney and Sam? Didn't it occur to anyone that an attack like this could happen?"

Clenching his jaw, Joe Morrison turned away. Glancing out the tinted side window of the limousine, he had to admit what the old man said was true. The Kansas City bureau had screwed up. Whether they believed the threats to be valid or not, Sydney should have received some kind of protection.

"All I can say is we fucked up." Slowly, Morrison returned his sad eyes to Kahn's. "Is the kid doing okay?"

"Yes," Jake responded. "Sam saw to it that Lydia received the best of medical care. Her heart condition has vastly improved. She's a regular kid now, not restricted in any way. She and Sydney have grown very close during the past year, but we all live in dread that Hassan will return. Is there any word on him?"

Joe shook his head. "The last trace we had on him was in London. He disappeared from there."

"At least you nailed his brother. Personally I favor the death penalty, but life without the possibility of parole inside Leaven-worth Prison is a close second choice. I understand that it may take years to unravel the black market organ scheme. Right?"

Morrison nodded. "Dr. Scoffield provided plenty of information on the Kansas City operation in return for a lighter sentence, but he couldn't shed much light on the corruption of the network for organ sharing. The investigation continues."

As the car veered onto Verona Circle, Morrison remembered a different time when the elite cul-de-sac was lined with fancy cars—not funeral black—for a party at the elegant colonial house belonging to the doctor and his pretty wife. It was that night Morrison kept a vigilant eye, not on the party but on the opulent mansion next-door where a sad little girl watched the festivities from an upstairs bedroom window.

Now the foreboding mansion stood vacant, and the lovely white colonial home was boarded up with the windows on the garage side shattered, along with the lives of the widow and child left behind.

As the limousine came to a halt, bile soured Joe's mouth. He had arrived late last night and had not yet come face to face with Sydney. If Jake Kahn thought the FBI guilty, would Sydney think any less? Straightening his tie, he followed Kahn through the front door into the parlor. What struck Joe immediately was the cold draft in what had been the warmest, most inviting room in the house.

"Jake, Joe, how good of you to come."

Sydney spoke in a flat monotone that Joe had never heard

before. As he approached, it became difficult to gaze into her haunted eyes.

Without her veil to shield her, Joe had expected her beautiful hazel eyes to be swollen and red from tears shed in private. Sydney's eyes, far from swollen, were vacant. And her creamy skin was so pale as to be nearly transparent. Having lived a life filled with more sorrow than joy, Joe Morrison took Sydney in his arms and tried to hold her close, but she abruptly pulled away, wanting no man's pity nor even Joe's strength.

Searching for the right words to say, the man of so few came up short. "I'm so sorry . . . ," he began.

"Thank you for coming, Joe. And you too, Jake. Please, sit down."

Awkwardly, Morrison paced to the rear of the handsome salmon and green salon, preferring to stand while Kahn sank into the richly upholstered couch.

Staving off a chill, Sydney turned her back upon the two men and gazed into the empty hearth. She quivered, "I guess you never know how much you love someone until you lose them." Turning back, she confronted Jake and Joe. "I killed Sam, you know."

Startled, both Morrison and Kahn tried to protest, but Sydney waved them away. "No, listen to me! I'm the one who killed my husband. Sam warned me about the danger we were in, but I ignored him. That bomb was meant for me. You know it and so do I."

A stony silence engulfed the drafty room.

"All I have left now is Lydia. I can't put her in any more danger. That's why I've asked you here today."

Sydney drew a deep breath as she dared to ask, "Where is Ali Hassan?"

"I'm sorry, Sydney, but I have no idea," said Joe.

"How safe are we here?"

Morrison paused. "How safe is anyone . . . anywhere?"

Sydney cried, "I don't deserve platitudes, Joe. Give me a straight answer."

"I did," he retorted. "After what happened to Sam, I can't guarantee that anywhere is safe, Sydney."

Bitterly, Sydney turned her focus away from Joe to the gruff, portly man who'd been perhaps her best friend and greatest mentor.

"I have to leave here, Jake. I've got to have time to sort things out and build a new life . . . without Sam . . . for Lydia and me. It can't be here. The memories would destroy me."

Sydney turned her back on her friends and walked to the far side of the room. There, on an end table hidden from view, was a computer disk. She handed it to Jake.

"This is my research on the story that got Sam killed. I can't go on with it. It's not worth the risk to Lydia. I haven't heard from my informant since the night Sam was killed. They probably killed him too."

She paused. "You know how much this story meant to me, Jake. I thought somehow that it would be my ticket to the top. Well my so-called 'ticket' cost me the only man I've ever loved. Do what you will with the computer disk, but please be careful. Perhaps now is not the time to go public with this story. It's too dangerous. Besides, without the testimony of my source, there's no way to corroborate the allegations. The arson fires in the City Market will be dismissed as unsolved cases. So be it. At least no one else has to die."

Sydney's strong composure melted. Standing alone in the middle of the impeccably decorated room, her body trembled as the tears, held in check for days, tried desperately to erupt. Jake Kahn came to his feet and, opening his burly arms, enfolded Sydney in a protective embrace. Sam's widow acquiesced to the gentle sincerity of the old man's comfort, but eventually she had to pull away.

"For your sake and for Lydia's, I know that you're making the right decision, but where will you go?"

"Back home to Kentucky where I belong. My dad owns a small horse farm near Lexington. It's the one place I know we'll be safe."

With a voice choked with emotion, Kahn had to ask, "Will you be back?"

Brushing a tear from the lovable old bear's cheek, Sydney shook her head. "There's nothing left for me here."

Morrison replayed Sydney's words in his head. Her simple declaration disturbed him more than anything else she had said. "It's the one place I know we'll be safe." He opened his mouth to speak but the softer side of his nature stopped him. She had suffered enough. Perhaps she needed the comfort and the illusion of peace her father's home offered. What he truly wanted to say, what he should have said, was to take no one, nowhere, for granted. Instead he kept his thoughts to himself. It was a decision he would later regret.

c h a p t e r 4

As the small commercial jet touched down at the Lexington airport, Sydney's stomach churned. Remembering another plane, a different night, she recalled her move to Kansas City with Sam. Then, she had been reluctant to leave the security of Velours for a bigger city. And not knowing a soul or having a job, she had no idea what the future would hold. During the course of the two years there, however, she found all the happiness one woman deserved. With a devoted husband, a child she adored, and a career more challenging than she could have imagined, Sydney, sitting on top of the heap, had taken her world for granted.

Now all that was lost, and she was forced to write a new chapter in her life. This time, though, it would be without Sam.

Taking a deep breath, she stood and, retrieving their two bags, led Lydia from the plane. As they walked across the tarmac, she searched the huge picture window for Mack's weathered face. Seeing no one through the glare of the glass, she hurriedly urged Lydia forward.

Nearly running inside the terminal and beyond security, she scanned the crowd. Mack Lawrence was nowhere in sight, though she heard a familiar voice calling, "Sydney, over here!"

Elbowing his way through the throng of people, a wisp of a fellow waved enthusiastically.

Her spirits sagging, Sydney mouthed the name "Billy."

Billy Ray Jones embraced her in a tight hug. As quickly as she could, Sydney broke away.

"Where's Mack?"

Oblivious to her marked disappointment, the former jockey answered, "Your daddy's not feeling well today. He asked me to meet you."

Sydney forced a smile.

"And who do we have here?" Jones inquired, his thinning blond hair askew but his brown eyes dancing.

"Billy Ray, I'd like you to meet my daughter, Lydia. Sweetheart, this is one of your grandpa's dearest friends."

Wiping his sweaty palms on his jeans, the friendly man took the girl's delicate hand. It was difficult for the child to warm to a stranger, particularly a man. She was only fourteen and yet she had already experienced the loss of the two men in her life who mattered most. Ali Hassan, her biological father, had abandoned Lydia to Sydney's care when he fled the country. Thinking she'd never see her daddy again, Lydia experienced his abandonment as a death. She had, over time, embraced Sam as her new father. Now he too was gone.

Since the jockey and the child were the same height, they eyed one another curiously.

"What a pretty little thing you are," Billy drawled, his thick Kentucky accent bringing a smile to Lydia's lips. "Not like your mama at this age, I must say."

"Whatever do you mean, Billy Ray?" countered Sydney in mock indignation.

"How old are you, Lydia?" he went on.

"Fourteen, sir," she replied.

Turning, Jones smiled a broad, toothy grin.

"At fourteen your mama here was a skinny, gawky girl with freckles all over her face and a wild mass of copper tangles. I never saw her in a dress, just jeans and dirty boots." Turning, he eyed the stunning woman—dressed richly in a smart wool skirt and creamy sweater. "You've turned into quite a prize, Miss Sydney."

An uncomfortable moment of silence passed between the

two old friends, with neither of them knowing what to say. Then Billy Ray seized the luggage and nudged them toward the door.

"Where's the rest of your things?" he asked.

Sydney shrugged. "This is all we need for now. The rest will be shipped after the house sells."

Stepping outside, Sydney paused and, inhaling deeply, savored the rich Kentucky air. It was a magnificent day in early March. The weather was crisp and cool, not frigid like what they'd left in Kansas City. The sun was shining brilliantly. For the moment, Sydney's mood brightened.

When she saw Mack's old station wagon parked in the first lot next to the terminal, Sydney smiled, truly smiled, for the first time in days. Some things never changed. Mack Lawrence was a man who required little, but he had two possessions he refused to give up. One was his truck—a beat-up old red thing—and the other was what he called his good car, a blue 1982 Oldsmobile station wagon.

Reveling in the familiar things of home—the air, the sunshine, even Mack's old car—Sydney knew that she'd made the right decision to return. She climbed into the rear seat and gazed out the window as Billy Ray pulled away from the airport.

At first, Lydia seemed not the least bit impressed by her new surroundings. Having been shuffled from place to place as a small child, she was prepared for yet another boring city of concrete, steel and glass. Instead, exiting the airport, she was greeted not by a skyline but by one continuous plank fence merging into another, and acre upon acre of luscious grass.

The stunned look upon the child's face caused Jones to grin. "I bet living in the city, you've never seen anything quite like this, have you, Lydia?"

Gazing at the magnificent horses dotting the endless fields of Kentucky bluegrass, the child replied, "Oh no, sir, never!"

It was with a great deal of pride that Billy Ray bragged, "I've traveled around enough to know that there's no finer place on earth."

Sydney glanced at the countryside and smiled. She, too, had traveled the world, more than most people dare to hope. Billy

Ray Jones was right. To those who loved horses and understood this way of life, there was no place more compelling on God's green earth.

A human being born and bred here viewed life, beauty, and even opulence differently from the rest of the world. Here a man's worth was measured not in terms of his estate, but rather in the quality of his barn and the stud value of his horses.

Here, in this strip of paradise between Lexington and Versailles, where an owner routinely spent more on his stables than on any mansion in Mission Hills, each farm was more magnificent than the next.

Here, horses were not sold by the pound but by bloodlines and confirmation. And the elaborate farms were not merely corporations but self-contained cities unto themselves, where a good horse vet was worth more than a brain surgeon, and the head trainer more valued than any mayor.

"Are you from Kentucky, sir?" Lydia inquired, her interest peaked by the unique character of Billy Ray.

"No, darling, not originally," he answered softly. "I came here quite by accident. But thanks to Mack Lawrence, I found a home."

Listening to his melodic drawl, Sydney warmed inwardly as childhood memories came flooding back. Had there been a time when the little fellow had not been around? No, not that she could easily recall.

She was about ten years old when she first met Billy Ray Jones, the year her father was invited to be the guest veterinarian at the Kentucky Derby. A young jockey from the East had been invited to race his remarkable mare the first Saturday in May in the year 1966. Bred and raised on a horse farm in Virginia, the mare's name was Lady Pink Floyd. The jockey—Billy Ray Jones.

It was the young jockey who had first recognized the yearling's ability. It was he who trained the filly to run and prepared the mare for the greatest race of her life. It was he who insisted upon riding her to glory himself. And tragically, it was he who went down with his mount when she stumbled just meters from the finish line.

Her right foreleg was shattered, but gamely the mare tried to rise and make it to the end, collapsing just short of the winner's circle. His own arm fractured in the fall, Billy stumbled to his mare's side. There, cradling her head to his heart, he waited for the vet to arrive. He knew what was to come; there was no alternative. It was Mack Lawrence who arrived to put the horse down with a merciful, lethal injection.

Locking eyes with his precious mare, Billy said good-bye as she drifted away in peace. Within seconds, her pain ceased. His would last much longer. Taking the boy in his arms, Mack Lawrence had allowed him to shed his tears with dignity. Then he had taken Billy to the hospital and stayed with him throughout the night. Mack brought him home the next day and put him to work immediately helping him in his practice. Slowly the boy's arm mended, and with it, his broken spirit. And by Mack's side, where he remained, Billy Ray Jones learned the art of healing.

"Do you race horses now?" Lydia inquired.

"No," Jones responded firmly. "I learned my lesson the last time at the track. It's not so important how fast a horse can run or anything else it does for man's pleasure. Being God's creatures, horses have a right to a good life, too . . . just like any man. Helping an animal live to the fullest, that's what counts."

As the miles ticked by, Sydney's attention drifted. Nothing had changed all that much, but somehow everything seemed different. Then she understood what was wrong.

"Billy, some of the farms we've seen look deserted, not a horse in sight anywhere. What's happened?"

"It's the economy, Miss Sydney. Everything went down the tubes a few years ago. Didn't Mack tell you?"

Sydney was much too ashamed to respond. For the past several years she'd been so absorbed in her own world that she had little time to care about Mack's.

"It all began when them foreigners came over here. They bought up the farms and began building their own stock. The Arabs in particular had money to spend. Cost was never an object. They drove the price of horses sky-high, and for a time everyone around these parts prospered. But once they had the quality of breed they wanted, they began shipping their horses overseas.

Oh, they still buy here from time to time, but not near in the quantity they used to. Folks got spoiled what with the inflated prices. They didn't want to believe their good fortune might end. So they borrowed against their farms to expand their stables. When them foreigners pulled out, everything collapsed. Some of the oldest and best farms went broke."

It was when Billy signaled a turn off the main Lexington-Frankfort Highway onto the smaller Midway Road that Sydney's heart began to beat faster. Soon, very soon, she would be home.

Billy Ray glanced in the rearview mirror. There was a car—a nondescript blue Ford—that had trailed them since the airport. Presuming they were on their way to Frankfort, Billy Ray had said nothing. But making his turn, he looked for the tailgating car to speed on. When it, too, veered onto the much quieter road, Billy Ray spoke up.

"Sydney, is there some reason you're being followed?"

Thinking of Joe Morrison and his concern for their safety, Sydney grimaced. "It's nothing, Billy Ray. We have . . . friends . . . looking after us, that's all."

His eyes riveted upon the car, Billy Ray was far from convinced. Cautiously, Jones eased the Oldsmobile to the soft shoulder of the road, forcing the Ford to veer sharply around them. He stopped the car and waited until the Ford crested the hill and disappeared.

Then he turned to Sydney and said, "See that monstrosity of a place across the road? Now there's an example of what I was talking about! Look at the bridge leading to the main house. The sheik who bought the farm paid over a million bucks just to build a fountain and a bridge to impress his guests when they first arrive. Why, he doesn't even stay here year-round! He's a big shot from a place called Dubai. He employs a staff of fifty full time just to keep the place up when he's gone. Now tell me, who in the hell around here can compete with that kind of money?"

A wave of fear swept over Sydney as she studied the magnificent farm. There was so much she didn't understand about the Arab culture, particularly the treatment of women. Throwing her glance to Lydia, she vowed to protect the child she loved from the heritage that was, by birthright, hers.

Jones eased the station wagon back onto the highway for the final few kilometers home. Leaning up over the driver's seat, Sydney whispered, "Slow down, Billy Ray, there's something I want to see." Billy Ray slowed the car. He didn't have to be told why; he knew what she wanted to see. Holding her breath, Sydney waited for the main house to come into view.

"Tell me, Billy," she whispered huskily, "is it still the same?"

"Just wait and see," he answered, smiling. He brought the station wagon to a halt at the drive where the stone wall gave way to a wide opening.

Peering down the lane, Sydney gasped, "There it is, Billy Ray. There it is!"

The dream home of her youth was still the most splendid mansion Sydney had ever seen. Framed by lush magnolia trees, the plantation home stood like a forgotten monument to the old South. Four stories high and supported by huge white columns, the house was divided into thirty rooms. Seeing the antique wicker furniture gracing the verandah that encircled the house, Sydney exclaimed, "Oh, Billy, it's still so beautiful!"

But eyeing the garden and the adjoining outbuildings, Sydney noticed a difference, an unnamed difference she had not noticed before. As a youngster she had played here often with the owner's children. Like one of their own, she was welcomed in the main house, particularly in the warm, inviting kitchen where the cook always saved them a special treat.

Before she was twelve, Sydney had memorized every inch, every detail of the estate. And if the truth were known, secretly she had always dreamed one day it would be hers. It was natural that she would sense the change.

"Something's different, Billy Ray. What is it?"

"The Jacksons are gone, Sydney. Moved out nearly three years ago. Unfortunately, they were among the first to go belly-up."

"The Jacksons . . . gone?" she stammered. "They were one of the oldest, most prosperous families. What went wrong?"

"It was just like I was telling you, Sydney. The Jacksons mortgaged the place to build a fine new stable. Unfortunately, things didn't work out."

"Didn't work out? That's it?"

It was because of the Jacksons that Sydney had grown up here where the air was fresh and values firmly entrenched. Way back in the sixties, shortly after Mack had begun his practice, he was covering for another vet when he was called to the Jackson farm to try to save their stock. A mysterious virus had swept through the main barn, threatening their prize studs, and with them the entire operation. It was a treacherous situation, even for an experienced veterinarian, much less one fresh out of school like Mack. Drawing upon his skill and raw guts, somehow he came through and, nursing the stallions day and night, managed to save most of the barn. The Jacksons were eternally grateful.

They wanted Mack to remain and so they deeded him several acres on the west side of the estate and helped him build a fine brick home. Here, in God's country, where a good horse vet was the most precious commodity of all, they crowned Mack Lawrence king and enriched his practice a hundredfold.

It was because of the Jacksons that the Lawrences had prospered and Sydney had been allowed to become all that she was. And now . . . now Billy Ray was telling her . . . like yesterday's garbage . . . they were bankrupt and gone!

"Who owns the place now?"

"He's a real nice man, Sydney. I work for him most of the time. He's a fine horseman even though he's got a bum leg. He's fixed the place up real good. His name is Kerry Donavan."

Bitterly, Sydney turned away.

"Take us home, Billy Ray."

Nodding, he started the car and, passing the main gate, turned onto the small gravel road leading to Mack's place. As the car bumped along the rocky path, Sydney wondered what else about her home she would find different.

It was then that the horrible truth dawned. Mack had failed to meet them at the airport. No matter how sick he was, that was totally out of character for him. Once again, she'd missed the obvious signal. What in the hell was really wrong?

Forcing Billy Ray's eyes to lock with hers in the mirror, Sydney asked quietly, "What's really wrong with my father?"

A sad, sick look clouded the man's eyes. "Oh God, Sydney, hasn't he told you?"

"Told me what?" she repeated harshly.

"Mack's got cancer . . . lung cancer. He won't take chemotherapy, and so the doctors only give him a few months to live. That's why it's so important you've come home."

"Hurry, Billy Ray, hurry!" she urged silently as if a few minutes would make up for all the years she had neglected her father.

Spraying gravel in every direction, the station wagon ground its way along the rocky path toward the house. Billy was driving as fast as the unpaved road would allow.

At last, the rambling brick house came into view. Squinting against the afternoon sun, Sydney scanned her surroundings in seconds, somehow believing the true nature of Mack's condition would reveal itself at the front door.

There were horses, as always, grazing in the side pastures. Fewer in number, perhaps, but healthy and well cared for. The lawn was mowed, the bushes manicured. The five-bedroom ranch house looked exactly as Sydney remembered. The white shutters were freshly painted, the windows washed, contrasting pleasantly with the perfectly shaped and aligned red brick. For a few precious moments, she tried to convince herself that Billy Ray was mistaken.

Bounding from the car, Sydney ran for the front door, leaving the others scrambling in her wake.

"Mack!" she cried. "Where are you?"

Pausing only momentarily in the hallway, she raced through the dining room leading to the kitchen. There, at the table, she found the emaciated man who had once been her healthy, robust father.

As Mack slowly and painfully came to his feet, Sydney cried, "Oh God, Mack, why didn't you tell me?"

Mack, at sixty, had never been a large man but now he seemed shrunken and frail. There were dark circles under his bleary eyes. His hair was dull and gray.

But throwing open his trembling arms, he smiled and whispered, "Come here, little girl, and give your daddy a hug."

Tears filled her eyes as Sydney rushed to her father, losing herself in the comfort of his embrace. Since Sam's death, she had thought of little else but the feel of Mack's strong arms about her. And even though his arms were no longer strong, and his bony ribs pricked her flesh, her father's loving hug was as warm and reassuring as she knew it would be. And after those first terrifying moments, Sydney realized that the woman in her might have to care for the man, but the child in her had once again found her daddy.

chapter 5

Sydney prepared Mack's favorite meal, fried chicken and mashed potatoes, for their first Sunday together. Only after the dishes had been washed and dried did Sydney steal a few minutes to wander outside alone. Wrapped snugly in Mack's down jacket, Sydney savored the brisk north wind as she slowly ambled down to the stable. She leaned against the white picket fence and studied the horses absently grazing in the field.

She recalled a time in her own life when she had been free of worry, free of concern. Back then, school and chores were her only responsibilities, and taking horses over higher and higher fences her only real ambition.

She had been a mere baby when they moved into their new brick home and Mack established himself here in his practice. By the time she was six her mother was gone, dead of uterine cancer. Now, nearly thirty years later, the memory of her mother had faded, but she had a warehouse full of recollections of Mack and the horses and growing up in the country where life was simple and people were genuinely good.

How things have changed, she thought sadly.

Since leaving home, her life had become a never-ending stream of responsibilities, beginning with her career and followed by her marriage to Sam. Now she had Lydia to consider and, with Mack's illness, a small horse farm to run. And what the hell did she really know about that?

Well, she certainly had the money to hire good help. And that she planned to do straight away. With Billy Ray only able to work a few hours a day, they needed a full-time foreman. She'd placed an ad to run in today's paper. They'd already had several calls. Tomorrow the interviews would begin. In the meantime, since it was the Sabbath and Billy Ray had the afternoon off, she had stalls to clean and horses to put away.

Approaching the barn, she slowed. "What in God's name do I think I'm doing?" she mused, glancing down at her city attire. She didn't even have proper clothes to wear for the dirty job at hand—just gabardine slacks, an outrageously expensive sweater, and Ralph Lauren flats. Only Mack's insulated jacket kept her from a look of total absurdity. For the past decade, she'd been placed in front of the camera where all that mattered was a pretty face, nice clothes, and a damned good story. It had been years since she'd mounted a horse or cleaned a stall. Had she forgotten everything her father had taught her? More importantly, did she care? After all, she had fled the tranquillity of the farm when she was twenty to forge an exciting life and build an important career. Despite Sam's death, could she really give it all up for good?

"And for what?" she asked, her spirits sagging. Piles of manure and a few acres of land? Coming home to find herself had been an illusion, for what she found here was more of a burden than what she had left.

"What am I going to do?" she wondered aloud. "Dear Lord, what am I going to do?"

With the afternoon sun at her back, Sydney entered the barn. Silhouetted against the door, it was difficult at first to see, so she paused to gather her bearings. Her eyes were slow to adjust to the darkness, but her other senses had sharpened. Down toward the far end of the barn she detected the distinct sound of movement. Yet before leaving, Billy Ray had turned all the horses out to pasture. Who or what, then, was in the barn?

Not knowing what she might encounter, Sydney slowly edged her way down the aisle as the rustling of straw grew louder. Her heart pounding, she struggled to focus. The stalls were empty, the horses gone. But there was definitely something, probably a rat or even a raccoon, in the single stall at the end of the barn where the door remained open.

. Grabbing a pitchfork, Sydney inched her way along. Taking a deep breath, she raised her makeshift weapon as she stepped in front of the half-open door and peered into the stall. Startled, she screamed.

There was no rat, nor even a raccoon. Instead, she found a man, a stranger, cleaning the stall. Who he was, she didn't know. Billy Ray had said they had no help and no one was expected until tomorrow.

"Who are you?" she demanded. "What are you doing here?"

Slowly, the man turned to face her. He was a tall, yet slender fellow with a small waist, narrow hips and piercing azure blue eyes. He was dressed in worn tight jeans, a tattered knit sweater, and black, muddy Wellingtons. His hair was not unkempt, but thick and full, falling just below his collar, a length to which Sydney was most unaccustomed. And his full head of wavy hair was a strange combination of pleasing colors—dark burnished chestnut streaked with gray.

Sydney guessed the man to be somewhere in his early forties. He had handsome rugged features, a musky masculine scent, and a mysterious air about him that disquieted her more than a little bit.

"What are you doing here?" she repeated.

"What does it look like I'm doing?" he countered, his annoyance clearly evident. "I'm shoveling shit. Would you care to help?"

And with his impudent response, Sydney thought she understood. The man had the slight brogue of an Irishman and suddenly everything made sense. In discussing their plight, Mack had assured her that there were a number of competent Irish lads looking for jobs. They were hard workers who labored for a pittance. But this was ridiculous. This man—more polished than his station would suggest—had gone to work without even bothering to apply.

"Look, mister, I appreciate your effort, but the job was only posted today. I'm afraid you'll have to come back tomorrow and apply like everyone else."

The corners of the stranger's mouth curled slightly. "Oh really? And who, in the meantime, will finish the stall? You?"

Breaking into a grin, the man stared boldly at the woman's slender figure. Much too boldly to suit Sydney.

Drawing herself to her full height, she replied, "And what makes you think I can't? For your information, my name is Sydney Lawrence. My father, Mack Lawrence, owns the place."

The stranger scoffed, "I see. Well then, hoist your fork and let's finish up. We have about eight stalls left to clean."

"Look, I told you! Interviews won't begin until Monday. Now please leave and come back tomorrow."

His lips quivered with amusement as he cocked his head. "Well, madam, you hardly seem dressed for the job at hand, and your ridiculous suede shoes will be ruined. But if you insist, I'll leave it for you."

The arrogant man moved slowly toward her, but as he started to edge past her, he paused with his face just inches from hers and their shoulders brushing ever so gently. Savoring the moment, he smiled knowingly as something stirred deep inside of Sydney, a hot, burning sensation she tried to ignore. And in that moment, for whatever reason, she feared the power of this man and desperately wanted him gone.

"I must say I'm disappointed," he said. "Your father is a gracious man. I had expected his daughter to be no less."

Her cheeks flushed crimson. She shouted, "How dare you speak to me like that! Don't bother to come back tomorrow. There's no job here for you!"

Feigning abject disappointment, the Irishman dropped his head in despair.

"I guess I'll have to apply elsewhere. Sorry to bother you. Good day."

Unable to take her eyes off the man, Sydney watched him saunter down the aisle. Holding his head high and his shoulders erect, the stranger walked with great dignity, although he had a distinct limp. Suddenly a sickening wave of nausea swept over her. Just where had she heard about the distinguished Irishman with the limp?

"Wait," she commanded. "Who are you?"

Slowly, the tall, handsome fellow with the piercing azure blue eyes pivoted to face her.

Bowing formally, he mocked her yet again. In the slow practiced drawl of a Southern gentleman he answered, "My name, madam, is Kerry Donavan. I own . . . the estate . . . next-door."

April 10, 1992
3:35 p.m.

As the sun began to dip into the west, a gleaming black limousine sped down the Lexington-Frankfort Highway. It was a lovely Friday afternoon in April, and although the air was a bit nippy, the promise of a warm spring lurked just around the corner.

The short twenty-minute ride from the airport had been a rather strained one as the chauffeur studied his sullen passenger in the rearview mirror. Frustrated by the man's aloofness, he decided to crack the ice just as they turned from the highway onto the smaller Midway Road.

"I trust you had a good flight, sir."

"Yes," the passenger replied. "Good flight, just long and tiring."

"Will you be staying with us awhile?"

The stranger's eyes locked with those of the driver. A brief smile crossed the man's swarthy features before the corners of his lips curled into more of a sneer.

"I should think my business in Kentucky might require a week, at the most two."

"The staff is fully prepared for your visit, sir. Sheik Mohammed has made it abundantly clear that nothing is to be spared for his guest's comfort."

Just as the limousine signaled a right turn into the long, winding drive of Sheik Mohammed al Maktoum's estate, an ordinary scene across the road caught the passenger's eye.

"Stop here," the man nearly shouted.

The chauffeur brought the car to an abrupt halt. Gazing at the bridge leading to the main house with the elaborate waterfall and colorful gardens, the driver sought to direct his passenger's attention to the splendor that lay ahead. But the stranger's eyes were focused on the attractive, auburn-haired woman standing at the end of the lane where the yellow school bus with the flashing lights came to rest.

He'd had the woman under surveillance for months. Now the grim foreigner tensed as he waited for the bus to deliver its goods and move out of the way. It was then that he saw the face he'd waited over two years to see. But the face he saw was no longer that of an innocent child; rather, the little girl had matured into a lovely young woman. And, having missed the transition, he was enraged.

Exhaling sharply, his eyes glazed for a moment. With his attention riveted upon the scene, he watched intently as the woman draped her arm protectively about the girl's shoulder. They turned and slowly meandered down the lane. Straining to see, he waited until the tall, slender figure and the smaller one passed completely out of sight. It was only then that he dared to speak.

In a choked, husky voice, he barked, "Drive on!"

■

"Mack, this is ridiculous! The last thing I want to do is have tea with that man! He's the most arrogant, conceited son of a bitch I've ever had the misfortune to encounter!"

Amused, Mack countered, "And from what I hear, missy, encounter him you did! Now if you ask me, all that's water under the bridge. Mr. Donavan has graciously invited us to tea and I have accepted. So wash your face, comb your hair, and let's go."

"You don't understand . . ."

"Oh, I understand quite well, my love. You're eaten up by grief and despair. For the past month, you've hidden in this house trying to avoid facing life. I've permitted you to get away with it because I knew you needed time. But it has to end."

Sydney opened her mouth to protest, but seeing the determined look in her father's eyes, she ceased. Arguing with Mack Lawrence was pointless, for if the daughter was stubborn, the father was impossible, and so she attacked the issue from a different angle.

"You've not been feeling well, Daddy. You have no business going."

Gripping his chair, Mack hoisted himself to his feet. Standing erect, he eyeballed his daughter directly.

"I'm not dead . . . at least not yet, Sydney. So please don't bury me before my time. Kerry wants me to have a look at his mare and I intend to do just that. Now, will you drive me, or should I trudge through the field?"

Knowing full well her father was just mulish enough to walk the mile through the pasture to Kerry Donavan's place, Sydney gave in. "Oh, all right! Come on, Lydia! Let's get this nightmare over with!"

After helping Mack into the front seat of the station wagon and seeing Lydia securely fastened in the back, Sydney gunned the motor and sped down the lane, spraying a cloud of dust and gravel behind her. Darting out onto the Midway Road, she veered sharply onto the blacktop drive leading to Donavan's estate. And, as always when she saw the mansion, her heart skipped a beat. But she was so angry at being forced to come that there was no way she would acknowledge—even to herself—how glad she was to see the place up close again.

The huge overhanging trees formed a canopy along the drive as she slowly approached the house. Yes, the beloved magnolia trees were still as she remembered, and the azaleas had begun to bloom.

"What's he calling the place now? Shadow Lane Farm is gone."

"He knows that, Sydney, perhaps better than anyone. He hasn't found the name yet. In the meantime, people around here just call it 'Donavan's Place.'"

Bringing the car to a halt, Sydney forced her gaze to the front door. There on the verandah stood the ruggedly handsome man whose mere presence made her angry. Steeling herself, she came around to assist her father and, linking arms with Lydia, marched with a defiant gait toward the front door.

"Good of you to come, Mack," the Irishman called, bowing slightly. "And Sydney, how . . . nice . . . to see you once again."

Grinding her teeth, Sydney shot the man an icy stare, for his sarcasm was too much to bear.

Dismissing Sydney with a bemused glance, Donavan directed his attention to her daughter. "And who do we have here?" he inquired.

"My name is Lydia, sir."

"Well, my name is Kerry," he replied, stooping to shake hands with the exquisite young woman. "Please come in. Tea and cakes are waiting."

Cursing under her breath, Sydney followed the two men and Lydia into the foyer of the main house. Immediately her eyes glanced up the winding staircase, and, despite her ill humor, a slight smile crossed her lips. For many an hour, she, together with the Jackson children, had polished the mahogany railing with their rumps as they slid one after the other, from the top of the winding staircase to the bottom.

Throwing open the door to the drawing room, Kerry Donavan invited his guests to follow. In an instant, Sydney felt she had journeyed not only back in time, but also from one continent clear across the ocean to another. No longer was she in a Southern mansion, but rather in an Irish country estate several thousand miles away.

The drawing room was huge. The walls were painted a pale ivory, and an intricate red, oak leaf-patterned plasterwork etched the coffered ceiling. Thick brocade burgundy draperies graced the floor-to-ceiling windows. But it was the huge Venetian mirror at the end of the salon that really captured Sydney's fancy.

Throughout the room, English and Irish antiques vied for attention, and a smattering of original artwork dotted the walls. What attracted Sydney more than the abundance of fine pieces was the roaring fire in the fireplace, inviting one and all to gather about snugly in front of the flames.

Catching the look on Sydney's face, Kerry hurried to explain. "Please forgive my absurd indulgence. In my country, we burn fires all year long. Here, though, I've learned I must stop the practice after spring."

"Stop the practice or suffocate," Mack countered, grinning.

"In Ireland, our homes are not centrally heated, and as the air can remain quite chilly throughout the year, most homes are never without a bit of a flame to warm the toes. Now please, sit down and let me ring for tea."

With Lydia firmly planted by her side, Sydney took a seat on the pale green, moire sofa across from the patterned one that Mack had chosen, leaving Donavan a choice of one of the four Chippendale chairs grouped about. Sydney could only hope that he would choose the seat farthest away from her, for no matter how charming his manners or how magnificent his furnishings, she wanted nothing to do with the man or his mansion.

In a matter of seconds a short, plump woman Sydney guessed to be in her mid-sixties arrived, carrying a tray of cakes and a steaming pot of tea. Sydney glanced yet again about her. Despite the exquisite decor, there was something about the drawing room that she found rather queer. Nowhere was there a photograph of home or family; nowhere was there a personal memento of the real man.

It was the sound of his melodic brogue that finally jarred Sydney from her curious trance.

"A bit of cream, Sydney? Or would you prefer only sugar?"

"Lemon, if you have it. No cream."

Taking the cup of tea from his housekeeper, Donavan served Sydney's tea himself. Pausing deliberately as he handed her the cup, his azure blue eyes perused her body as a blind man's fingers might caress his Braille. And her body reacted to the boldness of his glance with a warm rush below her waist.

Feeling her cheeks flushing, Sydney averted her glance while Kerry, reveling in her discomfort, merely smiled and walked away. It was then Sydney decided to fight back. No man had the right to make her feel so vulnerable and out of control.

There was only one way she knew to get even. The bastard obviously had a past, and Sydney Lawrence was determined to make him squirm.

Mack's words of warning just before leaving the house haunted her. "Now listen here, missy! Kerry Donavan is a private man, so be sparing with your incessant questions. Mark my words and let him be."

Well, Sydney reasoned, Kerry Donavan had just crossed the line of impropriety, and the rules of the game had now changed.

Taking a deep breath, she steadied her frazzled nerves and waited for her adversary to settle in the nearest chair by the fire, just across from her. Only when he was comfortable—and unaware—with the cup of tea raised to his lips, did she smile coyly and begin.

"Tell me about yourself, Kerry. What brought you to Kentucky?"

His eyes narrowed slightly. He paused, then slowly completed his sip of tea before responding.

"I'm afraid there's nothing much to tell, Sydney. My love of horses, of course, brought me here."

"But where do you come from originally?"

Donavan hesitated. Mack cleared his throat, begging for Sydney's glance, but she refused to look at him. Finally Kerry replied, "I come from a place called Lisnagry, just outside the city of Limerick. Are you familiar with Ireland, Sydney?"

"Not at all," she drawled politely, bringing the rim of her own cup briefly to her lips, "but I hear there's no more beautiful country on God's green earth. And with the Irish love of horses . . . well . . . ," Sydney allowed the implication of her words to blanket the room. "What in heaven's name could have enticed you here?"

Sydney watched the man's face chill before her.

Deliberately, he replied, "I suppose there comes a time in every man's life when he needs a change."

"But your family, what about them?"

Lest he crack the delicate antique cup, Donavan set the fragile piece of china upon the table. Rising, he walked to the hearth. Ignoring Sydney, he stoked the fire then paced to the rear of Mack's sofa. Only then did he dare to speak.

"What is past, Sydney, is in the past. My reasons for coming here are not important. What is important are my plans for the future. Would you do me the honor of accompanying me to the stable to see my mare?" Piercing her with his pointed gaze, he concluded, "I'm sure Mack and Lydia won't mind. They can finish their tea in peace."

Giving her no chance for refusal, Donavan approached Sydney menacingly and decidedly extended his hand. Helping her to her feet, he propelled her out of the drawing room and down the back hallway to the rear door. Once outside, despite his limp, he picked up the pace, forcing her to match his stride.

Pausing only once to savor the sunset, he gazed across his spacious fields then, throwing a veiled glance to her, said, "I understand that you were very fond of the Jacksons. Is that why you resent me so?"

Sydney turned away, avoiding his eyes, and when she failed to respond, he sighed and directed his focus straight ahead. "As you know, Sydney, this is not an overly large farm by bluegrass standards—five hundred acres, more or less. I bought the place because I loved the house and because of the stables. And with the farm in bankruptcy . . . well, the price was certainly right."

Resuming their walk, he permitted the silence to comfort them. Approaching the stable, he halted, allowing Sydney to note the perfectly manicured hedges surrounding the barn, the brass lanterns and fixtures adorning the building, and the impressive weather vane atop the peaked roof.

"This is the new stable where I house my mares and foals. I keep my stallions in the original stable just below. Come, have a look for yourself."

Entering the barn, Sydney gasped, for she had never encountered an operation quite like this before. At least double in size to Mack's house, the stable was built in a rectangular configuration.

Along the length of each side of the building were ten stalls made of a finely sanded oak lumber, each the size of a standard bedroom, with a door facing the aisle and a window opening to the outside.

Taking her by the elbow, Kerry led her into the interior of the barn.

"I was appalled when I first saw the stable because it had been designed to please the spectator, not the horse. I pulled down the crystal chandeliers and ripped up the ludicrous carpet. Instead, I wanted to utilize the center of the barn, and so we constructed a lounge with kitchen, dining, and sleeping quarters for the grooms so an attendant can be with the horses at all times. Of course, we have neither the staff nor the stock to warrant such a vigil just yet.

"We have our own heating and air-conditioning units," he went on, "a separate feed room, three wash stalls, a tack and saddle closet, and, of course, medical facilities."

Unlocking the door to the large room adjacent to the lounge, Kerry switched on a light and smiled.

"Mack helped us design this space so he could treat any medical emergency right here on the spot and the horses wouldn't have to be moved. He could even perform surgery if necessary."

Completing their tour of the building, Kerry added, "I intend to build this operation into a top breeding farm. Funny though," he mused a bit sadly, "despite all the work, I've not yet named the place."

Speechless, Sydney turned toward Kerry with a new measure of respect. But there was an obvious question that went unanswered. Only half the stalls were filled. He had gone to so much trouble, and yet his operation had barely begun.

Reading her mind, he responded, "I'm brand-new at this game, but I have a real sense of the future. There are only a few of us now to work the place, and it will take time to hire the right staff. More important, it will take precise, careful planning to build my stock. That's why every horse is vitally important, but the one I want to show you . . . this one is the very best of all. My future rests with her."

Directly across from the lounge in the stall on the south side of the building, Kerry Donavan presented his prize mare.

"Sydney, meet Dare to Dream."

Kerry reached through the narrow bars of the stall and affectionately patted his horse's muzzle.

"This lovely mare is one of the few good horses that Sheik Mohammed failed to buy. I discovered her at my first Keeneland auction. Fortunately for me, the sheik got distracted during the bidding and his advisors let him down. So I bought her and bought her well."

Glancing at her swollen belly with the genuine satisfaction of a contented owner, he added, "And soon, very soon, she'll foal my first Kentucky Derby winner."

Admiring her gleaming chestnut coat, Sydney asked, "She's beautiful, Kerry, but what makes her so special?"

"She's a daughter of Alydar. You do remember Alydar, I presume?"

The sarcasm of Donavan's remark was not lost upon Mack Lawrence's daughter. Despite the time she'd been away, there was no one who was in anyway associated with horses who did not know the significance of the lineage of Alydar—the horse that lost the triple crown to his rival Affirmed, but had thus far soundly beaten him in the breeding shed.

As he gazed at his beloved mare, Sydney, for the first time during their brief and uncomfortable encounters, saw the Irishman's guarded shroud disappear and his rugged features soften.

And without thinking, Sydney edged closer as the chestnut mare thrust her white muzzle forward for a pet. Absorbed in the horse's trusting eyes, Sydney forgot for the moment her dislike of Kerry Donavan. Even Kerry warmed a bit as in a kinder voice, he said, "Now perhaps you can understand why my past is not really so important. It's the future that I dream about—and the present that I cherish."

Tuesday, April 21, 1992
7:45 a.m.

It was truly a magnificent spring morning as Sydney and Lydia strolled down the lane to await the school bus. Glancing at the exquisite young woman by her side, Sydney smiled. Even though she missed Sam terribly, the bond between Lydia and her grew stronger every day, giving Sydney's life renewed meaning. And slowly, as the bleakness of winter gave way to spring, Sydney found herself coming back to life as a mother, if not yet as a woman.

Against the backdrop of a puffy blue sky, the sun rose above the horizon, turning the luscious grass greener before their very eyes, while the sweet smell of flowers permeated the crisp, cool air. Yes, it was the kind of day that made you forget for a moment your pain, your defenses, even your keener sense of danger. Perhaps that's why Sydney failed to notice the car parked across the road obscured by a thick clump of trees.

The somber man sitting in the rear seat was not pleased. Neither was his driver, nor the burly, well-armed man beside him. It was Jamil, the driver, who ventured to speak in a voice that was both timid and respectful.

"I'm sorry, sir, but as you can see, the child is never left alone. Every morning the woman walks her down the lane. Every afternoon, she greets her. Aside from that, they go shopping twice a week, take the older man to the doctor, and on Sunday they go to church. Even at school the child is constantly monitored."

The one in the back—the commander—replied, "Be vigilant, Jamil. Our moment will come."

With some trepidation, Raoul Sabid, the armed guard, countered, "But, sir, you said yourself, time is running out. How much longer can we wait?"

The man with the cold eyes smiled, but it was not a pleasant grin. By nature, he was a brutal man. By trade, he was a terrorist arms dealer. Originally, he had gotten into dealing weapons in order to raise money to overthrow the government of Iran. But, with the current political structure in the Middle East, his primary goal had been unachievable, at least at the present time. Now he remained in the business of supplying terrorist training camps with weapons simply for the money and the power it afforded him.

His bodyguard was right. Every day they remained in the States, they were losing money in the Middle East. But Ali Hassan had a plan.

"How right you are, Raoul. My patience is wearing thin. My daughter is worth the wait. But with every passing hour, the woman becomes more expendable . . ."

■

Taking her time returning home, Sydney stooped to pick a wildflower. As always when she said good-bye to Lydia, she felt abandoned. Taking a deep breath, she steeled her emotions because the day that lay ahead promised to be an unpleasant one. Mack was failing. It was clear to see that his days were indeed numbered.

Even now he lay in bed asleep, having been awake most of the night. A simple cold had turned into a deep, chesty cough, signaling yet another infection. Perhaps this too would pass as the other episodes had. But for now he was too weak to care for himself.

■

2:00 p.m.

The afternoon passed uneventfully, and Sydney enjoyed a few quiet moments with her father. Despite her fears, Mack had rallied during the past few hours. And so, after lunch and a brief nap, he summoned his daughter for a chat. There was something weighing on his mind, a matter he was determined to discuss.

"You've got to think beyond today, my girl. Being here with me hour after hour is no existence for you or for Lydia. You're wasting yourself here. There's too much life in you to just give up. Take a good look at yourself in the mirror. My glamour girl is gone."

And at that, Sydney had to smile, for indeed, while settling into country life, she'd changed. The expensive clothes had been closeted away and the fancy hairdo was no more. Instead, today like every day in recent weeks, she was attired in jeans and a work shirt, tennis shoes and no makeup. Her hair was pulled back in a ponytail, with tiny, untamed wisps of copper curls falling casually about her face. From working outdoors with the horses, she had the beginnings of a pleasant freckly tan, and all in all she wasn't entirely displeased with her new, fresh look.

"Please, Mack, let me be. I need time to figure things out. I like being here with you, and country life agrees with Lydia. Aside from missing Sam, I've never seen her happier than being around the horses. So stop fretting. Don't you see? For the first time since Sam's death, I feel safe."

Leaning forward, Sydney tucked the covers under her father's chin. Hearing wheels squealing in the drive, he motioned for her to listen.

At the sound of a sharp rap upon the door, Sydney shouted, "I'm coming!" Yet rather than diminishing, the pounding only grew louder.

Annoyed, she threw open the door. She was confronted by the last person she wanted to see.

"Where's Mack?" the intruder shouted.

"In the bedroom, but wait! He's much too sick to have visitors!"

The harried man pushed past her. Cursing, she followed. "Who in the hell do you think you are?" she demanded.

Kerry Donavan rushed to the foot of the bed. "Mack, I need your help! It's Dare to Dream. I think she's gone into labor."

Struggling to rise, Mack countered, "Can't be. It's much too early. She's not due for another month."

"I know, but she's refused to eat. And she's dropped. Her udder's enlarged and her nipples are waxing. It's time, Mack. You've got to help me!"

Sydney stepped between her terminally ill father and her rude neighbor. "What do you think you're doing?" she shouted. "Would you take a look at Mack? He's too weak to even get out of bed! Where's Billy Ray?"

"I sent him to town for supplies. He won't be back for hours."

"Well, surely there must be someone else who can help you!"

Donavan's stone-cold eyes were piercing. "I have no one." He returned his gaze to the old man. "I'm sorry, Mack, but there's no time to find another vet. Please, tell me what to do."

Summoning his strength, Mack threw off the covers and tried to rise from the bed. Falling back on the pillows, he knew it was useless.

Determined to spare her father further indignity, Sydney intervened. "Nevermind, Mack. I'll go with you, Kerry. It's been awhile, but I know how to assist at a birth."

His eyes darting between Mack and Sydney, Kerry remained immobile. Jerking his arm, Sydney shoved him out of the room. "Let's go. We're wasting time here."

Donavan had no choice but to follow. Gunning his truck, they sped down the lane to his farm. It was a tense, dismal ride to the stable. The uncomfortable silence was broken only when the Irishman turned to Sydney and asked, "Do you really know how to help her?"

"I used to go with my father when I was a little girl. I've assisted on several deliveries. It's been awhile, Kerry, but I remember. Everything will be okay."

Sydney could only hope that her words were true and that Dare to Dream's delivery would be an easy one. It was when they entered the barn that she knew her wish was in vain.

The lovely chestnut mare was pacing frantically in a mindless circle, pawing at her hay and snorting in pain. Around and around she went, and then, collapsing to the ground, she waited for the next agonizing wave of contractions to begin.

"Get warm water, blankets and iodine," Sydney commanded, "and hurry!"

Kerry returned in minutes with everything they needed. Laying them off to the side, he went to his precious mare. Drenched in sweat, she curled her lip in agony as she arched her back.

"How long has she been like this?" Sydney inquired.

"I came to check the horses about an hour ago. She refused her feed and she kept shifting her weight to find an easier position. When I saw that her nipples were covered with colostrum, I knew it was time to get help."

Donavan looked the mare over thoroughly. It was clear to see that she was fully dilated and proceeding to the next stage of labor where the contractions would come more frequently and last longer.

"Look!" Kerry exclaimed, as a white patch appeared in the birth canal. It was the white cellophane membrane enveloping the foal. Kneeling down beside him, Sydney waited for the next contractions to push the bag out a little farther. Breathing a sigh of relief, they saw first one front hoof and finally another, and then what they thought to be the nose.

"Thank God," Sydney whispered. "At least she's positioned correctly." Had she not been, it would have been hopeless for anyone but a skilled veterinarian to save her.

In a shaky voice, Donavan exclaimed, "Something's wrong, Sydney! The fit's too tight!"

And so it was that all hopes for an easy delivery were dashed and their second fear came to pass. Indeed, the foal was too big to be pushed easily through the birth canal. It became clear that, to save the mare and the foal, the man, the woman and the horse had to work together. Again, the chestnut horse struggled to rise, but this time it could not be permitted. To survive, she had to remain quiet and in place.

"I'll hold her head down while you get ready," said Sydney. "When she begins to push, you pull—but very, very gently, Kerry. Too much and you'll tear her insides apart."

Sydney knelt by the mare's head and gently stroked her mane. Their eyes connected as a horrible wave of pain engulfed the terrified animal.

"Now, Kerry, now!" Sydney cried, as the mare struggled to push her foal through the canal. But Kerry was able to move the cellophane bag half an inch . . . if that . . . no more.

"Again!" Sydney cried, but it was useless, and with every agonizing push, the mare grew weaker. Feeling the horse's pain to her very core, Sydney tried desperately to soothe her. But, panicking, Dare to Dream turned away, and once again struggled to rise as she threw her head back in despair.

And in that moment, Sydney understood why. It was not she who had a history with the horse, only Donavan. It was not she who could reassure her; only he could.

"Change places with me, Kerry. She needs you."

As rapid beads of sweat poured from his brow, Kerry shook his head no. "You're not strong enough. Look how little the foal has moved, and the longer it's in there, the greater the chance it will suffocate."

"I know," Sydney argued, "but if the mare gives up, the battle's lost anyway. Let me try."

Quickly switching places with him, Sydney crouched on her knees with her hands in position. She glanced up to find Kerry cradling his mare's head, speaking to her in the same soft, melodic brogue he might a small baby. Sydney was touched for she had never seen the tender side of Kerry. Locking eyes with her master, Dare to Dream stopped her frantic pawing and eased, but as the next wave came, both Donavan and Sydney tensed.

Sydney dug in as the water sac broke, spraying her with a dark, muddy brown fluid.

"Now!" Kerry shouted. "Now!"

With all her might, yet as gently as she could, Sydney pulled. And the foal moved, not one, but several inches. Alas, with time ticking by, it wasn't enough.

"Again," he cried. "Again!"

And, grabbing a towel for greater tension, she pulled yet again, nearly screaming from the strain. Falling back, she cried out as the first shoulder appeared. "It's coming, Kerry, it's coming!"

They worked in tandem as the fiercest contraction yet gripped the mare.

"Now!" he shouted. "Pull!"

Summoning more strength than she thought she possessed, Sydney gave it her all as, with the final push, the foal sprang forth, breaking free from the white membrane and drenching her with the mare's blood.

"It's alive, Kerry. It's alive!"

Instinctively Sydney reached for a warm towel as she cradled the foal to her heart. And, seeing it gasp for its first breath, tears of relief clouded her eyes and began to fall.

It would be awhile before the third stage of labor, the expulsion of the placenta, would begin. In the meantime, Kerry wearily rose to his feet, allowing his mare to succumb to fatigue. Anxious to see the new foal, he asked, "Is it a filly or a colt?"

But Sydney did not answer. Once the tears she'd locked inside for months burst forth, there was no stopping the sobs that were to follow. For the foal and the miracle of life. For loving Sam and for losing him.

Kerry approached slowly, not knowing what to do. Oh, he understood her pain, because he'd experienced that depth of sorrow himself. Yet he'd never been able to release it. His tears were still buried in his heart. Gently, he removed the trembling foal from her grasp.

Sydney was oblivious to her surroundings, to Kerry, even to the time of day, as she cried her heart out. Only when there were no more tears left to cry did she remember where she was. Only then did she think about Lydia.

"Oh my God, Kerry! What time is it?"

"Nearly four o'clock."

"The bus," she stammered. "I'm late."

Jumping to her feet, she glanced down, first at her blood-soaked clothes and then at her sullied hands. Helplessly, she looked to Donavan, not knowing what to do.

"You look fine," he assured her, "now go. I can handle things from here."

As he attended to the foal, he watched her stumble to the doorway. In the course of an hour, something very precious had taken place between them. Drenched in dirt, blood and sweat, with wisps of hair clinging to her face, Sydney Lawrence had looked more beautiful, more real, than Kerry Donavan cared to admit. And he had glimpsed a depth of character—call it raw guts and sheer determination—that he never dreamed lurked beneath her veneer. He wouldn't tell her. He didn't know how. But the new information was there, locked deep in a place he shared with no one.

At the entrance to the stall, she halted as a most important question crossed her mind. Turning back to Kerry, she had to ask, "What is it?"

With pride and a great deal of relief, he responded. "It's a colt, Sydney. A fine, strapping colt."

"I'll bring Lydia back to see him."

Satisfied, Sydney turned on her heel and left the barn. Stepping into the brilliant sunshine, she closed her eyes and lifted her tear-stained face to the source of the warmth. For the first time in months, she felt free.

■

3:45 p.m.

The driver of the car checked the time just as the school bus crested the hill. Glancing up the lane, the three men expected to see the woman. Where was she? With flashing lights, the bus came to a halt at the end of the lane leading to the gravel road.

"Start the car," commanded Hassan in the back seat of the sedan.

Stepping off the bus, Lydia searched for Sydney, but didn't find her. For a moment she seemed confused, even a little frightened.

Just then, Sydney came to the junction where the stone wall gave way and the road came into view. Waving frantically, she called to Lydia, but the noise of the car's racing engine drowned the sound. Seeing the car, Sydney froze, but only for a fraction of a moment. Then, as her heart caught in her throat, she found her legs and frantically ran down the drive.

The car came to an abrupt halt, blocking the lane, and Ali Hassan jumped out. Startled, Lydia wheeled around as a look of disbelief crossed her face.

Throwing open his arms, Hassan cried, "Come to Daddy, Lydia! Come to Daddy!"

The girl instinctively turned away, searching for the woman who had become her mother. Seeing Sydney, she started toward her.

Enraged at his daughter's betrayal, Hassan grabbed Lydia by the hair and jerked her to him. He drew back his open hand and slapped her hard, then dragged her, kicking, to the car. The bodyguard in the front seat leaped out and, leveling his gun, aimed at Sydney. Dropping to her knees, she screamed, *"Lydia . . . no!"*

The roar of the engine was not enough to diminish the child's cries. *"Mommy . . . help me!"*

Shoving the girl to the floor of the car, Ali Hassan climbed in behind her. His face was a mask of bellowing rage as he cried, "I've come to bring you home, Lydia! With me . . . where you belong!"

Federal Prison
Leavenworth, Kansas
11:30 p.m.

Joe Morrison shuddered as the heavy gate clanged shut behind him. Despite the fact he'd spent the better part of his life in law enforcement, here in the penitentiary he felt every bit as much a prisoner as the ones in stripes. In silence, Joe was escorted down the hall to a small, olive green conference room adjacent to the warden's office. There he waited for the only man he knew who could help them.

He fumbled for a cigarette. Then after rolling it between his thumb and index finger, he lit up. He studied the swirling cloud of smoke hovering directly above him as he pondered the meaning of existence. Life, at times, he decided, was pure piss.

The door opened and a bent old man entered. For a moment Morrison thought they'd brought him the wrong prisoner. This shell of a human being looked twenty years older than the one who had been convicted for masterminding the conspiracy to steal human organs a little more than a year ago.

"Sit down, Rajid. We have to talk."

Morrison studied the prisoner who shuffled to the seat on the opposite side of the table.

"Prison life doesn't agree with you, Farhad. You look too thin. Is there anything I can do to help?"

"Help!" the man hissed. "You're the bastard who put me here! What in the hell could you do for me now?"

Joe Morrison leaned forward, flicking the ash from his cigarette to the floor. His next words had to be measured carefully.

"There's a great deal I could do for you, my friend. In exchange for the right information."

Farhad Rajid eyed the FBI agent with contempt. He spat on the floor and snarled, "I want nothing from you."

"You're being much too hasty, Rajid. Bad things happen to small, defenseless men in prison. Have those big ugly slugs been fucking you?"

What little color the man had retained drained from his face. Lowering his glance, he refused his enemy the satisfaction of seeing the devastation in his eyes. In Iran, he'd been born to a family of privilege. In here, he was at the mercy of anyone strong enough to take him. And for that, he would never forgive Joe Morrison.

"Look, Farhad, I know that you haven't had an easy time in prison. The warden tells me that you're especially hated because of your heritage. Seems prejudice knows no bounds, even within prison walls. I can't commute your sentence, but I do have the power to make life better."

Despite his loathing for Americans in general, and Joe Morrison in particular, the prisoner was forced to ask, "How?"

"You give me the information I want and I'll get you a private cell. That way no one can hurt you."

For the first time during their brief meeting, a flicker of light flashed across the man's eyes.

"And what would you want in return?"

Morrison crushed out his cigarette on the floor. Folding his hands on the table, he took a deep breath.

"One thing . . . Rajid . . . that's all I require. Tell me where your brother is and it's done."

The expression on the smaller man's face changed from a sneer to a satisfied grin. Then, falling back in his chair, he opened his mouth and bellowed. To him it was a laugh, but to Morrison it was a hideous screech.

Returning his smoldering eyes to Morrison, he slammed his fists upon the table. "My brother came back to reclaim that which is his! My people have won! Our cause will triumph while you and all like you will perish!"

"Save the rhetoric, Rajid. It's time to think about yourself. Your brother can do nothing for you now. You're at the mercy of strangers in prison." He nodded at the tiny, barred window. "You'll never see your homeland again, or even daylight outside prison walls. You'll spend the rest of your life here at Leavenworth. Why not make it easier?"

With a sound that was not quite human, Rajid replied, "There is nothing you could do to make me betray my brother."

"No, you're right," Morrison replied calmly. "We don't resort to torture like you bastards do. Have it your way, Farhad. Perhaps in time, you'll come to enjoy life's little *pleasures* in here."

Farhad Rajid leaned forward, only this time he spat, not on the floor, but in Joe Morrison's face. Morrison came to his feet slowly. He didn't call the guard. He simply took out a clean white handkerchief and carefully wiped Rajid's spit from his face. He walked around the table. Rubbing his knuckles, he balled his fist and laid the bastard out flat.

■

It was nearly four in the morning before the FBI Learjet touched down at the Lexington airport. Morrison had been in contact throughout the night with his office and the local police who met his plane and drove him to the Lawrence farm.

As they turned off the Lexington Highway onto the Midway Road, Joe recalled the last hours of the day that had just passed. It had been an unusually quiet afternoon at FBI headquarters in Washington. So much so that Joe had scheduled a few uninter- rupted hours at his desk to finish some long overdue reports. He absently grabbed his extension when it rang shortly after five o'clock.

It had taken several seconds for his jumbled mind to register what the hysterical woman on the other end of the line was saying. Right before Sydney's eyes, Ali Hassan had returned to reclaim his daughter. Collapsing to her knees on the gravel road, Sydney had waited for the bodyguard to shoot her. When he didn't and the car sped away, she was disappointed.

Forcing herself to her feet, she stumbled to the house and called for help. The local police were unfamiliar with her and with Lydia's situation. It made no sense to them that an Iranian child had been wrongly abducted by the man she knew to be her father. By the time they verified Sydney's story, it was too late. Ali Hassan and his party had disappeared.

■

Sydney had turned to the only man she trusted. But after checking in with the policeman stationed in front of Mack Lawrence's home, Joe Morrison feared that, in this situation, he was useless.

"How's the woman?" he asked the guard before being escorted into the living room.

"She's a mess," he replied, "and so are the others who have stayed with her since it happened."

"Who's here?" Morrison queried.

"Her father, an employee named Billy Ray Jones, and a neighbor, Kerry Donavan."

A flicker of surprise crossed Morrison's face as he heard the name of the man he knew only by reputation.

"They're expecting you. Go right in."

Entering the room slowly, Joe immediately sought Sydney as the others, not knowing him, stared with vacant eyes.

"Sydney," he said softly. "It's Joe."

Seated next to her father on the sofa, Sydney raised her swollen eyes to Morrison. She was still in shock and numb from exhaustion. But breathlessly she whispered, "Did you see him?"

Joe grabbed the nearest chair and drew it opposite Sydney,

not far from Billy Ray Jones. Only Kerry Donavan remained apart from the group, standing by himself in front of the fireplace. Joe took Sydney's hand in his own.

"I saw Rajid, but he wouldn't talk," he said. "Rajid knows where Hassan is, but nothing would make him betray his brother. We're on our own, honey, and it doesn't look good."

It was Mack who ventured to speak in a stronger voice than his illness allowed—this was his daughter whose life had been shattered. He struggled to help.

"The police have had hours. What have they done? Surely someone saw Hassan at the airport. Have all departing flights been checked?"

"Yes," Morrison replied. "No one traveled under the name Hassan, but that's what I expected. Being a wanted felon, the only way for the bastard to re-enter the country was with phony papers. I'm sure he arranged a passport for Lydia as well. By now they could be anywhere."

"We have to go after them!" Sydney cried as fear overtook exhaustion.

Glancing to the floor, Joe's gaze avoided hers. "Look at your father, sweetheart. How could you leave him?"

"You leave me out of this!" Mack countered angrily. "Finding Lydia is more important!"

Undeterred, Joe continued. "The journey to find Lydia could take months. Even then there's no guarantee we could snatch her. I'm not even sure we have the right to try."

A flush of color returning to her cheeks, Sydney cried, "What in the hell do you mean, Joe? I have every right to Lydia. She's my daughter."

"Listen to me, Sydney. It's imperative that you understand the situation. Yes, here in the States, Hassan renounced all claims to his daughter, and your adoption is perfectly legal. But in the Arab world, your decree is a worthless piece of paper. Even if you were Lydia's birth mother, you would have no rights. Under Islamic law, the father retains all claim and custody of his children. There's absolutely nothing you can do about that."

Tears welled in Sydney's eyes as she said, "What kind of a

father would abandon his child when she was critically ill? I'm the only mother Lydia has ever known! I have to find her!"

Even though he was not an educated man, the unfairness of the situation rankled Billy Ray.

"Surely between the FBI and the CIA, Hassan can be found. Then we just go in and get her."

"You've watched too many movies," Morrison countered, not unkindly. "What you need to understand is that with the current unrest in the Middle East, both the CIA and the FBI are stretched beyond their capabilities. In the scope of world affairs, the fate of one little girl is of low priority."

Mack tried to restrain Sydney as she exploded. "You're talking about my daughter, Joe! I don't give a damn about rights or foreign affairs. Hassan gave Lydia to me. We've formed a bond that no one can break. I'm her *mother* for God's sake! She's my daughter. . . ."

Sydney broke down sobbing.

Morrison leaned forward and took her hand, stroking it in his own awkward way.

"I know, honey, I know. But where in the world would we begin to look for Lydia? There are only two countries where Hassan can't hide. One is here in the States. The other, because of his history with the shah, is Iran. Beyond that, with his wealth and connections, he could go anywhere in the world. It's hopeless, Sydney, and I'm sorry. But the sooner you understand the score, the sooner you can put all this behind you. You've got to get on with your life."

"Life!" Sydney cried. "What kind of life will Lydia have if we don't go find her?" Sydney sprang forward and grabbed Joe by the arms. "Remember the little girl you watched from the upstairs window at Hassan's mansion? My God, all I can think about is the haunted look in her eyes and the sadness I felt around her. What kind of life did Lydia have then, Joe? What kind of life would she have now with an arms dealer who's a wanted criminal?"

Joe glanced away. He couldn't look Sydney in the eyes. He'd never forget the face of that lonely little girl, surrounded by body-guards, watching life pass her by. But reality was reality.

Sydney fell to her knees in front of Joe, forcing his gaze back to her.

"I've lost everything," she sobbed. "First Sam and now Lydia. You couldn't do anything to save my husband. But please, Joe, I'm begging you to help me find Lydia!"

Joe felt his heart constrict and for a moment he couldn't breathe. Gently, he helped Sydney back on the couch next to her father, and then he walked away. Mack held Sydney tightly as she wept.

Fingering a cigarette, Joe had an agonizing decision to make. The easiest thing—and perhaps the kindest in the long run—would be to leave and do nothing. Chances were Sydney would recover. Chances were they'd all be better off.

Lighting his cigarette, Morrison glanced first to Sydney and Mack and then to Billy Ray. Finally he directed his gaze to Kerry Donavan. But the man who remained silent, turned away. Facing the mantel, Kerry stared at a photograph of Sydney and Lydia.

Joe inhaled his smoke deeply, then turned his attention back to the others.

"There's an underworld of terrorists that's stronger than any Mafia connection we have here in the States," Morrison said. "Even though their motives are vastly different, terrorists trade arms and train together much like the Green Berets and Special Forces from allied nations around the world. The Red Brigade trains with the PLO, and the IRA with Libya's Qaddafi. In no way are their causes sympathetic, yet Hassan probably sells arms to them all."

Billy Ray's eyes widened, as did those of Mack Lawrence. Kerry's hands tightened around the photograph. Only Sydney didn't seem to comprehend what Morrison was getting at.

"To find Ali Hassan," he continued, "we'd need a man with powerful ties to that underworld."

Mack leaned forward, urging Sydney to listen.

"Are you saying you know such a person?" he asked.

"I might," Joe replied.

Sydney's voice was quaking with renewed hope when she said, "I'd pay him anything, Joe! Just tell me where to find him!"

"I don't know the man personally, Sydney. You can't buy him, though, that I do know. To help you locate a child who's not even yours, the man would jeopardize everything he holds dear—his business, his safety, even his life." Morrison's voice trailed to a near whisper. "If it were me, I'd tell you all to go to hell."

"Please, Joe," Sydney implored. "Tell me who he is and where to find him!"

Feeling a lump in his throat that made it difficult to speak, Morrison searched the room for an ashtray. No, he didn't know the man personally. Yet, by his very words, he could be calling for his execution.

In a voice rising with anger, Mack demanded, "Sydney asked you a question, Joe. She deserves an answer. Where can she find the man you describe?"

Dropping his butt in a stale cup of coffee, Morrison walked slowly to the fireplace. He put his arm around Kerry's stooped shoulders and whispered, "I know what I'm asking. It's up to you."

Joe watched Kerry's knuckles turn white as he gripped the photograph. Then nodding, Kerry lowered his head in helpless, hopeless resignation. Finally he turned around and faced the others. But it was to Sydney alone that Kerry looked.

His eyes were filled with anguish when he said, "I'm the man you're looking for, Sydney. I'm the one who can find Hassan."

Friday, April 24, 1992
8:45 p.m.

Luckily the evening flight from Atlanta to Shannon was not heavily booked, so the man and the woman had the first-class section of Delta 11 nearly to themselves. A senior cabin attendant studied the odd couple from the corner of the galley. The 747 had been airborne for over an hour, and yet the man and the woman had exchanged only a few terse words.

She was dressed in a pale pink cashmere sweater and charcoal gray wool slacks. He was clad more casually in starched jeans and a navy sports jacket. She appeared reserved. Her burnished copper hair was caught at the nape of her neck and fastened with a large satin bow. His chestnut hair was wavy and untamed.

They were a fine-looking couple and yet they seemed troubled, distant, remote. Lovers, the cabin attendant decided. Disillusioned lovers who have come to know each other too well. Drawing the curtain, the attendant turned and busied herself with more important matters. She couldn't possibly know how wrong she was. For the woman was Sydney Lawrence, and the man, Kerry Donavan. Far from lovers, what concerned each of them so deeply was how little they knew about the other. For the next few weeks, they would have to depend upon each other like they had never depended on another human being before.

Yet the only thing she knew for sure about the man was that he had a past. And the only aspect of the woman that he understood was her desperate plight.

Glancing out the tiny window into the cosmic sphere of nothingness, Sydney sat in pensive silence, as she had since take-off from Atlanta. She tried to reconstruct the events of the last three days since Lydia's abduction, but the details were a blur. How she had progressed from that point to here, she didn't know. Somehow, with Joe Morrison's help, their passports had been validated, money for the trip secured, and new pictures taken in case different identities were needed. All Sydney knew for sure was that they were on their way to Limerick, Ireland, where Kerry had the connections to locate Lydia's whereabouts. Beyond that, they had no game plan.

Sydney didn't care about the peril. Her husband was dead, her child lost. And her father—the only human being she had left who mattered—had been abandoned to die alone. Sighing deeply, she turned away from the window, only to confront the blue eyes of the man who read her mind.

"You're thinking about Mack, aren't you?"

A simple nod was answer enough.

"We've left him in good hands," said Donavan. "With Billy Ray staying at the house, Mack will never be left alone. And my house-keeper will report to them every day to tidy up and cook their meals. You've done all you can, Sydney. The rest is up to God."

"God?" she repeated. "What kind of a God would let this happen? My only hope is that my father will survive until I return." When she turned to Kerry again, there were tears in her eyes. "Do you think I'm doing the right thing?"

Kerry Donavan stared at his companion. "The right thing?" he repeated. For him, this futile venture could only result in disaster. For her, disappointment and heartache. The only right thing he'd done for sure was book Delta, an American airline, for the flight, rather than Aer Lingus, the Irish airline, where his chances of being recognized were greater. Beyond that, there wasn't a damned thing right about this trip.

It had been an agonizing decision for him to leave the safety of his farm in Kentucky to journey back to a homeland where so many despised him. But Sydney's plight broke his heart and, if the truth be known, cut to the core of his deep well of guilt. Had it not been for his own blind obsession with his mare, Sydney would not have left her daughter alone on Midway Road.

Lost in his own bleak world, Donavan failed to hear the cabin attendant. Tapping him on the shoulder, she repeated, "Sir, would you like a drink?"

In his slight Irish brogue, Donavan replied, "Coffee for me. Just black. No cream."

"And you, ma'am?"

"Wine, please. Chardonnay, if you have it."

Leaving Sydney to her glass of dry white wine, Donavan sipped his own tasteless brew in silence. This woman, the stranger by his side, knew nothing of the ugly ghosts that haunted him. Few people in America did. For years Donavan had kept to himself, becoming a recluse so no one could touch him or uncover his past. Yet before this jumbo jet touched down at the Shannon airport, Sydney Lawrence had to know and comprehend his terrible secrets.

Finally, taking a deep breath, he plunged in. "We must talk, Sydney. In less than seven hours we'll land in Ireland. It's imperative that you understand the danger we face."

Setting her drink aside, she turned to face Donavan. If the Irishman was finally willing to talk, she at least had to listen.

"To understand what I'm about to tell you, you must have a sense of my people, my family, and me. Ireland is a rich and beautiful country, but the people are poor. The Irish have always had to work twice as hard for half as much, particularly under British rule. And the English have traditionally despised us. They endeavored to crush our spirits, but they never captured our souls."

Kerry paused as his features softened with what Sydney guessed to be a bit of Gaelic pride.

"The majority of Irish have far more heart than possessions. Yet in the midst of poverty, a unity of purpose always prevails. And in the sameness of deprivation, one knows one's place. A man belongs."

Sydney nodded, encouraging him to continue.

"I was born into privilege, Sydney, which was a rarity in my country, in my day. I was different from the other lads I played with and so I never felt I truly belonged. My family was wealthier than most people in Ireland dare to dream of being. I felt guilty and ashamed because of it."

Turning back to his coffee for a moment, Kerry conjured up a clear image of his father, a recollection he'd not permitted himself in years.

"My father was a bit of a genius, turning his Irish charm and business sense into a sizable fortune. We owned land, lots and lots of land, around Limerick. We had a stable of prize racehorses and more than a dozen prospering businesses. We employed several hundred people in our day."

"Were you an only child, Kerry?"

His reply surprised her. "I grew up with a younger sister, but I'm no man's child now."

"I don't understand."

It was in a strange, husky voice in which Donavan replied. "I'm not proud of what I have to tell you, Sydney. Permit me to go about it in my own floundering way . . ."

■

The year was 1969, and Kerry Donavan was in his third year of studies at Trinity College in Dublin. A rich, spoiled lad, Donavan, at twenty, was not all that different from his Yankee blue-blood counterparts during the late sixties. He was restless and bored. He was idealistic and searching for a cause.

Ireland is a small country—three hundred miles in length and two hundred miles in width at its widest point—but a nation divided into two. The South, the Republic of Ireland, is free and completely under Irish rule. The North is still part of Britain's empire. And, unlike the South, which has a Catholic population of 98 percent, the North has a significant Protestant hold.

The troubles began, as they usually do, in the name of God and religion. The Protestants hated the Catholics and the feeling was returned in kind. Because of their religion, the Catholics were discriminated against and confined to ghettos, particularly in Belfast. As jobs were withheld and money became sparse, tempers flared. Then, in 1969, the riots broke out and the killings began. Soon the English troops were called in to maintain civil order.

Since its inception, the Irish Republican Army had been a corps of honor. A rare breed of resistance fighters, the IRA had battled against all foes proudly in the name of Irish freedom. But when it came to the torment of 1969 and the bloody riots in the Belfast ghettos, the IRA was powerless to protect the women and children who were slaughtered.

And so it was that the old guard was put aside, and a new generation, a new breed, arose. They called themselves the Provisionals. They were young, ruthless and strong. And to them, like magnets, blind, idealistic youths like Kerry Donavan were drawn.

It all began so innocently . . . a few political meetings here and there followed by endless hours of discussion in the smoky Republican pubs of Dublin where the Guinness flowed and the boys from the IRA hung out. Because Kerry Donavan was Catholic, he was angry. And because he was wealthy, while so many of his brethren in the North were poor, he felt guilty, and therefore became vulnerable.

He offered the use of his name and his contacts, and soon even his influence, to raise money for the Provisionals under the auspices of Catholic Relief. What began as the brash escapade of a foolish boy would haunt Kerry Donavan throughout his adulthood, for in the process of becoming a man, the bright, impetuous son of a wealthy capitalist became the power broker for the IRA and the financial wizard behind the terrorist cause.

■

"I thought the IRA was made up of lower-class men and women who have no education, little hope for employment, and basically nothing to lose. What could possibly have attracted you, Kerry?"

"I don't know that I can explain, Sydney. Knowing Mack as I do, I realize that you grew up with a real sense of purpose and belonging. Your father gave you everything you needed, but at the same time you were taught the importance of work and making your own way. You learned that a dream is all there is, and it's your responsibility in life to make that dream come true. In my family, the dream had already been fulfilled. There were no new paths to forge, no mountains to climb, no adversaries to conquer. My father prepared me only to be his caretaker, subjugated to his authority, preserving the empire he had created. Never did the bastard tell me I had the right to achieve something solely on my own."

■

And so the boy from Limerick began living a double life. At first it was rather simple. In 1969, and the early years to follow, there was great sympathy in the South for the Provisional IRA. It was reasonably easy to raise money for the cause. By going, at first, only to people he knew, Kerry raised money—a good deal of money. Delivering the sums himself, he soon became acquainted with the IRA leadership in Belfast, and they with him.

They were impressed, not just because of who he was, but because of what he was capable of doing. As contributions increased, so did Donavan's acceptance into the inner circle of the IRA. Impetuous though he was, he had no desire to bear arms and fight the battle himself. He soon discovered that the power of the Irish pound and the American dollar was greater than any M-16.

It became his obsession to raise the money to buy the arms the boys in the ghetto so desperately needed. Graduating with a business degree from Trinity, Kerry did the expected thing and returned to Limerick to assist his father in running the family business.

Jockeying himself into position, Kerry made sure it was he who traveled to the States on family business where support in certain cities for the IRA ran high. It was not difficult to make his contacts, to secure funds, and to arrange for the shipment of arms. All he needed was the know-how to negotiate the deals, leaving his own name out of print so nothing could be traced back to implicate the Donavan family.

Maintaining bank accounts in several cities under assumed names, Kerry raised hundreds of thousands of pounds for the brethren. And with every pound he raised, his influence, his power, grew stronger. By the end, the leadership of the IRA was made up of an army council run by three—Gerry Adams, Martin McGuinness and Danny Morrison—and a silent, perhaps equally powerful, fourth—Kerry Donavan.

■

"What happened, Kerry? What changed?"

"Two events occurred in the space of a couple of years that altered the course my life. I met a lovely girl named Patricia, and my father had a massive heart attack."

Patricia McCarthy was a rare mixture of Irish and German beauty. She was tall and slender, with flowing golden hair, emerald eyes, and pronounced cheekbones. She had full, luscious lips and a rather pouty smile. And the first time Kerry Donavan laid eyes on her, he knew to what purpose he'd been born.

Patricia had been raised in Bonn with her mother, but she returned to Ireland in the spring of 1978 to visit her father. She was little more than a child herself, but Kerry Donavan was determined to have her.

Their passion was the kind experienced only once in a lifetime, for it was all consuming, with no beginning and no end. From the moment their eyes connected they became one, and life without the other was unthinkable.

They married in December of that same year, when she was eighteen and he twenty-nine. The following October, a baby daughter was born. Kerry Donavan was happier than any man had a right to be.

Five months later, Seamus Donavan suffered a massive coronary that nearly killed him. Clinging to life, he turned over the keys of the empire to his son. And suddenly, in the space of a few moments, Kerry Donavan had it all—the empire, his father's approval, and a new purpose for being.

Kerry took to running the family dynasty as if he'd been born to the president's chair. He was bright, creative, ambitious, and to many a financial magician. Under his steady hand the family business soared to even greater heights. But always shrouding the young genius was a cloud that few people saw or understood.

As with any terrorist group, one could not just abandon the IRA at will. Kerry knew this, and so did the army council in Belfast. And while it was unthinkable for a man now of Donavan's position and stature to be a member of the Provisional IRA, so it was unthinkable for him to betray his cause.

Sentiment for the Provisionals had long since soured in the South. Because of their brutal tactics and senseless bloodshed, no longer was the IRA a name spoken with reverence, but rather with disdain and true Gaelic scorn.

Kerry Donavan, as an angry boy, had spun a web of intrigue, a web from which he could not escape. Meeting in secret with the big three—Adams, McGuinness and Morrison—a bargain was struck. In exchange for a steady stream of funds, Donavan's identity would be protected, and to some degree his wishes respected. Donavan urged the council to use the funds not to buy arms, but rather to gain political influence. As a man now on the brink of middle age, Kerry realized that more could be achieved through diplomacy than through violence.

Kerry kept up his part of the bargain, secretly funneling thousands of dollars into the IRA cause, but terrorists are not honorable men. Like a whitewashed member of the mob, Kerry Donavan led his secret double life, forging blithely along on the golden road he had created, not realizing he was walking on land mines.

■

"May I serve your dinner now?" the cabin attendant inquired.

Not wanting to be diverted even for a few minutes, Sydney quickly replied, "No. We'll let you know when we're ready."

"But ma'am, we'll be landing in Shannon before you know it. Isn't there something I can get you?"

Sydney raised her eyes to the hovering attendant. The piercing directness of her gaze was enough to cause the woman to leave, this time for good.

Finally, after a short silence, she asked, "Kerry, what happened to your wife and daughter?"

■

Kerry Donavan's family had a tradition they'd established since baby Kate's birth. Every year in December they journeyed to London to shop. This Christmas was to be no different. And so, after three wonderful nights in London, they went to Harrods to complete their shopping.

The date was December 16, 1981. While Patricia took baby Kate to sit upon Santa's knee, the indulgent daddy lost himself in the toy department, buying everything in sight for the daughter he revered.

Meanwhile, an IRA team drove two cars packed with explosives to Knightsbridge in London and parked them behind Harrods. The street was filled with shoppers like the Donavans buying Christmas gifts. One half-hour before the bomb was to explode, a member of the IRA phoned in a warning, but it was hopelessly late. It was Christmas, after all, and Harrods was packed with happy, enthusiastic shoppers.

The police tried desperately to evacuate the store in an orderly fashion. But shepherded like a pack of wild animals, panicked people lost all sense of reason. Kerry searched frantically for his wife and daughter, but when the explosion rocked Harrods, he was hurled to the floor unconscious with his leg shattered. It was days before he regained consciousness. Upon wakening, the one question on his mind was the one no one wanted to answer.

Eight people had been killed in the bomb blast that nearly destroyed the famous London store. Among them was an Irish woman and her baby daughter. Patricia Donavan and Kate.

■

Sydney sat in stunned silence. Suffering. She thought she alone had defined the word, but watching the silent stream of tears etching their way down the Irishman's cheeks, she understood the meaning of shared pain.

"Oh God," she whispered. "I'm so sorry."

It was several minutes before Kerry Donavan found a voice with which to speak. Then finally he said, "I lost everything in that moment. Patricia, Kate, even the will to live. What hurt the most was the knowledge that I had killed them."

Kerry turned to Sydney, his face contorted with rage.

"Don't you see the divine irony? It was the money I raised that bought the explosives! I supplied the bomb that killed my own baby!"

"No, Kerry, no!" Sydney argued. "It wasn't your fault!" But even as she spoke the words, they both knew it was a lie. Anyone who had participated in the travesty was as guilty as the one who actually detonated the bomb.

"What did you do?" she stammered.

"When I left the hospital I returned home. I confronted my father and told him the truth. I cut off all supply to the IRA and exposed my sources. In short, I bared my soul."

"What happened?"

"I was ruined. My father disowned me, but before his will could be amended, he had another heart attack and he died. My sister, Barbara, and I inherited everything, but I had to leave Ireland. Once I revealed the truth and cut off the supply of money to the IRA, I was labeled a 'tout,' an informant. Do you know what that means? It means there's a price on my head for any man who blows it off!"

"Where did you go?" Sydney asked quietly.

"I wandered around Europe for a few years, then finally I settled in the States. I traded a bit of information with the FBI for a small measure of protection. I bought Shadow Lane Farm and you know the rest. Don't you see, Sydney? I have no family, not even a heritage. My farm and my horses are all I have left."

Sydney toyed with the hem of her sweater, avoiding for the moment Kerry's eyes. He had revealed so much of himself in such a short time, so much that the dynamics between them had changed. But there was something . . . something so crucial . . . that had not been said.

"You've been through so much, Kerry. Now finally you've made a decent life for yourself in Kentucky, far away from the awful past. Why . . . why now . . . would you jeopardize everything to help me?"

Reaching over, he gently covered her hand with his own.

"I feel responsible for Lydia's abduction. Had it not been for my obsession with Dare to Dream, you would not have been put in the position of having to help me, and Lydia would not have been left alone."

Instinctively, Sydney started to argue, but Kerry silenced her.

"I let my wife and daughter down, Sydney. In helping you and Lydia, maybe in some small way I can make amends for them."

The sharp descent of the aircraft, followed by the muffled voice on the intercom startled them.

"Please see that your seatbelts are fastened and your tray tables secured in their upright and locked positions. We'll be landing at the Shannon airport momentarily."

Both Kerry and Sydney turned their attention to the side window and the breaking of dawn in Ireland. Then Kerry said quietly, "Welcome to the land that despises me."

Susan M. Hoskins

Shannon, Ireland
Saturday, April 25, 1992
8:45 a.m.

Sydney tried to get up, but her knees buckled and she was forced for the moment to resume her seat. Was it weariness from the long flight, or Kerry's revelation that caused her legs to wobble? No, she decided, it was a pervading sense of doom that engulfed her. She realized that her blind obsession to reclaim what was hers could lead to this man's execution. *And what had he done to deserve that?*

Reaching into the overhead compartment above their seats, Kerry retrieved their two bags. Since they had no idea where they were going, or how long their journey would last, Donavan insisted that they travel light. Whatever was required for their trip could be purchased as needed. Mobility and speed were far more important than luggage.

At the moment the only thing he knew for sure was that they would remain in Ireland no more than a few days . . . just long enough to obtain the information they needed. At any time they might be forced to abandon their search and flee.

"Sit a moment and collect yourself," he said, seeing the ashen color of Sydney's face. "There's no need to rush. We'll let some of the others out first."

And so they did. Blending into the throng, they exited the plane and followed the scores of travelers down the corridor to the top of the stairs.

"Mind the steps," he warned, as they started down the steep flight of stairs. Kerry grimaced as his stiff left leg began to throb.

"Are you all right?" Sydney asked.

"It's the remnants of the blast, I'm afraid. My leg was shattered pretty badly. It pains me when I sit too long. I'll be all right soon."

At the bottom they halted as the crowd waited for the immigration process to begin. Kerry edged closer to Sydney. Taking her by the elbow, he drew her to him and whispered, "Steady yourself, girl, and be calm. Remember, we're on a pleasure trip when you're asked. Relax and try to smile."

Sydney struggled to calm her nerves, but it was deathly hot in the narrow passageway crammed with several hundred people inching their way toward the two booths. Kerry veered her sharply into the left line. There was something about the officer on the right that disturbed him, a sense that he somehow knew him.

The process was painfully slow, as one by one people had their passports stamped and their reasons for traveling checked.

Nearing their turn, Kerry reminded her of the plan.

"You go first. I'll be right behind."

It was not that Kerry Donavan was entering his homeland illegally, but he didn't want to alert the wrong people that he was here. When her turn came, Donavan nudged Sydney forward. Seeing the pretty woman with the hazel eyes standing before him, the immigration officer smiled. Sydney glanced to the man's name tag. It read Daugherty.

"Good morning, ma'am. Your passport, please."

Quickly she complied.

"Now your immigration card." Obeying, Sydney thrust the white card before him. "Is this your first trip to Ireland?"

"Yes," she replied levelly, "it is."

"Are you here for business or for pleasure?"

"Pleasure," she stated firmly.

"All right then," Mr. Daugherty said, smiling. "Pass on through. Have a nice stay."

Sydney measured her steps carefully. Pausing, she turned slowly to face Kerry. The seconds that followed were agonizing.

Donavan stepped forward. He was traveling under his own name and had a valid American passport. With a steady hand he slid his papers under the glass booth.

The immigration officer glanced first at the name and then at the picture. Only then did he slowly lift his gaze to confront the man he knew by name and reputation. His entire demeanor changed and his voice was tinged with scorn when he demanded, "Why are you here?"

Kerry's reply was direct and unruffled. "Pleasure."

Grunting, the immigration officer scrutinized Donavan's papers. Then, laying them aside, he selected another sheet filled with the names of those permanently barred from the country. The name of Kerry Donavan was not to be found, since his citizenship had never been revoked.

"How long do you plan to remain in Ireland, Mr. Donavan?"

"No more than a few days," he answered.

He paused and, eyeing Donavan directly, asked, "And where will you be staying?"

Kerry answered, "The Limerick Inn."

The immigration officer with the name tag Daugherty leaned forward. In a lowered voice he said, "If I were you I'd mind me back. Now get the hell out of my sight!"

Calmly, Kerry collected his papers and passed through the archway. But his cheeks were flushed as he grabbed Sydney by the arm and urged her forward. He didn't tell her that he'd been recognized. He didn't tell her that, knowing he was being set up, he had lied about where they'd be staying. He didn't tell her that the word was being passed; but deep in his gut, he knew that by the time they left the terminal, his enemies would already know he'd returned home.

■

With just their carry-ons to contend with, it was not necessary to delay a minute longer. Elbowing their way through the swell of people, they made their way toward customs. With his eyes averted, Donavan relinquished the lead to Sydney.

A middle-aged man in a primly pressed uniform hailed them. "Good morning. Do you have anything to declare?"

Responding as equally pleasant, Sydney replied, "No, sir, not a thing."

Seeing the growing crowd behind them, the man tipped his hat and waved them on. Having traveled enough to know the difference, Sydney was amazed at how easy the process had been. Kerry supplied the reason.

"We're used to Americans here. Most of the time they sneak into the country with a few extra cigarettes, that's all."

They rounded the corner and entered the terminal. For a moment all eyes were fixed upon them as an excited group of people surged forward to greet those they yearned to see. Through it all Kerry remained mute, refusing to glance up. On the outside he remained cool and aloof, but inside his guts were churning. More than anything, he was sad that, after nearly a decade away, no one was there to welcome him home. But time had not tempered the Irish loathing for a man who, with the best of intentions, had brought shame on himself and his family.

He steered Sydney to a quiet, darkened corner of the airport. His voice was a bit huskier than usual. "We need to take care of business as quickly as possible. Do you see the row of booths at the far end of the lobby?"

Sydney nodded.

"I want you to proceed to the car-rental stand at the end of the row on the right side. You'll see the name O'Shea Motor Hire. Present yourself to a man named Tony O'Shea. I went to school with him. He's a rogue of a fellow but a great guy. You'll recognize him immediately. He loves women. When he sees you, he'll be the one grinning ear to ear."

"Okay."

"Can you drive a stick shift?"

"It's been awhile," Sydney replied.

"Well then, ask for an automatic. Believe me, you'll have enough to contend with without that. But tell O'Shea you want a good deal. He's as fond of the Irish pound as anyone. Remind him that this is not the height of tourist season. Tell him you'll pay a hundred and fifty pounds for the week, no more."

The look on Sydney's face amused him.

"Car rental is very expensive in Ireland. There are a couple more things. First, charge the car to your American Express. That way we'll have full insurance. If he asks what you do, tell him you're from Kentucky and you raise horses. The Irish won't rent cars to writers or others with strange or creative careers. I guess they fear they'll be distracted on the road."

"Where will I meet you?"

"While you're making arrangements, I'll go to the bank and change our money into Irish pounds. Tony will bring the car around and get you started. Don't engage him in too much conversation and don't let on you're waiting for someone else. Just pull the car around to the front in the spot saved for departing passengers. And remember . . . for godsake . . . stay on the left!"

Trying to keep her instructions straight, Sydney hoisted her carry-on bag over her shoulder and marched ahead. As she approached the row of car-rental booths, she felt the stare of eager, curious eyes upon her. Blushing slightly, she sought the small booth labeled O'Shea Motor Hire and the handsome man named Tony O'Shea.

Susan M. Hoskins

"Jesus Christ!" Kerry roared. "Watch the road! The left . . . stay on the left!"

"I can't do this!" Sydney cried. "You have to drive!"

Finally, after seeing the self-assured, confident woman lose all sense of reason, Kerry, rather than screaming, burst out laughing.

"You think it's so damned easy!" Sydney shouted. "Everything about this car is reversed . . . the lights . . . the heater . . . and where the hell are the wipers? My God, does it always mist like this?"

"Pull over, Sydney. Just pull over! No . . . not so sharp! *Ease* the car to the side of the road."

Screeching to a halt, Sydney threw the automatic into park and angrily shut off the engine.

"My God, why can't you people drive a car like everyone else . . ." Sydney realized the utter stupidity of her own words and, despite her rage, she too burst out laughing. "This is ridiculous!"

Donavan resumed his instructions in a gentler voice. "Driving in Ireland is really quite logical if you just remember to keep the steering wheel aligned with the center markings. That's all you have to do for now. I'll explain the rest as we go."

"I can't . . . I just can't do it!"

"Look," Donavan countered rationally, "I've been told by other Americans that the first ten minutes out of the airport are the most frightening. Now get a hold of yourself and . . . ease . . . back out onto the highway. No, Sydney! The signal's on the other side!"

Falling back in his seat, Donavan struggled to remain calm. Rattling the woman beside him would only serve to get them both killed. Glancing at her sideways, he shook his head. Deep down he had to admit she was a remarkable woman. But she was a disaster behind the wheel.

"There, that's better," he soothed. "Like it or not, you've got to know how to navigate while we're here. What if I'm not with you and there's an emergency? We're only fifteen minutes from Limerick, so keep going. I'll say my prayers while you hang on."

"Why is that idiot honking, Kerry? I'm doing what you told me! I'm staying by the center line!"

"Move over to the shoulder of the road, Sydney. He's trying to overtake you, that's all. There, that's it. Let the others whiz by. We've got all day."

Sydney steeled herself to accomplish the seemingly impossible. "It can't be that difficult," she reminded herself. "Stay on the left . . . just stay on the left."

The next few miles flew by with no further incident. Slowly the palms of her hands stopped sweating as Sydney relaxed her death grip on the wheel.

Halfway to Limerick, Kerry Donavan grew solemn. "Slow down," he ordered suddenly. "See the place up ahead packed with cars? Turn in there but don't get too close. Stay well out of sight."

Sydney did as she was told.

"What's Setright's Cross?" she asked, seeing the sign above the door.

The preoccupied man beside her did not respond. "Drive around to the back!" he commanded.

Sydney guided the car to the rear of the pub while Kerry studied the license plates of the other vehicles.

"What are all the cars doing here?"

"Okay," Donavan directed. "Let's go."

"I asked you what this is all about. Why won't you give me a straight answer?"

"This is a local IRA hangout," Kerry sniped. "I want to see who is still around. Now let's get the hell out of here!"

Sydney waited for Donavan to cool down; then she asked, "So what could you tell from the cars?"

"Most of the same boys are here as when I left. Oh, I saw a few new license plates, and some old ones missing. But basically the same bullshit continues day after day, year after year. I'm sorry I snapped at you. But seeing Setright's Cross brought back a lot of bad memories. It's a part of my life I wanted to forget. Now I'm here and I can't."

The Irishman and the American continued on in silence. Finally, Donavan broke the spell.

"Things change so quickly. There's a new roundabout at Kurn. When I last saw the place it was a secondary road—practically bog and dirt. We'll be coming into Limerick shortly. Perhaps I'd better drive. I've been away so long, I have no idea what to expect."

Sydney pulled to the side of the road and gratefully relinquished the wheel. As he tore off down the highway, she allowed herself the pleasure of a roaming eye. What she saw was breathtaking.

In children's books she had read, Ireland was painted as a land of mystical fantasy, with gnomes and leprechauns abounding, and green—everything was supposed to be green. But the storybooks had painted only a partial picture. Everything here was indeed green, from the sloping hills to the trees and grass. Yet the color was far from a mundane shade of murky moss. No, the countryside here was a mixture of brilliant hues of varying degrees of emerald and jade. And rather than fanciful characters dotting the hillsides, there were scores of cattle and sheep grazing as they had for generations.

Entering the city limits of Limerick, Sydney immediately sensed a different pulse. The small narrow roads were teeming with older, more compact versions of the Toyota they had rented. Passing a Catholic school, she saw a playground filled with uniformed children scampering about while women, bundled in heavy coats and scarves, braved the cold misty rain on foot, presumably to go to market.

A man on a bicycle caught Sydney's fancy. He was elderly, how old it was hard to tell. There he was, perhaps seventy or eighty years old, pedaling across the bridge for all he was worth. He passed a woman he seemed to know. Not skipping a beat, he tipped his hat as he veered sharply around her, then proceeded on his merry way.

Two young women with prams also were crossing the bridge, with three other toddlers scampering beside them. And the children were magnificent with their carrot-colored curly hair, freckly faces, rosy red cheeks, and adorable flashing smiles. Suddenly Sydney felt a terrible ache in her own heart for the child that was missing and for the children she'd never have with Sam.

Turning away, she could watch the brilliant scene no longer. Only then did she become aware that Kerry had been speaking.

"My God, Sydney, how things have changed during my absence. Look at that sign. 'New traffic system.' Now what in the hell do they mean by that?"

Kerry's babbling continued. The sequence of his thoughts made no sense.

"Now, about the roundabout. You must be careful when approaching roundabouts, and believe me they are everywhere. The arrows will indicate what turn to take, but you have to be mindful that anyone already in the circle has the right of way and you must yield."

It took a moment for Sydney's mind to register the frantic, scattered quality to Kerry's speech. Her eyes fixed upon him, she knew instinctively something was wrong.

"Good Lord in heaven, will you just look at that park! And that huge building! Why, I think it's the Irish equivalent of a shopping mall. See, Sydney, it says Arthur's Quay. Why, it's as nice as anything I've seen in Lexington."

Cautiously, with a great deal of trepidation, Sydney's hand fell to her side, then slowly inched its way toward Kerry. But her touch stopped short of his, for she had no idea what was wrong, and even less idea what to say.

"What I love about Limerick is the spattering of new against the backdrop of the old. We live in a throwaway society in the States. We want to build a bigger monstrosity, so we raze the old to make way for the new. Here we cherish the past and we hold on to it . . ."

Like a wisp of wind, Sydney breathed his name, but Kerry Donavan was too engrossed in his own jabber to hear. Finally, at the traffic light, he paused and turned to face her. His eyes were glassy, his angular jaw set tight. It was then that she realized what was wrong. The anguish of being exiled and the dread of returning home consumed him. Life in Limerick had flourished quite nicely during his absence. He was back now, if only for a short time, but there was no place for him here. His name was Kerry Donavan and his heritage was Irish, yet he was, and always would be, a despicable stranger in a foreign land.

Reaching out, she simply laid her hand atop his leg and whispered, "It's okay, Kerry. It's okay."

The blare of horns behind him forced Donavan's attention back to the road. His brow drenched in sweat, Kerry realized that he was succumbing to his own frazzled emotions. Steeling himself, he curved around behind the new development and briefly onto the Dublin Road. He signaled a right-hand turn and continued straight ahead a short block until he reached Ellen Street. Seeing a car-park just ahead, he pulled in and, retrieving a ticket, took the first available space. Only then did he shut off the engine. Burying his head on the wheel, he collected himself while Sydney waited for him to recover.

Finally he turned to her and, in a calm voice, gave her the instructions she needed.

"The shop is straight ahead on the left. Go in and ask for Mary Margaret O'Sullivan. If there are people milling about, simply make conversation. Pretend you're interested in antique jewelry. You know what to do after that."

Sydney nodded, then stepped out and proceeded down Ellen Street to the first main shop on the left, the shop called The Attic.

It was nearly eleven o'clock on a Saturday morning, and the shop was quiet. Sydney took a moment to get her bearings. The tiny shop was much to her liking, with an assortment of fine antique jewelry in the cases, and other knickknacks adorning the walls. Two women were seated side by side at the desk, pouring over a set of books. The frail woman on the right glanced up and said, "Good morning, madam. Is there something I can show you?"

Sydney smiled and, trying to remain calm, said, "I'm looking for Mary Margaret O'Sullivan." It was then that the woman on the left looked up. Grinning mischievously she quipped, "Well, right or wrong, I guess you've found her. What can I do for you?"

The warmth of the woman amused Sydney, yet Mary Margaret's keen eyes sized Sydney up in a heartbeat. Such bold scrutiny disquieted the American. With difficulty, she found her voice. "Miss O'Sullivan, my name is Sydney Lawrence and I bring greetings from a friend in the States."

"Oh," the woman replied, "and who might that be?"

Sydney studied the woman a moment before answering. She was a short, stout, impeccably dressed lady on the downward side of fifty. She had silver-streaked hair, a more than ample bosom and intelligent navy blue eyes.

Sydney leaned toward the desk. "The horseman from Kentucky sends his regards."

The woman's hands instinctively flew toward her breasts. "You know him?"

"Yes," Sydney replied, "I do."

Realizing that they were not alone, Mary Margaret O'Sullivan composed herself quickly. "Would you join me for coffee across the way?"

"Yes," Sydney answered without a moment's hesitation.

Nearly bolting from her chair, O'Sullivan grabbed her handbag and hurried out.

"Take over, Dorothy. I'll be back in time for your lunch."

Once outside, Mary Margaret drew Sydney closer and whispered, "Is he well?"

"For the most part," Sydney replied. "And he's here."

"Oh, dear God," O'Sullivan stammered. "How could he be so foolish? Doesn't he realize the danger?"

Sydney laid her hand gently atop the older woman's trembling arm.

"You're the only person in Limerick whom Kerry completely trusts. Please, Miss O'Sullivan, we have to talk."

Mary Margaret O'Sullivan took a deep breath and drew herself to full stature, which at best was a modest sixty-four inches. Taking the taller, younger lady decidedly by the arm, the pleasantly plump woman marched purposefully across the street toward the popular Irish pub known as the Lucky Lady.

"Where's Kerry now?" the woman demanded.

"He told me to secure a quiet spot in a corner, out of the way. He said to order drinks and that he'd join us as soon as the coast was clear."

A frown wrinkled Mary Margaret's brow.

"Is he drinking again?" she asked sternly.

"Well . . . no . . . I don't think so," Sydney replied, for she knew so little about Kerry's habits that she had no idea if he indulged or not.

"After his wife and baby were killed, Kerry hit the bottle pretty heavy. Booze and grief nearly destroyed him. Last I heard, he'd given up spirits for good."

At the entrance to the Lucky Lady, O'Sullivan paused.

"You look like you could use a good stiff shot yourself, and Lord knows, I could as well. I'll order gin and tonics for us and brewed coffee for him. You hold the table over there in the dark corner."

And before Sydney could argue, Mary Margaret left her standing in the middle of the spacious pub while she marched to the bar. Luckily, the establishment was rather quiet, as the lunch crowd had not yet arrived. Only a few people were scattered about. Selecting a booth in the small private room to the right, Sydney took the chair facing the door, leaving room for Kerry and Mary Margaret O'Sullivan.

Taking a minute to collect herself, Sydney glanced around the warm, inviting pub. Nearly four hundred years old, the former whiskey warehouse had huge, wide-planked, wooden floors and antiques stuffed in every crevice. In the center of the larger room was a roaring fire with huge, elevated round tables and whiskey barrels for stools. Here, where patrons would sit in the cozy nook off the beaten path, more business was conducted in the small booths than in any office building downtown. In a matter of minutes, Mary Margaret returned with two glasses filled with gin, ice and lemon, two bottles of tonic, and a steaming cup of brewed coffee.

Pouring the tonic over ice, she handed the gin to Sydney. Toasting the American's glass with her own, she hailed, "Cheers, and welcome to Ireland." Collapsing in her chair, Sullie, as she was known to her friends, raised the glass to her lips and swallowed a good, healthy swig of gin. Only then did she see the look of sadness clouding Sydney's features.

"Now what in the hell is this all about?" Sullie asked.

Following Mary Margaret O'Sullivan's lead, Sydney raised her own glass, and although it was much too early in the day to indulge, she gratefully allowed the strong liquor to warm her.

"It's a long story, Miss O'Sullivan."

Throwing up her hands in disgust, the vivacious antique jewelry dealer stopped her. "Not another word, Sydney, until you promise to call me Mary Margaret or Sullie like the rest of the blokes around here do. The term 'Miss O'Sullivan' makes me feel old, and today, after this, I already feel like both me feet are fallin' in the grave. Now forgive me, Sydney, and get on with your tale."

"My husband was killed in February . . . *Sullie*. I moved back to Kentucky to be with my father, Mack. He's dying of cancer. Kerry owns the horse farm next-door to ours."

Sydney was struggling to remain calm and rational. She took a deep breath, then continued. "I adopted a child named Lydia after her father fled the United States as a wanted felon. He's an Iranian arms dealer named Ali Hassan. Lydia's birth mother is dead." Sydney's eyes brimmed with tears as she said, "I'm the only mother Lydia has ever known."

Sydney had to pause. Tears spilled down her cheeks.

"Hassan abducted Lydia on Tuesday. They could be anywhere in the world by now."

Sydney took a deep breath and collected herself. "Kerry has the contacts to find them."

Mary Margaret eyed Sydney up and down. "Are you involved with Kerry?"

"Good God, no!" she cried, nearly spitting out her drink.

Mary Margaret O'Sullivan set her gin and tonic upon the table. She had not yet made up her mind about the pale, thin, American woman. There was a certain fervor in Sydney's voice when she spoke about Kerry Donavan. And whether she came to loathe him or to love him, it would be with a heart filled with passion.

"Kerry Donavan is a good man," said Sullie. "He made some tragic mistakes. But don't we all?"

"How well do you know Kerry?" Sydney asked.

"I've known Kerry from the time he was a wee brat. I knew Patricia as well, and I was godmother to baby Kate. To tell you the truth, Sydney, I love Kerry and his sister, Barbara, like they were the children I never had. And God knows, sometimes . . . I wish I didn't."

Sydney's glance traveled beyond Mary Margaret as a familiar presence entered the pub. With her back to him, Sullie did not see or hear him approach. Laying his hands softly atop her shoulders, Donavan bent down and whispered, "You're the most beautiful sight in all of Ireland, Mary Margaret O'Sullivan."

Tears came to Sullie's eyes as she reached up and gently stroked the man's calloused hands. Kissing her cheek quickly, Kerry released his grip and seated himself by her side.

"Who's here?" he asked abruptly.

"No one to be bothered about," Mary Margaret replied. "You're very bold to come back to Limerick like this. Why didn't you warn me?"

"If I'd warned you, I wouldn't have had the fun of this surprise."

Reaching across the table, Donavan grabbed his cup of coffee. Bringing the hot, steaming brew to his lips, he turned to his friend of many years.

"You're a good girl, Sullie, to remember how much I loathe the bloody instant stuff. Now tell me, is the booty for my head still as high as when I left?"

Mary Margaret eyed Kerry unhappily. "Some things never change, genius."

Donavan broached another subject. "Tell me about Barbara. Is my sister all right?"

O'Sullivan thoughtfully sipped her gin before responding. "She's in reasonably good form, Kerry. Have you written her lately?"

"You know I'm too Irish for that, Sullie. If I can't say something face to face, then it isn't worth saying. Besides, her worthless husband doesn't make it easy."

"Now you bite your tongue, Kerry Donavan. For whatever else Liam is, he's been good to your sister. The scandal with you and the death of her father nearly destroyed the poor girl. He's provided her a safe haven."

"And helped himself to her money in return!"

Feeling like an intruder in their past, Sydney chose to direct her attention elsewhere, leaving the two friends to thrash out their disagreement.

Gazing about the pub, she noticed a man enter the Lucky Lady with a twill cap perched precariously atop his head and a copy of the *Irish Times* tucked neatly under his leather jacket. She wasn't sure why he caught her notice except that he had a bright rosy complexion and a broad Irish grin.

Pausing in the doorway, his gaze darted about the pub. Casually, the man glanced to the darkened corner of the private room where Donavan, Lawrence and O'Sullivan were sitting. First he noticed Sydney and he grinned lustily. Then he recognized the familiar outline of the antique jewelry dealer and he nodded. Only then did his eyes roam to the left. A strange look crossed his features as his gaze came to rest upon the rounded back of Kerry Donavan.

Throwing his glance back to Sydney, he tipped his cap and took a seat, calling out loudly for someone named Sean. For an instant, Sydney was gripped by terror. When Sean approached, the man ordered a sandwich and a pint of Guinness, then settled back, donned his glasses, and unfurled his paper. His attention remained fixed upon the written word. Finally satisfied, Sydney turned away from the fellow at the bar. She was weary, bone weary, from the flight. The man had not known Kerry. She was imagining things, that's all.

"What's wrong, Sydney?"

The sound of Kerry's voice startled her.

"It's nothing, just jet lag."

"Whatever are we thinking, Kerry? The poor girl must be exhausted."

Mary Margaret's eyes, softer now, saw beyond Sydney's pretty face to the pained human heart within. She'd seen the same depth of despair only once before . . . and that was in the eyes of the man she loved so dearly . . . the one who sat beside her now. Remembering Kerry's pain, she decided to do whatever she could to help Sydney.

"All right, Kerry, what do you want from me?"

"I need two things, Sullie. First, can you locate Paddy McDowell?"

Shamelessly, Mary Margaret wrinkled her nose in disgust.

"Yeah, sure," she said. "The weasel hangs out on O'Connell Street. What do you want with him?"

Kerry glanced at Sydney, then said, "He's the only one of the old gang I trust."

"Done," Sullie acknowledged. "What else?"

"Would you call Barbara? See if Liam is out of town. If so, I'd like to see her."

Mary Margaret O'Sullivan grabbed her handbag, pushed back her chair, and stood.

"Gin and tonic, Sydney?" she asked.

"No. No thank you, Sullie. Another one of these and I'll be under the table."

"Okay then," Mary Margaret said. "I'll be right back."

In a matter of minutes, she returned. Throwing her handbag upon the table, she clapped Kerry on the back and said, "It's done. Liam's out of town for the next few days, and Barbara wants to see you. Paddy McDowell will meet you there this afternoon, at five o'clock."

Squeezing her plump, fleshy arm, Donavan whispered, "Good girl, Sullie." He motioned for Sydney to stand. "Let's go. We both need some sleep."

Before departing, Sydney reached across the table and clasped Mary Margaret's sturdy hands. "Thank you, Mary Margaret."

Having come to the conclusion that Sydney was genuine, and a woman perhaps worthy of her Kerry's notice, Sullie smiled sincerely. "You're welcome, Sydney. God bless."

Mary Margaret exited the Lucky Lady first, followed next by Kerry Donavan, his head lowered, his eyes averted. It was Sydney Lawrence who brought up the rear. At the door to the pub, Sydney came to an abrupt, tingling halt as a cold chill inched its way up her spine. Turning toward the bar, she confronted the man with the twill cap.

His paper set aside, his cold eyes never wavered. Cocking his brow, he returned Sydney's glance and Sydney knew Kerry Donavan had been recognized. What she didn't know—what she couldn't know—was who the man was. Once upon a time, Kerry Donavan had had a pal named Eddy. Now, he had an enemy. A ruthless adversary by the name of Ed Maloney.

The man perched atop the stool watched the woman leave,
then turned his attention briefly to his pint of Guinness. Draining
the last bit of foam, he dug in his pocket for a couple of Irish
pounds and threw them on the bar. It was unthinkable that he
would dally at the Lucky Lady merely to pass time with his
cronies. He had a mission now.

Eddy Maloney was not an extraordinary man, and that fact
alone had plagued him all of his life. The fourth of five sons, he
had been outstanding in neither academics nor sports. He was a
disappointment to his father, except for the one area alone that
bound them together. For generations the Maloney family had
staunchly supported the ideals that founded the Irish Republican
Army. It was with honor that his grandfather bore arms during the
uprising of 1916, which ultimately won the Republic of Ireland
its freedom from Britain. His father, likewise, supported the
cause, as had his sons who followed. It was not the firstborn, but
the fourth who most ardently devoted himself to the cause.

Ed Maloney had grown up poor like most of his contem-
poraries. His father owned a small farm just down the road from
the Donavan estate. Throughout school, Kerry and he had been
the best of buddies, yet as they grew to manhood, a thick cord of
jealousy strangled their friendship. Kerry Donavan had it all—
wealth, acclaim, success—while Eddy Maloney struggled to
survive. Even with the cause they secretly shared, it was Kerry

Donavan's name that was whispered with reverence in the inner circles, never Ed Maloney's.

Exiting the Lucky Lady, the short, stocky fellow paused and, glancing to the sun peeking through the clouds, inhaled the brisk air. It had been a brutal winter in Limerick, but finally it seemed as if spring had come.

No, Ed Maloney had never been known for his stunning good looks. He had drab brown hair and undistinguished features. He had the ruddy complexion and paunch of a man who overindulged in brew, and he had pinched murky eyes that never trusted and rarely danced.

Yet glancing down the street to the Toyota pulling out of the lot, Ed Maloney smiled like a man who'd been born with it all. He donned his twill cap and reverently bowed his head. Today, on this one ordinary day, nestled in the calendar of so many others, he'd finally been blessed by fate. By simply being at the right place at the right time, the fourth of five Maloney sons had been chosen to settle the score. He made the sign of the cross and humbly thanked God for the sacred mission to which he'd now been entrusted.

Oblivious to the eyes that were watching them, Kerry drove off in gloomy silence. It was Sydney who ultimately tried to break the spell.

"I like Mary Margaret. I see why you trust her so."

It was with a weak nod that Donavan agreed. "Mary Margaret O'Sullivan is the finest woman I know on either side of the Atlantic. She has a heart as big as Ireland itself, and if she were destitute, she'd give away the last blouse she owned. I consider her the best friend I have. I don't mind risking my life, but I hate putting hers in jeopardy."

Succumbing to his bleak mood, Sydney pondered his words. Because of her, they were all in danger. No matter how much she loved Lydia, she had to ask herself if it was worth it. But it was her daughter's life . . .

Negotiating the roundabouts, they soon came to a popular pub on the right.

"Mark this place, Sydney. The pub's called Finnigans. If you happen to be driving, our turn is next."

Making his way to the center of the busy highway, Kerry veered off sharply to the right and then around to a curving winding road.

"Be mindful of traffic here. The roads are narrow."

Passing a fairly new housing development on the left, they wheeled sharply right as the landscape changed before their eyes. The rows of tiny brick houses gave way to acres upon acres of green fertile land. And the estates—separated by huge stone walls instead of white wooden fences—were impressive, reminding Sydney of the Kentucky horse farms they'd left behind.

The sign before them read "Ashroe Riding School 5 miles."

Speeding down the narrow road, the Toyota swerved to the shoulder as a stunning woman with flaxen hair nearly collided with them in her Mercedes station wagon. Sydney silently prayed that she'd never have to negotiate these dreadful roads alone.

Kerry came to a brief halt at the crossroads where four passageways converged at the church. To the left was a small, thatched-roof cottage, and just behind the church an ancient graveyard with massive tombstones. Sydney wanted to ask about it, but seeing the strained look on Kerry's face, she decided to remain mute. For now, the encounter that lay ahead was all that seemed to matter.

About a mile past the church, Kerry slowed the car. He signaled a left turn and eased onto the blacktop drive leading to the main house.

Sydney turned her attention to the centuries-old, majestic trees lining their path. Before long the huge oak trees relinquished their place to the splendor and flourish of the eucalyptus leaf. To the left and to the right were formal English tea gardens setting off the Georgian mansion in the center.

As the serene stone edifice built in the late 1600s came fully into view, Sydney whispered, "Oh my God!" Kerry swore as well, but it was not to the house that his attention had turned but to the petite, raven-haired woman standing in the archway of the front door.

Cautiously, Kerry brought the Toyota to a halt. Not knowing what to say or do, Sydney remained silent by his side. The woman in the doorway remained frozen, neither smiling nor frowning, only staring with vacant eyes.

Painfully, Kerry extracted his tall, lean frame from behind the wheel of the Toyota. His leg was still stiff and throbbing, so his limp was more pronounced than usual as he trudged to the front door.

He glanced about for the yapping dogs to greet him or the sound of horses whinnying in the pasture. But there were no familiar sounds of life here at the home he had abandoned. The playful white Labrador retrievers had long ago been replaced by pristine English tea gardens and a manicured lawn.

Sydney watched him make his way toward the sister he'd not seen in ten years. She was dressed in a black wool skirt, a starched white lace blouse and smart pumps. Her indigo hair was severely knotted in a bun. Her skin seemed sallow, her lips too bright a shade of red. Sydney was awed by differences in the brother and sister.

Only when he was close enough to touch her did Donavan speak her name. "Hello, Barbara," he whispered.

"Oh my God, Kerry," she said. "Is it really you?"

Grabbing her brother, she crushed her cheek against his as they embraced. Not able to surrender to the moment for long, Donavan pushed his sister gently away.

"Let me have a good look at you, Barbara."

Wilting under his scrutiny, Barbara glanced away. It was then that she saw the stunning American woman standing by the car.

"Oh, dear Lord, Kerry! How rude of us to ignore your guest!" Barbara Donavan Thompson smoothed the lines of her skirt and approached Sydney. Offering a delicate, manicured hand to Sydney, she said, "My name is Barbara. Mary Margaret told me when she rang that Kerry would be bringing a lovely American named Sydney. Any friend of Kerry's is certainly a friend of mine."

Barbara led the way into the foyer, and then, throwing open the door, into the parlor.

"Please make yourself at home. Shall I serve tea now, or later?"

Sydney followed Kerry's sister into the drawing room. Even though the salon was magnificently decorated with its huge Waterford chandelier, sterling silver pieces atop the Chippendale sideboard, and huge gilt mirror hung just above the hearth, she shivered against an unexpected chilly draft. The opulent surroundings somehow seemed sterile, and she felt an indescribable wave of sadness for herself and for Kerry, but especially for Barbara.

Barbara took a seat on the pale yellow sofa and beckoned Sydney to her side. Kerry stood by the fireplace as if to warm his hands. But there was no roaring fire to soothe him, only a few pictures on the mantel.

He started to retrieve the one with the exquisite blond woman cradling her baby daughter, but then he let it be. Clearing his throat, he returned his attention to his sister.

"Barbara," he said, "we have to talk."

"Of course, dear, once we've had our tea." Starting to rise, she ignored Kerry. "Sydney, do you prefer your tea with cream or lemon?"

With a firm hand Kerry interrupted. "Barbara, we must talk now!"

Jerking a fragile antique chair to the sofa, he plunked down directly in front of his sister.

"Where are the servants?" he demanded. "Did Liam get rid of them like the horses and the dogs?"

With more emotion in her eyes than Sydney had seen before, Barbara countered, "No, he did not! George is nearly seventy now, and Martha not much younger. I gave them the afternoon off so we wouldn't be disturbed."

Seemingly embarrassed by his accusations, Kerry glanced away. "I'm sorry," he mumbled, "but the place just doesn't feel the same."

"What did you expect, brother? You don't live here anymore. The house belongs to Liam and me. We entertain a great deal, so we've made some changes. You can't expect . . ." Then, a different thought crossed her mind. "Why are you here, Kerry? Why have you come home?"

"Sydney and I need your help," he replied. "I have important business in Limerick. Mary Margaret said that Liam is out of town. I'd like to stay here with you if we could."

"Do you think it's safe?" Barbara queried. "Yes, Liam is in Switzerland for a few days, but he'd be so angry if he knew you were here."

Through gnashed teeth, Kerry responded, "Be that as it may, this is my home and you are my sister!" Throwing his gaze in Sydney's direction, he said, "This woman has lost her child and I intend to find her. It will take a day, at the most two, to determine where she is."

Kerry paused and, taking a deep breath, allowed his eyes to wander about the parlor of the home where he was raised. Memories crammed every crevice of this room, which was merely one of twenty. Returning his weary eyes to Barbara, he whispered, "I haven't seen you in nearly a decade. And after tomorrow . . . I might not ever see you again. I'd like to spend this little fragment of time here with you, Barbara. I'd like this one last chance to come home."

Younger than Kerry by three years, Barbara had been different almost from the time she was born. A timid, insecure child, she never could handle the pressure of being who or what she was. When she was a young girl and the stress of life overwhelmed her, it was to her big brother that she turned. And always he had been there for her, to soothe her hurt and to fight her battles. Barbara felt abandoned when Kerry left Ireland in disgrace. That's when she turned to her father's attorney, Liam Thompson, for guidance and direction. But even now at forty, it was not to her husband that her heart truly belonged, but to her brother. She acquiesced.

"All right. You and Sydney may stay, but not here in the main house. With Mama gone, the granny flat is free."

Diverting her attention from Kerry, Barbara retrieved a strand of fallen hair and patted it neatly back into its severely knotted bun. Turning to her guest, she confided. "It's not that I wish to be rude, Sydney, but even with the privacy of the guest quarters upstairs, it's much too dangerous for you in the main house. The servants have been with me a long time, but you never know . . . whom you can trust . . . and who might betray you."

c h a p t e r 14

Losing herself in the seduction of the flannel sheets, Sydney drifted in and out of slumber. Her dreams were gentle, flowing from one pleasant scene to another. Three hours had passed since weariness had overcome her. Now, in the twilight between sleep and waking, Sydney became aware of the feel of the pillow beneath her head and the down comforter atop her.

Opening her eyes, she found herself under the intricate lace canopy of a four-poster bed. It was a woman's room, which she knew by the gentle pinks and easy yellows. She couldn't remember where she was or why. It was the pungent, musty smell of quarters that had not been lived in which finally brought her back around.

Upon seeing the charming apartment tucked at the rear and just under the main house, she had asked Barbara the question she'd wondered all afternoon.

"Why do you call it a granny flat?"

"It's a common expression in Ireland. When Liam and I moved into the main house, we renovated the servants' quarters for Mama. She furnished it herself with her own precious belongings. And really, for a time, I think she was quite content."

"What happened?"

"Papa's death and Kerry's troubles were too much for her to deal with. Her mind simply snapped. She committed suicide four years ago."

"I'm so sorry . . ."

Barbara's response caught her off-guard. "Oh, don't be sorry, Sydney. At first, her suicide was a terrible embarrassment. But then I realized that if God was merciful, Mama was in a much better place now, where life can't hurt her anymore."

And queerly, Sydney was struck, not by the sorrow of the mother's plight, but by the envious yearning in the daughter's heart to journey to that special place where her own splintered mind couldn't find her.

Throwing the covers aside, Sydney forced her aching body from the bed. Her limbs felt heavy from the long flight and from the short, too deep, repose. Glancing about with eyes only half-open, she noticed a soft light illuminating her room. She wondered whether it was dawn or dusk.

Kerry had allowed her to pack only a few necessary belongings, but he had insisted that she bring a heavy dressing gown for Ireland. Silently she thanked him for his advice as she fumbled for the emerald green robe at the foot of the bed. It was spring after all, yet with no central heat in the flat, the air was damp and chilly as Sydney wrapped the garment securely about her quivering body.

Rubbing the sleep from her reddened eyes, she stumbled down the short hallway toward the sitting room of the granny flat. The sound of a hearty discussion stopped her. There were two animated voices vying for attention, both male, both Irish. One she recognized as Kerry's but the other voice she didn't know. Pausing at the doorway, she listened.

"Just find the child, Paddy, that's all I ask. Our friendship is worth that much, is it not?"

"Aye, Kerry, it is. But your foolishness in this adventure astounds me. Have you any idea what will happen if you're discovered?"

There was a long, difficult pause before he responded. "It's something I must do. Will you get on it yet tonight?"

"Aye," the man answered, "I will. I'll contact the boys in Belfast right away. I should have your answer sometime tomorrow, if I'm lucky. I'm afraid it will cost you a pretty pound, Kerry. The boys don't give anything away free."

Slipping naturally into the slang of his compatriot, Kerry agreed, "Aye, I'm prepared to pay for this and for any papers that we might need." Reaching into his back pocket, Kerry handed Paddy an envelope bulging with Irish pounds. "This should more than cover any expenses. If me hunches prove correct, Paddy, Sydney and I will need a new identity and different papers." Showing McDowell the contents of the envelope, Donavan continued, "Here are our new pictures and a list of possible names. Once you locate Hassan, we'll finalize the details."

Sydney peered through a crack in the door as the men stood and embraced. They were an unlikely pair, these two. Kerry's height and stature contrasted sharply with the smaller man's brittle demeanor. Donavan had said little about the nervous wisp of a man Mary Margaret had called "the weasel." But catching a glimpse of him now, Sydney grinned at the accuracy of Sullie's description.

Short and feeble looking, Paddy McDowell was somewhere near sixty. He looked haggard, with black greasy hair and the stubble of an unshaven beard. As he pivoted just slightly toward the door and turned his face toward Sydney, the hideous, puffy red scar that disfigured his face from his forehead across his left eye to the bottom of his jawline came fully into view. Seeing this, and the cold dead resolve in his lifeless eyes, Sydney shuddered.

"I'm trusting you with me life, Paddy. For godsake, don't let me down."

It was with a deep measure of respect and genuine friendship that the man answered.

"Your trust rests well with me, Kerry. But be careful, me friend, and stay well hidden. You were recognized at the airport. The word is out on the street that you're back."

As the two men moved away from the sitting room, their voices became muffled. A few minutes later Kerry returned, his face drawn into a worried grimace. Acting as if she'd just awakened and not heard Paddy's dire warning, Sydney glided into the sitting room yawning, pretending to rub the sleep from her eyes.

"What time is it, Kerry?" she inquired.

"Just after six. Did you rest well?"

"I did, but I could have slept another twenty hours."

"With jet lag, it's best to only briefly nap and then get up for the remainder of the evening. By ten o'clock, you'll be ready for a good night's sleep and well on your way to a full recovery."

Walking to the hearth, Kerry stoked the wood then, turning, beckoned Sydney to him. "Come, sit with me by the fire. Barbara had a function to attend this evening, but she fixed us a light supper. Would you care for a glass of wine first?"

"That would be nice."

Wrapping her robe tightly about her knees, Sydney sat on the terra-cotta tile directly in front of the roaring fire as she allowed her eyes to roam about, seeking a sense of the woman behind the surroundings.

The granny flat, as it was termed, was a small, homey space, much more to Sydney's liking than the sterility of the main house. The flat boasted a living room, dining room, small kitchen, two bedrooms and a bath. Studying the woman's choice of colors and the placement of her treasured possessions, Sydney tried to get to know Kerry's mother, the woman who had played perhaps the greatest influence in his life.

Mai Donavan, who would have been in her seventies, was a woman who loved rich pinks, sassy yellows and various shades of blue. Sadly for Sydney, these were Lydia's favorite colors, too. Mai's favorite fabrics were richly flowered, brightly colored chintz, and a muted rose satin. She loved primitive Irish oak antiques and shiny brass pots.

Sydney surmised that she passed the lonely evening hours doing needlepoint and embroidery, as there were pillows of various shapes and sizes casually strewn about.

She was a woman, Sydney decided, who had lived for her husband and who adored her children. Their pictures were everywhere. Mai Donavan's flat was neat and clean, but there was a sense of living here—unlike the main house—where a spattering of dust and dirt could easily abide with cleanliness and organization.

When Kerry returned from the kitchen, Sydney said, "Your mother must have been a remarkable woman."

Squatting by the fire, Kerry handed Sydney her glass of wine.

"Mai Donavan was a no-nonsense woman who hated pretension. She'd not be happy with the changes on the estate. She loved the dogs and the horses. She made our home an exciting place to live . . . not some doll house."

Understanding the unspoken implication, Sydney had to ask, "Why do you hate Liam so?"

Kerry's eyes narrowed as he sipped his tea.

"He's an arrogant English bastard with a vile temper. When I left Ireland, he moved in like a vulture. He only married my sister for her money and he's been squandering her assets ever since." Grimacing as if his mouth had soured with bile, Kerry turned away. "Enough of him. Drink your wine."

Savoring the dry tartness of her white wine, Sydney smiled. "Thank you for remembering, Kerry. A glass of wine in the evening helps me to relax. Sam and I . . ."

Sydney allowed her words to disappear into an embarrassed whisper. What she had started to say was that she and Sam looked forward to a glass of wine together in the evening as a time to reflect upon their day and plan their days ahead.

Closing her eyes, Sydney tried to force images of Sam Ellis from her mind. But it was hard to push the man she had loved from the forefront of her thoughts. Resolving to get on with her life, she jerked her attention back to the present and the man before her.

Swallowing hard, she opened her eyes and spoke. "I heard voices when I awoke, Kerry. Was that Paddy McDowell?"

"It was," he replied.

With trepidation, Sydney queried, "Does he think he can help us?"

Donavan sipped his tea while thoughtfully gazing into the

fireplace. "Yes, he does, but not without some tricky maneuvering and a good deal of finesse. He's certain, though, that the information can be obtained."

"When will we know?"

"If we're lucky, we might know something tomorrow. I haven't said anything to you before, but in general I have a pretty good idea where they've gone. Before we left the States, Joe Morrison thoroughly briefed me on Ali Hassan. And after reviewing his profile, there's one thing I know for sure. He's one hell of a shrewd businessman. If my hunches prove correct, we'll find him dealing arms somewhere in the Persian Gulf. The war may have ended, but the ultimate power struggle has only just begun. A well-connected arms dealer could name his price and make a bloody fortune."

"So you think he's taken Lydia to the Persian Gulf?"

"I'd bet you my last Irish pound. Where is the only question."

Kerry set his cup of tea upon the floor.

"I feel certain he's not in Iran, but God forbid he's headquartered in Iraq. Both Jordan and Syria are risky; and because of Qadaffi and the IRA connection, I'm a dead man if he's sheltered in Libya. Depending on where he's gone, our mission is a go or it's over. I'm sorry to be so blunt, but that's the way it is."

Seeing Sydney's crestfallen expression, Kerry changed his approach. "Come on, girl, drink up!" he said. "Let me get you another glass of wine. We can't do a damn thing until tomorrow, so we might as well enjoy tonight. We're comfortable here and we're safe. Nobody will bother us."

Rising stiffly, Kerry shook out his sore leg and made his way to the kitchen for the wine. Then, towering above her, he refilled her glass. "I'd say that over the past few hours, you've glimpsed a hell of a lot into my black soul. Yet I know so little about you. Let's have dinner and talk. Who can say, Sydney? This might be the last time we have to relax and get to know each other."

And so, over poached salmon and fresh asparagus, in front of the roaring fire, Kerry Donavan and Sydney Lawrence, two vastly different people who might never have sought each other out, opened up and shared. Mainly, it was Sydney who talked and

Kerry who listened to stories about her childhood in Kentucky and her struggle to become a television journalist. Finally, over apple tarts and cream and fresh brewed coffee, she broached the subject of Sam.

Was it the wine or the sheer seduction of the fire that made her face flush and her body tingle? Whatever it was, tucked away in this granny flat in a foreign country with a man she barely knew, Sydney's defenses began to crumble at the same time her senses came alive. From the smell of the crackling firewood to the sweet-sour taste of the apple tart upon her lips, everything looked better, tasted better, and smelled better than it had in a long time.

But there came a time when all the stories she cared to share had been spoken, and the fire waned to a pile of glowing cinders. The bottle of wine was empty, and suddenly Sydney was wearier than she could possibly imagine.

Kerry stood and pulled Sydney to her feet. He steadied her when she stumbled, and without thinking, he drew her near. Secure in his arms, she lifted her gaze to his face.

His voice grew husky as he whispered, "You look exhausted. We'll both feel better after a good night's sleep."

First he kissed her left cheek, then, as was European custom, her right. But he couldn't bring himself to release her. Not now. Not after their hours together. Instead he cupped her face—her fresh, freckly face, glowing pink from the fire—as his lips sought hers.

Laying them gently upon her warm mouth, he enveloped Sydney in his arms, crushing her against his chest until the beating of their hearts was the only sound she heard. Her lips parted naturally with no thought, no formality.

Succumbing to the strength of his embrace, lost in his touch, Sydney forgot who she was, and why. In that moment, abiding only in his kiss, her past meant nothing, her future was of no consequence. She was simply a woman in the arms of a man.

Trembling, Sydney pulled away and rushed down the hall.

"Oh my God!" she cried. "What am I doing?"

Slamming the door to the bedroom, she burst into tears as she threw herself on the bed.

"Oh, Sam," she implored, "forgive me!"

She wiped Kerry's kiss from her mouth as she struggled to remember the feel of Sam's lips, so gentle, upon her. But no matter how hard she tried, the thrill of Kerry's sensual mouth—seeking hers, teasing hers, crushing hers—would not let her be.

Kerry arose first the next morning, shortly after eight o'clock. The sun was already up, but what a long day it would be as they awaited word on Lydia's fate. Unshaven, with his thick chestnut hair askew, Donavan sat at the kitchen table, dressed only in an undershirt and jeans. He sipped his coffee and brooded.

Sydney Lawrence was the first woman who had stirred his fractured heart since the death of his wife. But where Patricia had been kind and even-tempered, keeping Kerry on an even keel, this flaming-haired hellion had the power to enrage him with a word or to melt him with a glance.

Lost in his thoughts, Kerry failed to hear Sydney's steps in the hallway. Wrapped in her heavy robe, she nudged the kitchen door open. Kerry glanced up, but quickly turned away.

In a tentative voice, she ventured, "I'm sorry about last night."

"Think nothing of it," he responded coldly. "It is I who should apologize for being so bold. Believe me, Sydney, it won't happen again."

Sydney sat down at the kitchen table and reached for the thick brew Kerry offered. Clutching his own mug, Kerry rose to leave.

"Wait, Kerry! Listen to me. What happened last night had nothing to do with you. It's Sam . . . I can't forget Sam!"

An insistent knock at the door interrupted their conversation, which as far as Kerry was concerned was just as well.

"There's a phone call for you at the main house," said Barbara, poking her head in. "The man said his name was Paddy."

Bolting for the door, Kerry started for the main house, with Sydney right behind.

"Stay here with Barbara," he commanded.

Sydney started to argue but backed down. It seemed like an eternity as she waited for Kerry's return. She sat in silence, allowing Barbara to prattle on in a feeble attempt to pass the time. It was fifteen minutes later when the door to the granny flat opened.

Whispering the name of her daughter, her eyes sought Kerry's. But throwing his glance first to Barbara and then to Sydney, Kerry refused her the satisfaction of a reply.

"What did you find out?" Sydney cried. "Tell me!"

Pausing only for a moment in the doorway leading to the second bedroom, he said, "We must be ready to travel tonight. That's all I can tell you for now."

As the bell tower in the center of town tolled ten o'clock, Mary Margaret O'Sullivan parked her van and hurried down Ellen Street toward her shop. Mopping her brow, she fumbled in her handbag for keys. It was not that it was unusually warm this morning, it was rather that the antique jewelry dealer had already worked up a sweat. With summer tourists arriving in six short weeks, she had a great deal to accomplish—dated inventory to sell and new stock to purchase. A woman who loved life and lived for her work, Sullie as always had a busy agenda. Even though it was Sunday, she had scheduled Dorothy to come in and help her inventory the shop.

Mary Margaret had slept fitfully, locked in a nightmare about Kerry Donavan. Over and over, she saw his bullet-riddled body lying in the street and no one stepping forward to claim him. Finally, at first light, she'd arisen and gone to Mass, hoping that the comfort of church would soothe her. But the bad feelings of last night remained with a disturbing premonition that wouldn't let her be.

She glanced about the shop and wondered what to do until Dorothy arrived. There was jewelry to polish, knickknacks to rearrange, and books to be balanced. But before settling in, she returned to the front door and glanced first to the right and then to the left. The street was quiet.

Because she was hot and perspiring and didn't want to stain her red silk blouse, Mary Margaret left the front door to the shop open. This would prove to be a mistake, because, unbeknownst to her, the man who had stalked her all morning had ducked into the protective archway of the shop next-door.

Lighting a cigarette, Eddy Maloney smiled. It was a lovely spring day in Limerick. Leaning against the brick wall just to the left of the open door, he waited, keeping his ears open and his eyes alert. Sooner or later, the unwitting shop owner would lead him to his prey.

Mary Margaret set her handbag behind the desk and opened the ledger. Not one to enjoy playing with figures, balancing the books was the one task she avoided. But her accountant would not be put off much longer.

The ring of the phone startled her. Stuffing the pencil she had just picked up behind her ear, she answered. The voice on the other end caught her off guard, and it took a minute to figure out why he was calling.

"Hi, yes, top of the morning to you, Michal."

"And the balance of the day to you, Sullie. I rang your house and when you didn't answer I thought I might find you here. But it's Sunday, Sullie, a day of rest. You're working much too hard."

"Aye, that I am, Michal. Maureen and the kids okay?"

"Yeah, sure. They're in great form, and the wife sends her regards. You know the favor you asked me to do, Sullie? Well, I'm calling to deliver."

Mary Margaret grew suddenly alert. Michal Flynn was an associate in Liam's law firm. She reached for her package of Rothmans and deliberately lit one.

"He's back?"

"That he is, Sullie. I just got word that Liam is returning to Limerick a bit sooner than he planned. His plane should be landing about now."

Mary Margaret mumbled, "Oh dear Lord . . ."

"What's wrong, Sullie? Why did you want to know when Liam returned?"

Quickly O'Sullivan composed herself. "Oh, it's nothing, Michal. Barbara is planning a bit of a surprise for Liam's birthday. She didn't want her man coming home unexpectedly and catching her in the act of party preparations."

There was a long pause on the phone. "I thought Liam's birthday was in June."

"Oh, it is, but you know our Barbara. Things have to be planned weeks in advance. Tell me, Michal, do you think he'll go straight home?"

"Wouldn't surprise me, Sullie. I'm not sure why he decided to return today. He'd been negotiating a deal in Geneva. He wasn't due home until the end of the week."

"Well, thank you, Michal. I'll let Barbara know her man's on his way. Blessings to you. And by the way . . . could you keep this phone call our little secret?"

"For you, Sullie, anything."

Mary Margaret replaced the receiver, then checked the time.

"Where in God's name are you, Dorothy? Oh, to hell with business! I can't wait!"

Jotting a brief note to her assistant, Mary Margaret grabbed her handbag and fled the shop. Her mind was focused on warning Kerry, and so, she paid no heed to the man loitering on the blind side of the building.

Grinning, Eddy Maloney snuffed out his cigarette and followed her to the car-park. And, as the bright blue van sped toward the Dublin road, Maloney—jumping into his brother's waiting car—followed a discreet distance behind.

■

Mary Margaret flew down the back roads out of Limerick toward Lisnagry to warn Kerry about Liam's return. Liam hated his brother-in-law with a vengeance for his past association with the IRA and the shame it had brought the family. He vowed to see him dead if he ever set foot in Ireland again. He was a man with the contacts to carry out his threat. Veering sharply off the narrow road, Sullie sped up the drive toward the house. At the last second, though, she wheeled her van to the left and followed the path to the rear of the mansion, back by the deserted stables. Bursting through the door of the granny flat, she paused to catch her breath.

She found Sydney sitting alone at the kitchen table. Seeing the impeccably dressed woman drenched in sweat and gasping for air, Sydney exclaimed, "My God, Sullie! You look terrible! What's wrong?"

"And blessings of the day to you, too, missy! I shouldn't say you look in top form yourself."

Sydney feigned a smile.

"Tell me, Sydney, where is the genius?"

"He's been gone for over an hour. He went with Barbara to visit his mother's grave. I should think they'd be back by now. Did you try the main house?"

"No," Mary Margaret replied. "I came directly here." Mary Margaret desperately tried to compose herself. "Get your things together, girl. It's time to get you out of here."

"What do you mean, Sullie? What's wrong?"

"I've just learned that Liam's on his way home. Came back from Geneva earlier than expected. He hates Kerry. If he finds him here there will be bloody hell to pay! We have to find you and Kerry a safer place to stay."

Mary Margaret took charge, gathering Sydney and her belongings quickly together. Then, fleeing the granny flat, they searched the grounds for Kerry. But their search proved futile. And so Mary Margaret and Sydney had no choice but to wait. Finding themselves alone in the drafty drawing room, the two of them counted the minutes. Praying to the Almighty that Liam would be delayed, Mary Margaret smoked nearly a pack of Rothmans while Sydney paced the floor aimlessly from one end of the room to the other.

Sydney was drawn to the picture of Patricia on the mantel. Clutching the photograph, she studied the blond woman's features one by one. Unwittingly, for reasons she didn't comprehend, she found herself in competition with a dead woman. It was a competition she couldn't hope to win. For while Sydney Lawrence was attractive, never would she be termed gorgeous, breathtaking, even sweet—the adjectives that slid off her tongue when gazing at Patricia Donavan.

"What's wrong, Sydney?" said Sullie. "Don't tell me it's nothing. Is it Kerry?"

Sydney opened her mouth to deny it, but found she couldn't. She sat down on the sofa next to Mary Margaret.

"Yes, it is Kerry. We had a wonderful evening together last night. It's the first time we ever . . . talked. I had a little too much to drink. When I got up to go to bed I stumbled, and he caught me . . ."

"Go on," Mary Margaret urged.

"He kissed me."

A wry smile crossed O'Sullivan's lips. "And?"

"And I . . . kissed him back. What I mean is . . . oh, God . . . Sam's only been dead a few months! How could I have let another man touch me?"

Mary Margaret shook her head. "Who are you trying to fool, Sydney? Me or yourself? Yes, your poor dear husband is dead, but you, my friend, are still very much alive. What you're feeling for Kerry has absolutely nothing to do with Sam."

"No, Sullie, you're wrong! You didn't know Sam. If you had, you'd understand. He was the nicest, kindest man I've ever known."

Crushing her cigarette in the ashtray, Mary Margaret gently took Sydney's hand.

"Listen to me, girl, and listen well. What bothers you about Kerry Donavan is how he makes you feel. I don't know you well, Sydney, but I do know this. You're a woman who needs to be in charge. Everything about you says power and control. I'd venture to say that you wrapped your Sam right around your little finger. Am I right?"

Sydney was silent.

"With Kerry Donavan, you have no control," Sullie continued. "And that, my darling girl, terrifies you."

Sydney stood and walked to the far side of the room. "I'm sorry, Mary Margaret, but you're wrong. You have no idea what you're talking about."

Sullie stood up as well, smoothing the wrinkles from her skirt. "Time will tell, Sydney. Time will tell. What are you so afraid of? Could it be you've never really loved a man before?"

Sydney wheeled around. "How dare you say that. I loved my husband!"

"I'm sure you did, Sydney, but not in the way that I mean. Like it or not, Kerry Donavan makes you . . . feel . . . things, way down deep inside." Clutching her own heart, she whispered, "If you allowed yourself to be swept away . . . just where would his love take you?"

The man behind the wheel of the black Mercedes drove slowly through Limerick before turning onto the Dublin highway. He was edgy, damned edgy, and his brow was damp with sweat. He stared straight ahead as he negotiated the narrow streets, refusing to acknowledge the people he knew along his route with even a brief nod or the hint of a smile.

Professionally his trip to Switzerland had been a lucrative one. He had successfully negotiated a deal with the Red Cross to lease a fleet of airplanes that would profit his client nearly a quarter of a million pounds. An Englishman never too reticent to seize an opportunity, he had flown to Geneva just after the media broke the story of the cyclone in Bangladesh. One man's tragedy, Liam Thompson believed, was another's opportunity. So it was for Liam Thompson and his client, Global Aviation, a company that leased aircraft to third-world nations or to countries with special needs.

But if the daylight hours had brought him career satisfaction, then the hours after dark had fulfilled the promise of sheer delight. The wisest move he'd made on this journey was to book a quaint, charming hotel away from the glare of downtown Geneva and away from public scrutiny. There he had immediately befriended the greedy concierge who, in turn, for a price, served him well.

Always richly groomed and preened, Liam Thompson, at forty-eight, was a man of few vices. Rarely did he drink, and then only the finest wines, and he'd rather choke than allow a cigarette to touch his lips. A vain man whose looks were second only to his brilliant mind, he forbade himself the luxury of overindulgence in any type of food or drink, with the exception of oatmeal and raisin cookies. Liam Thompson, with his finger-waved, platinum hair, and delicate, almost pretty features, prided himself on being a man of singular vice, but that one pleasure was rapidly causing him problems.

This time it was a young French boy of fourteen. The price of the child was five thousand pounds for the week, and in the beginning the pleasure had been worth every sou. For as smooth and virginal as the lad was, he knew what to do with his tongue to deliver indescribable waves of pleasure to every crevice of Liam's hungry body.

This child was as he preferred them—nearly hairless, with no trace of a beard, and a voice that had not yet matured. He was blond and fair, with innocent blue eyes and a mouth as sweet as the pectin of any fruit. The boy was the mirror image of Liam at the same age.

For the first few nights, Liam had spoiled the youngster, named Pascal, with the richest of gourmet foods and the best of spirits. After satiating the boy's hunger, he had taken him to bed and allowed the youth to demonstrate his gratitude . . . neatly, cleanly, with the full exuberance that only a child craving to please would dare offer.

Liam Thompson was born into a matriarchal family where, for generations, the women were leaders and the men were workers. Liam developed the personality of a perfectionist, trying harder and harder to gain what he thought of as *love* from his domineering mother. No matter what he did, he never measured up. After years of feeling unloved, Liam developed a deep hatred of women.

He married Barbara for her money and the status she offered. On the surface, he tried to meet her needs, offering her guidance and protection. But because she was female, he never felt satisfied or loved in return. He never felt like a man. That's why he turned to young boys for sexual satisfaction.

Then, last night, everything changed. The boundaries between the boy and the man dissolved. Rather than seeing the boy as Pascal, a poor French boy desperate to please, Liam saw Pascal as himself at that age—desperate for love but unable to attain it. That's when everything changed.

With brute force he thrust himself upon the boy harder and harder, using his superior strength to subdue the child in a desperate attempt to prove his love. But the boy lashed out, screaming at Liam to leave him alone, calling him a perverted faggot. It was then that Liam's mind went dark. He had no conscious thoughts. He would not recall the acts that followed.

Blind rage has only a beginning. It has no end. The torture ceased only when, spent with fatigue, Liam collapsed. When he came to, the child lay dead. The bed was soaked with the boy's blood that had flowed from the child's rectum.

Shaken, Liam struggled to gather his wits. He couldn't believe the boy lay dead. For an instant, he wondered who had done this terrible deed. Then he realized he was naked with the boy's blood covering his penis.

In desperation, Liam offered the concierge fifty thousand pounds to make the situation go away. The child was a teenage prostitute with no known family. Liam didn't want to know the particulars, only that the body had been disposed of and the hotel records of his stay destroyed. Liam had left Geneva on the first available flight to Shannon. On the surface, everything had been taken care of. He made a plausible excuse to his client that an emergency called him away. He would conclude their business from Ireland. The client was satisfied, but Liam was nervous. A situation like this could come back to haunt him.

Just past Finnigan's, Thompson turned off the main Dublin Road on the way to his estate in Lisnagry. He vowed to be more careful in the future. Bedding young boys was one thing, killing them quite another. He deluded himself into believing that the child was better off. He wouldn't have to suffer through a life of desolation. He could rest in peace.

Nearing home, he thought about his wife, Barbara, the lady whose fortune made his pleasure possible. He hated her and all she represented.

Just before his turn into the driveway of his estate, Liam noticed an old, beat-up car hidden in the foliage just across the road. His mind registered that something was amiss. He pulled the Mercedes to the side of the drive where, undetected, he could get a better look at the two men in the front seat.

When Liam peered closer, he realized that the intruders were his unsavory neighbors, the Maloney brothers, who lived in a shanty down the road.

Well they were no one to be afraid of, he thought, and boldly strutted down the drive and across the road to their car.

Startled, the two men had no time to react.

"Good day, lads," said Liam, leaning down and peering through the open window. "May I ask what you're doing here?"

Eddy Maloney shot his brother a glance that warned him to be silent.

"Nothing," Maloney replied. "Just catching a bit of nap before heading home."

"Come come, now," Liam chided. "You can do better than that. If it's hunting on my property that you want, you're out of luck. You know I forbid it."

Eddy Maloney started to make excuses, then realized there might be a better way. Stepping from the car, he beckoned Liam closer.

"Sir," he said, "if we might talk . . ."

Liam Thompson stood his ground, immobile, as a brief hint of fear crossed his soft features. Seeing the look of apprehension, Maloney understood.

"Sir, I mean you no harm. I have a bit of information . . . information of interest to us both."

Knowing the brothers and their family, Thompson felt in no immediate danger.

"Get on with it, Mr. Maloney. I haven't got all day."

Eddy Maloney looked Liam Thompson straight in the eye. "Your brother-in-law has returned. Kerry Donavan is here. Right now."

Liam Thompson stared at the man, barely registering the news.

"Kerry Donavan . . . here? You must be mistaken."

"Saw him with me own eyes yesterday at the Lucky Lady with the jewelry dealer. Followed Mary Margaret O'Sullivan here this morning when she got word that you were returning home earlier than expected."

"Son of a bitch," Thompson muttered to himself. "But what are you doing here?"

Maloney thrust his hand into his bulging jacket pocket and withdrew a gun. "I want him, Mr. Thompson. I want him bad. He betrayed the boys. There's a bounty on his head."

The color drained from Liam's face. "What in God's name are you thinking, man? You can't kill him here! The news would be all over the papers! I can't have it. Kerry Donavan's link to the IRA damned near ruined me. A man in my position can't tolerate another scandal. Be quiet a moment and let me think."

Composing himself quickly, Liam Thompson struggled to formulate a plan. "You want him, Maloney? Well then, he's yours. But not here . . . not like this. Let me get him off the place. I'll have him followed. We'll set him up somewhere else." Thinking what he would do to the handsome Irishman if he could, Liam managed a sick, twisted smile. "Go home now and wait for my call."

Gripping his revolver, Maloney didn't budge, and for a terrifying moment, Liam wondered if the IRA terrorist might not shoot him on the spot just to get him out of the way. In a stronger, more commanding voice the Brit shouted, "Are you deaf? Go home, Eddy Maloney! I'm a man of my word. You'll have your precious bounty. And a thousand more pounds to boot. But we'll do it my way, good man . . . not yours!"

Susan M. Hoskins

chapter **17**

Acid soured his stomach as Liam crossed the road back to the estate. He thanked the God of his Anglican Church for giving him the wisdom to handle the hotheaded terrorists as well as he had. But the light of his own brilliance quickly faded as he searched for a way to deal with a much keener and sophisticated foe.

Thompson had known Kerry Donavan for most of his adult life. And if the truth be known, his brother-in-law was one of the few men he truly respected, yet even now deeply feared. Kerry Donavan had the keen eye to see through Liam's cool exterior and the guts to destroy him. If push came to shove, the Irishman had the temper, coupled with the brute strength, to annihilate Liam Thompson.

Meanwhile, lighting yet another Rothman, Mary Margaret O'Sullivan paced the drawing room, pausing at the window that overlooked the garden and the drive. It was then she saw Liam's vehicle approaching. She felt her face blush and her heart begin to pound. Dealing with Liam Thompson now rested upon her rounded, overburdened shoulders.

"Liam's home," she told Sydney. "Say nothing. Do nothing. Leave it all to me."

Mary Margaret took her seat upon the sofa, placing Sydney in the wing-tip chair to the right. There, in silence, they waited. They heard footsteps on the porch, then the jingle of keys and a smooth tenor voice call out, "Barbara, darling, where are you? I'm home."

Her voice quivering slightly, Mary Margaret returned Liam's greeting from the drawing room. "Liam, my pet, Barbara isn't here at the moment. But come in and give Sullie a hug. How in the world have you been keeping?"

Thompson entered the archway of the drawing room. Seeing Mary Margaret O'Sullivan, he responded in kind, with a smile carefully etched on his cherubic face. But there was a hint of disdain for the woman in his eyes. To a seasoned journalist like Sydney Lawrence, it was a look that did not go unnoticed.

He bowed slightly to Sydney and said, "Good day. I don't believe I've had the pleasure . . ."

"This is a friend of mine from the States," O'Sullivan quickly interceded. "Sydney, please meet Barbara's dear husband, Liam." But denying Sydney the opportunity of a reply, Sullie grabbed Liam by the sleeve of his suit jacket and jerked him down on the sofa beside her.

"Liam, darling, we need to talk."

Displaying a look of proper bewilderment, the Brit countered, "Oh, dear Lord, Sullie, has something happened to Barbara?"

"No, pet, no," Sullie assured him. "Barbara's in great form, but we have a bit of a dilemma. I would ask only that you hear me out and that you remain calm."

"Yes, yes," Thompson urged. "Get on with it."

In a quiet voice, Mary Margaret simply stated, "Kerry's here at the estate. He and Barbara have gone to visit Mai's grave."

His voice rising with only the slightest hint of emotion, Liam repeated, "Kerry, here? But why, Sullie? Doesn't he realize the danger?"

Sydney leaned forward to answer, but Mary Margaret abruptly brushed her aside.

"Let me tell you what I can, Liam. This woman's child has been abducted. Kerry is in Limerick for the sole purpose of locating the missing girl. As soon as he receives the information he seeks, he'll depart. A few hours more, that's all he needs."

"Well, he simply can't be discovered here," replied Liam in

his firm, well-modulated voice. "You should know that, Mary Margaret. To risk my reputation and good name is unthinkable. I'm afraid Donavan and his lovely companion will have to leave."

"Of course, Liam, of course. No one knows he's here at the estate. Barbara dismissed the servants with pay for a few days. Believe me, Kerry has been most discreet. I can assure you of that."

"Yes, well, yes . . . ," Thompson hesitated, knowing full well that Kerry Donavan's whereabouts were already a matter of public knowledge.

"Please try to understand, Liam. This was the only way Kerry could spend some time with his sister. It may be the last chance they have to see each other for the rest of their lives. No matter what you think of Kerry, you can't blame Barbara for stealing a few precious hours with her brother. As soon as they return, we'll leave. Please, Liam, just don't make a scene."

Sullie's eyes narrowed and her voice took on an edge Sydney had not heard before.

"I want your assurance, Liam, that there won't be any . . . retribution . . . for Barbara's actions."

His mouth turning under slightly, Liam Thompson met O'Sullivan's stare. Then he shrugged with a look of total amazement. "I have no earthly idea what you're implying, Sullie. You know that I've never been anything but . . . kind . . . to Barbara."

Mary Margaret's voice was low and her eyes stern when she said, "Just promise me, Liam."

With all the tension in the drawing room, no one heard the door to the kitchen open as Kerry and Barbara returned from their trek to the family cemetery nearly a mile away. It was the sound of their laughter echoing in the hallway that finally caught Sydney's notice.

Gesturing to her Irish friend, she warned, "They're back."

Mary Margaret O'Sullivan threw a final glance to Liam. "Mind me words, man, for I mean them with all me heart."

"Ah, Kerry, I can't tell you how much this time has meant to me," Barbara was saying, as arm in arm they meandered down the marble hallway. Gazing up at her brother, a hint of tears brightened her eyes. Just outside the doorway to the drawing room, Barbara spoke the words she'd locked away for years. "No one on the face of the earth means as much to me as you do, Kerry. You've always held the piece of my heart no one else can touch."

It was the coppery highlights of Sydney's hair that caught Barbara's notice as she cast her eyes to the drawing room. "Good Lord, girl, you scared me to death!" she cried. "What are you doing sitting here all alone? My heavens, have we been gone that long?"

It was then that Mary Margaret O'Sullivan stood. Starting to move toward the door, Sullie gestured wildly for them to back away.

"Kerry, dear, if we might have a word . . ."

Despite her sterling intentions, O'Sullivan's ploy proved to be a dismal failure. Taking great relish in the power of a surprise, Liam Thompson regally came to his feet and, turning benevolently, threw open his arms to his wife. "Barbara, dear, I'm home. And look what a surprise I've found!"

Barbara's eyes grew large with fear. What little color she possessed drained from her porcelain cheeks.

"Don't be upset, darling," Liam soothed. "We'll discuss the matter . . . after . . . your guests have departed. In deference to Mary Margaret, I've agreed not to make a scene, but I'm afraid you'll have to leave, Kerry. You're not a welcome guest in my home."

Kerry's eyes were smoldering. "This is *my* home, you son of a bitch, not yours!"

Liam's expression remained cold as steel, but his left eye began to twitch. "Get out!"

Kerry surged forward. Mary Margaret stepped in between the two men.

Barbara reached out and gently touched her husband's arm. "Please, Liam . . ."

Without thinking, Liam pushed her away, hissing, "Shut up!"

Barbara stumbled and nearly fell.

Kerry balled his fist to strike Liam. Mary Margaret cried out as she tried to restrain him, "For the love of God, Kerry, get hold of yourself. For Barbara's sake, don't do anything you'll regret!"

Kerry threw his glance to Barbara. The look of terror was unmistakable in her eyes.

"Please, Kerry," she whispered.

Donavan struggled to regain his composure. Barbara was trembling, and there was a depth of fear in her eyes that he had never seen before. Liam displayed no such fear. Mary Margaret's eyes were pleading. It was then that Kerry thought he understood both the warnings and the terror.

He stepped back out of Mary Margaret's grasp, then quickly surged forward again. Grasping Liam by the lapels of his shirt, he shoved him backward, and watched him stumble and fall.

Towering above him, he said, "If you ever lay a hand on my sister, I'll kill you. Do you understand?"

"Well, you've done it this time, genius! What in the name of God were you thinking, threatening Liam?"

Kerry Donavan sat scowling in the passenger seat of Mary Margaret O'Sullivan's dark blue van. Staring glumly straight ahead, he brooded in silence, refusing to answer her bait. A woman not to be ignored, O'Sullivan trudged right ahead.

"For the love of Jesus, Kerry! Don't you realize the danger you've put yourself in?" Glancing in the rearview mirror at Sydney following in the rented car behind them, Sullie shook her head with disgust. "And what about your lady friend there? You've thrown her to the dogs as well. As if she doesn't have enough on her mind! Don't you know by now that Liam Thompson is not a man to tangle with? More than likely he's got every thug in town out looking for you. The booty on your bloody head has probably doubled."

Kerry's sullen expression turned angry.

"Liam Thompson is a spineless pervert, Sullie. He doesn't have the balls to come after me. He's not *man* enough to fight me! He knows I'd beat the crap out of him!"

"I've taken you for many things, Kerry Donavan, but never for such an idiotic fool!"

"I want the truth, Sullie. Has that son of a bitch ever hurt my sister?"

Mary Margaret dared not answer. Her eyes remained fixed on the road straight ahead. No answer was answer enough.

Flexing his strong, calloused hands, Donavan said, "I *will* kill him, Sullie."

Turning off the main Dublin Road, O'Sullivan carefully guided the van through an alley to the rear of Ellen Street, back behind her shop. Shutting off the engine and signaling Sydney to come to a halt as well, Sullie turned and confronted Donavan with grave concern. "What now, Kerry? How are you going to connect with Paddy McDowell?"

"I asked Barbara to field his call and get word to you where and when our meeting will take place. I suggested that she call you here at the shop."

"Meantime, what should I do with you?" said Sullie.

Kerry Donavan turned to his friend of many years and feigned a repentant smile. "Feed us dinner, I hope. I'm starved."

"You're shameless!" Sullie replied, grabbing her handbag and carefully descending from the van. Gathering Sydney and Kerry up like a flock of lost chickens, she clucked, "I'll hide you in the attic. It'll be a bit dirty, but at least, please God, if I can keep your bloody faces hidden and your mouths shut, I might be able to keep you safe."

Back at the estate, Barbara Donavan Thompson trembled with fear. Liam remained on the floor, his cheeks red with rage. Waiting until Kerry, Sydney and Mary Margaret had safely departed, she approached her husband cautiously. "I'm so terribly sorry, Liam. Let me help you up."

As Barbara extended her quivering hand, Liam lifted his black gaze to hers and met her glance. Then, grabbing her arm and springing to his feet, Liam—with pure hatred spewing from his eyes—drew back his hand and slapped Barbara across the face with such ferocity that she stumbled and fell against the sofa.

"You fucking bitch!" he cried, rushing toward her. "How could you have done this to me?"

Towering above her, he slapped her again and then again until, whimpering like an abused child, she begged for mercy.

"Please forgive me, Liam. I was only trying to help my brother."

His breath stinking hot upon her, Thompson spat the words in her face, "I wish your brother dead and you with him! Now get the hell out of my sight!"

Paralyzed with fear, Barbara remained where she was, too frightened to move. Turning his back on her, Thompson marched to the bar and poured himself a stiff shot of brandy. It was not yet one o'clock, but he had to get himself under control.

Swallowing the hot burning liquid, his raw nerves began to settle. He poured himself a second shot. Then in a calmer voice he said, "You may not leave the house, Barbara, and I forbid you to have any contact with your brother. It would be foolish to disobey me. The consequences would be most unpleasant."

Barbara spent the afternoon in her room praying to God for forgiveness. Having been beaten throughout the years, she had come to believe that her husband's brutality was somehow her fault. She had lived her life out of a sense of duty first to her father and now to her husband. She never felt she measured up in either man's eyes. She could not bear children so she had failed at being a mother. In her mind, the only value she had left was that of being a good wife. She vowed to try harder to please Liam and to hide her shame from the outside world. Appearances, after all, were everything.

At 4:30, she arose from her bed to start Liam's supper. She chose to prepare his favorite dinner—veal scallopini, fresh buttered carrots, new potatoes and a tossed green salad. It was just before five when the first of two phone calls rang through.

She stared at the phone for a brief second, but, not wanting her husband to be disturbed, she grabbed the receiver before the second ring. The voice on the other end sent shivers up her spine, not because of who he was, but because of what it meant she had to do. The man's message was terse but clear. Liam's ominous threat played heavily on her mind, but her brother needed her. Risking everything, she dialed the number to Mary Margaret's shop, relieved that she heard the antique jewelry dealer's voice by the third ring.

"Sullie," she whispered, "it's Barbara. No . . . I'm fine . . . really

. . . I am. No, dear, he didn't hurt me, but Liam is very angry so I must make this brief. Tell Kerry that Paddy McDowell will meet him at Gerrad's Place shortly after six o'clock. But be very careful, Mary Margaret. Paddy warned that the roads are being monitored and the boys are roaming the city in packs, checking pubs. And one more thing, Sullie. Tell my brother that I love him."

Replacing the receiver gently, Barbara backed away from the phone, frightened. She had done what she promised, but she could do no more. In time, God might forgive her for disobeying her husband, but Liam Thompson never would.

Poor Barbara. She had no way of knowing that Liam had awakened from his nap early. She had no way of knowing that he had picked up the phone just a fraction of a second before she had. Cupping the mouthpiece, he had listened as Paddy McDowell revealed the plan. Depressing the receiver, he waited patiently while Barbara relayed the message to Mary Margaret, as all along he knew she would do. But there was one thing that puzzled him that didn't make sense. Paddy McDowell had said to meet at Gerrad's Place. There was nowhere in Limerick by that name. Nevertheless, when Barbara had completed her phone call to the antique dealer, Liam Thompson made one of his own, just as he had promised, to the IRA man named Eddy Maloney.

It was just past 5:30 when Barbara finished preparing Liam's supper. Everything had to be perfect, from the veal scallopini to the fresh flowers she picked from the garden to adorn his tray. She would not dine with her husband this evening, for she knew he was still much too angry with her. She started up the stairs with his tray alone, prepared to eat later by herself in the kitchen.

At the top of the stairs she heard the phone ring. With her hands full, there was no way she could answer it. No matter, she thought, Liam caught it by the third ring. When Liam was on the phone, he did not like to be disturbed. And so, like the good and dutiful wife she was, Barbara waited patiently outside the slightly cracked bedroom door.

"What in God's name do you want?" Liam growled. "How dare you call me here. I've already paid you dearly. I won't permit you to extort more." After a long pause, he said, "Fifty thousand pounds was enough to dispose of the body and destroy any evidence. The boy was a prostitute. His life had no worth!"

The bedroom door was ajar. Barbara tried not to listen, but the sharp edge to Liam's voice pierced her troubled mind. At first his words made no sense. She listened more carefully.

"All right, I'll pay what you ask. I'll wire the money into your account tomorrow. Just make damn sure no one links this murder to me! Do you understand? If I go down, you go down with me! Now leave me the hell alone!"

Barbara suddenly chilled and her hands went numb. Hearing the clatter of china crashing to the floor, Liam bolted from the bed and ran after his wife, cursing. "Goddamn it, Barbara, come here!"

Stumbling down the stairs, Barbara Thompson sought only to escape. The horrible revelation was all she needed to know. Her husband was a murderer. He had killed a boy, a prostitute. She had to get away.

"Barbara, wait! You don't understand . . ."

"Murderer!" she screamed. "Murderer!"

The sound of his steps scrambling down the stairs terrified her as she ran for the front door. Five steps, that's all she had to freedom. Only five steps . . . but just as her hand touched the doorknob he grabbed her shoulder from behind.

"Listen to me, Barbara! I can explain!"

Trapped, in a final desperate attempt to escape, Barbara wheeled around and kicked Liam with all her strength, full force in the groin. Shrieking in pain, his eyes glazed with rage, Thompson lunged for his wife as she clawed her way once again for the door. Ripping her neat bun apart, he grabbed her by the hair and dragged her down the hall. He threw her into the drawing room, then bolted the door to prevent any escape.

Taking a deep breath, Liam steeled his nerves as his pain abated. Approaching his wife cautiously, he smiled benevolently.

"Enough of this, Barbara. You must be reasonable. You have no choice. Take hold of yourself, then perhaps we can find a workable solution."

Genuflecting beside his fallen spouse, Liam reached out and patted her shoulder gently.

"Be a good girl now, and I will explain."

There were no words Liam could utter that Barbara wanted to hear. For years the disturbed, raven-haired woman had endured his abuse, believing it to be her fault. She had labored years to create a fantasy of their life together, maintaining, at all costs, appearances to the outside world. But there was nothing he could say that would alter the truth of what he was. The illusions she had created shattered.

"I hate you," she cried, and then she spat in his face.

Wiping his wife's spittle from his mouth, Liam's mind started to dim. Reason was replaced by rage, blind rage with only a beginning, no end. Jerking her head back, he balled his fist as he smashed first her jaw and then her cheekbone. Rubbing his bruised knuckles, he kicked her hard in the ribs three times until he heard one crack and then another.

There were no cries of anguish from Barbara nor pleas for mercy, even as he kicked her again, this time in the head. When the pain became too much to bear, she simply closed her eyes and drifted off to a kinder place.

Liam was unaware of the passage of time. He would recall stumbling to the bar and pouring himself a double shot. He would wonder why his knuckles hurt. He would glance first at his hands and then at his clothing. He would be stunned that he was splattered with blood.

When he finally turned back to the center of the room, he would recoil in horror. He would have no memory of what had happened. But there lay his wife in a pool of blood, her features no longer recognizable. He would blame Kerry for Barbara's death. If Kerry had not returned home, Barbara would not have crossed him. He vowed to make Kerry pay.

chapter **19**

Racing down the Dublin Road were Mary Margaret and Kerry in the van, followed closely by Sydney in the rental car. The time was 5:45 p.m. Their destination was a pub in Ballina called Mad Molly's, owned by a friend of O'Sullivan's by the name of Gerrad McNamara.

Pondering the strange little character named Paddy McDowell, Mary Margaret turned to Kerry. "I must say your man used his head. How did he know that Gerrad's Place was my name for Mad Molly's?"

Kerry ignored Sullie's question. His eyes were focused on the people, the vehicles, and the buildings. Mary Margaret O'Sullivan had managed to keep them safely hidden in the attic of her shop this afternoon, but with a covey of loyal IRA on the prowl, Kerry understood that his remaining hours in Ireland were precious few indeed.

With the keenness of a hunted fox sensing the chase, Donavan focused his gaze upon the rearview mirror. Sydney closely tailed the van, allowing no other vehicles to come between them, her Irish driving skills, by necessity, vastly improved. No one seemed to be following them, but Kerry couldn't be sure. Paddy had warned that the roads were being monitored and, more importantly, the pubs checked.

Edgy, Donavan again glanced at his watch.

Time . . . time . . . time.

Time was running out. Where were they going? How would they get there? What would they find when they arrived?

Donavan threw a nervous glance to the right, past Mary Margaret to Finnigan's, the popular pub outside Limerick, just before the turnoff to Lisnagry. A familiar figure caught his eye.

"Slow down a bit, Sullie."

Obeying, O'Sullivan backed off the pedal while Kerry craned his neck to observe two men carefully checking cars. Gazing back toward the road, the IRA man Kerry knew from childhood patted his bulging pocket, then signaled the other to follow him through the front door. The lead man, the one in charge, was Eddy Maloney; the second, his younger brother, Patrick.

"Speed on, Sullie," he urged. "The bastards are moving our way!"

Time . . . time . . . time.

The IRA was closing in. Kerry's life was in dire jeopardy. Even Sydney was in danger just being with him. And even though she could stay behind, hidden in a safer place, the time to find her daughter was now or never. They had to leave Ireland tonight.

Hidden away in a lovely spot where the Shannon River pays homage to the hills of Clare, two towns are joined by a single bridge. Just across the bridge, on the Clare side, stands Killaloe, while on the near side sits the village of Ballina, in County Tipperary. Here, nestled near the Lakeside Hotel and the marina, was a small, unpretentious place by the name of Mad Molly's. The pub was known only by word of mouth and frequented mostly by locals, except when there was traditional Irish music featured. Buried off the main Dublin road by twenty miles, Paddy McDowell knew the pub was not one regularly visited by the IRA, nor would it be first on the list to be checked tonight. That was one of the two reasons he had chosen it as their meeting place.

No, one would never seek out this pub unless one knew the owner, a charming fellow by the name of Gerrad McNamara. A tall, lanky chap in his early fifties, Gerrad stood six feet one and weighed a lean one hundred eighty pounds. He had a roguish face and a wavy mix of brown unruly hair. An extrovert with a great sense of humor, Gerrad was known as an entertainer, a lover of women, and an expert boatman. If Gerrad McNamara didn't like you, he paid you no heed. No matter who you were or where you came from. But if he considered you a friend, as he did Mary Margaret O'Sullivan, there was no length to which he wouldn't go to help you. That was a fact Paddy McDowell counted upon, and the second reason he had chosen Mad Molly's.

On this particular evening, the normally tranquil village was aflutter. Known as a fishing and boating paradise during spring and summer, the two villages of Killaloe and Ballina joined forces to sponsor a huge, weeklong fair to kick off the fishing season beginning at dusk on Sunday and ending with a lavish parade the following Saturday. Tonight, booths were being erected and children's rides tested in the park adjacent to McNamara's tiny pub.

The sleepy village of Ballina had suddenly come alive. Teeming with excitement, everyone, it seemed, had come to pitch in and help with the fair. But soon the men would tire of their labor and, one by one, drift into McNamara's for a pint of Guinness.

The car-park adjacent to Mad Molly's was nearly full, so after hiding the van and the Toyota in McNamara's private drive on the blind side of the pub, Kerry and Sydney trailed Sullie cautiously through the side door. Mercifully, the pub was still relatively quiet. Gerrad stood, washing glasses behind the bar, preparing for the rush ahead. Only a handful of people graced the plain wooden tables near the fire. Two old men, fixtures at Mad Molly's, huddled together at the far end of the bar, while a smaller, younger fellow sat hunched over his pint with his back to the door.

Seeing Mary Margaret O'Sullivan, Gerrad threw down his towel and grinned. First he nodded to the man seated directly in front of him. Then he gestured to the table away from the windows in a secluded corner of the room. Finally he beckoned Mary Margaret to him and prepared to fix them all drinks, while Kerry, understanding the signals, ushered Sydney to the designated spot, back and out of the way.

"Good evening to you, darling Sullie," McNamara hailed jovially. "How have you been keeping?"

"I've had better days, pet," O'Sullivan sighed, pushing a stray lock of hair from her beaded forehead. "Would you ever fix me two gin and tonics with lots of ice, a Ballygwan for my friend, and a pint of Guinness for our pal, Paddy, when he arrives?"

"Aye, that won't be necessary," the slouched chap at the bar interjected. "I have me Guinness, Miss O'Sullivan, but I thank you just the same."

Paddy McDowell turned his scarred face toward Mary Margaret O'Sullivan and, without cracking a smile, evenly met her surprised gaze. Turning around, he acknowledged Kerry and then paused to check out Sydney. He climbed down from the stool but, before moving away from the bar, leaned closer to Mary Margaret. "Would you ever be so kind as to distract the American woman for a few minutes? I don't know how much time we've got, and I'd like a word alone with Kerry."

Perplexed by his request, Sullie merely nodded. Waiting until Gerrad had their drinks in hand, O'Sullivan and McDowell followed McNamara to the table in the corner. There, Kerry waited patiently to confer with Paddy, but it was Sydney who could not take her eyes off the man's disfigured face. It was not that she was fascinated by his appearance, rather that she was trying to read the information he'd come to convey. But, refusing to take a seat, McDowell denied her access to his inner thoughts or emotions. Suddenly Mary Margaret reached over and picked up Sydney's gin and tonic as well as her own. "Come with me, girl. Let's leave the men to talk."

"I'm staying right here," Sydney replied. "I want to hear what he's come to say."

Stubbornly, Paddy McDowell stood his ground, refusing to take his seat. It was Kerry who was forced to intercede.

"Go with Mary Margaret, Sydney. We don't have the time to quibble."

Again Sydney started to protest but, knowing it was futile, rose to her feet. How she hated men when they played their chauvinistic games, but she was in no position to argue. Time was simply too precious to waste.

Mary Margaret led Sydney just outside to the park that overlooked the Shannon River, the hills of Clare, even the bridge to Killaloe. The huge setting sun dominated the hills of Clare, blanketing the river and the surrounding countryside in an eerie coverlet of golden apricot.

Sydney's eyes were fixed upon the fair and the children's splendid rides. The merry-go-round in particular caught her fancy and would not let her be. The ride was not a phony plastic replica, but an old-fashioned, hand-carved masterpiece of wooden horses of every design, shape and color. And as the adults tested the ride for safety and the wonderful horses danced round and round and up and down to the music, the children standing nearby clapped their hands and shouted with glee.

Yet it was not the Irish children that Sydney saw, but the face of her own dear sweet Lydia. It was through Lydia's eyes that she experienced the vibrant yellows, ruby reds, electric blues and shimmering purples of the dancing horses whirling against the sunset.

"Oh, Lydia," she whispered aloud. "Where are you?"

Holding her still untouched drink in her right hand, Mary Margaret wrapped her free arm around Sydney's waist. Seeing her in grief, Mary Margaret O'Sullivan said nothing. There were no words she could utter that would mend this broken heart. Besides, she was angry. Sighing deeply, Mary Margaret silently asked God the questions only He could answer. "Why, God? Why do you let these things happen? Why must it be the children who suffer?"

She watched the people blithely crossing the bridge between Ballina and Killaloe. So trusting, she thought, the young and old alike going about their daily business, never dreaming what horror might befall them. People meandering about here and there—some in cars, others on bicycles, a few on foot—taking their time, most seemingly in no hurry.

Except for two men standing on the bridge, gazing frantically in both directions.

One looked familiar.

Where had she seen him before?

His shoulders hunched.

His pocket bulging.

His dark eyes darting in her direction.

Like a scene flashing from a passing car . . .

She remembered.

The face of the same man outside of Finnigan's.

Dropping her drink, she screamed, "Oh, dear God! They're here!"

Gasping for air, Mary Margaret grabbed Sydney by the arm, as together they ran with stumbling steps to the pub. Barging through the door and forgetting they were not alone, Sullie hurried to the table and cried, "They've found us, Kerry!"

Pushing back his chair, Kerry stuffed the papers Paddy had come to deliver into his pocket and stood. Seeing Mary Margaret in distress, Gerrad McNamara set his work aside and, signaling Molly to take over at the bar, joined the others at the table.

Trying to keep her voice low so as not to attract more attention, Sullie said, "I saw them, Kerry . . . that fellow you know and his brother. They're here."

"Where, Sullie? Where are they?"

"I saw them on the bridge."

Sizing up the situation quickly, Paddy asked, "Were they alone?"

"I couldn't tell. It seemed as if the one in charge kept looking around for others. Finally he turned and hurried toward Killaloe after the other one came this way."

Kerry turned to his compatriot. Laying a hand briefly upon his shoulder, he ordered, "Get out of here, Paddy! You can't afford to be seen with me now!"

Paddy McDowell realized the truth of his friend's warning. Throwing out his hand, he grasped Donavan's warmly.

"Be careful, Kerry. If the boys have come this far, they might already be blocking the road. You've got to find another way out."

Paddy McDowell donned his wool cap and, pulling it down to shield his eyes, moved cautiously to the entrance of the pub. Stepping through the front door, he glanced in either direction and then moved smartly down the hill, losing himself in the crowd at the fair.

"Mary Margaret, is there another road out of Ballina?"

Not knowing, Sullie turned to her friend Gerrad for the answer.

"I'm afraid not, my friend. Any other roads but the main one would come to a dead end. And your pal there was right. If the boys have come this far, they've probably got a lookout posted on the main road. No telling how many there are. They'll be checking the hotel and the bigger pubs first, but they'll get to us eventually. No, it would be too risky to attempt to outrun them on the road."

"Well then, what will we do?" Sydney cried.

"We've got to get to Dublin tonight," Kerry stated. "We'll just have to take our chances, that's all."

Gerrad McNamara removed his apron and, tossing it to a nearby table, declared, "There's only one way to beat them."

Three pairs of eyes turned to the lanky Irishman for the answer.

"I'll take you by boat. There's no one who can beat me on the water."

"You must be mad!" O'Sullivan wailed. "At this time of evening? My God, Gerrad, with the rocks and the dam . . . you could be ripped to shreds!"

"What choice do these people have?" McNamara countered. Glancing at his watch and then outside, he added, "Besides, if we leave now, there might be just enough daylight to make it!"

"It's no good," Donavan protested. "We can't involve you in this. Anyone helping me puts his own life in peril."

"Won't be the first time," piped Gerrad. "What do you say? Let's go now!"

Donavan's darting eyes sought the door. Any moment the boys with guns could come bursting through it.

"Okay," he said, "let's go! Sydney, hurry to the van and grab our things! Gerrad, is there another way out of here?"

"Aye, I'll sneak you out the kitchen and down the back steps to the marina. But hurry, my friend!"

"What do you want me to do?" Sullie inquired.

"Stay here," McNamara commanded. "From what I know about the IRA, the boys are ruthless but not insane. As long as you're not with Kerry, no one will harm you here in a public place. You're not the one they want. Just divert them as long as you can. But you have to promise me one thing or I won't go. No matter what, don't leave here until I return. Give me your word, Mary Margaret, or I won't leave you."

"You have me word," she swore. "Now go!"

McNamara turned and called for his wife, Molly. She joined the group still gathered in the corner. "Mind the pub while I'm gone, love, and keep a sharp eye on our girl, Sullie." Kissing her cheek quickly, he added, "I'll be back to help you close."

Molly McNamara did not like the glint in her husband's eyes. Someone was in trouble and her rogue of a man was intent on helping. Resting a finger ever so gently on her lips, he whispered, "Everything will be okay, love. I promise."

Alone now, two friends confronted one another, more than likely for the last time. It was an awkward, poignant moment, with precious seconds ticking by and neither one knowing what to say to the other.

"Where are you going?" Sullie asked.

"To a place called Dubai in the United Arab Emirates," Kerry replied.

"Dubai," Sullie repeated. "Yes, I've heard of it. A number of Irish lads have gone to Dubai to find work." With tears misting her eyes, Mary Margaret O'Sullivan threw open her arms and enveloped Kerry. "Take care of yourself, my love. And mind Sydney as well. She's a good woman. She deserves better."

Just then Sydney returned with their few precious belongings. Giving Mary Margaret a quick hug, Sydney said, "Thank you for everything, Sullie."

"Let's go," McNamara mouthed, gesturing for them to follow him behind the bar.

Grabbing his bag, Kerry turned to leave. But then he paused. "One more thing, Sullie. Look after Barbara for me. I don't trust Liam. Promise you'll let me know if anything goes wrong."

It was with a sincere nod that Mary Margaret O'Sullivan laid her hand upon her heart and swore, "I promise, Kerry. Now go!"

Gerrad McNamara hustled Kerry and Sydney through the narrow kitchen, then eased open the back door. Seeing no one, he
signaled them forward. The parking lot was full, the fairgrounds
packed. So many people wandering about, it was impossible to
tell who might be friend, who might be foe. McNamara took off,
running down the hill, with Kerry and Sydney in close pursuit.
Nearing the Lakeside Hotel, they slowed their pace. It would not
do to cause unnecessary notice. They forced themselves to walk
down the back steps to the marina.

The high-powered speedboat was buoyed in the third slot
near the end. McNamara jumped on board, then turned and
offered Sydney his hand.

Hoisting their bags on board, Kerry quickly followed. Gerrad
fired up the powerful engine, then guided them out of the slot.
Kerry's darting eyes quickly scanned the village. Yes, there they
were just as Mary Margaret had said—not Eddy Maloney or his
brother, but three other IRA loyalists exiting the Lakeside Hotel.

Turning his back on the village, he cried, "Get the hell out of
here, Gerrad!"

McNamara gunned the boat and sped away, spraying water in
all directions.

Falling into the seat beside Sydney, Kerry had to cup his
hands and shout to be heard above the engine's roar.

"Where are we going?" he cried.

"There's a village about an hour away called Portumna," McNamara shouted back. "I'll drop you there. The marina has a phone and you can call a taxi. The driver can take you on to Dublin, or perhaps you're still in time to catch a train. I'd take you farther myself, but we've barely enough daylight to get you there and me back here. There's no way to navigate the Shannon after dark. Nothing on the river is lighted at night . . . not even the buoys."

Leaving the villages of Killaloe and Ballina behind, they sped down the narrow rocky channel of the Shannon River. At twilight on the Shannon River, all is peaceful, as swans, ducks and geese gather to feed. As the piercing whine of the high-powered speedboat grew closer, the birds scattered in fright, spraying water and feathers in every direction. Sydney shivered as she was reminded of her own life—once so tranquil, but now shattered into pieces and scattered about at the very mercy of a fate that mocked her. She was cold and she was frightened. Putting his arm about her shoulders, Kerry pulled her to him. It was the gesture of a friend. It was the gesture of a man who felt and understood her fear.

■

It was all Mary Margaret could do to make her way back to the table. Her knees were like jelly. Sagging into her chair, she closed her eyes and prayed.

"For the love of God, keep them safe."

A familiar voice jolted her.

"Are you all right, Sullie? You look a might pale."

"No, love, I'm fine," Mary Margaret lied. "But would you ever bring me a gin and tonic? Me nerves are shot. I think I'll sit here awhile and collect me thoughts."

"Sure, Sullie, sure," Molly soothed. "Shall I clear the rest of the table?"

"Please, pet."

The Limerick antique jewelry dealer was a fixture at Mad Molly's and a damned good friend of Molly's husband. It disturbed the barmaid greatly to see the beloved lady so badly shaken. As quickly as she could, she returned to Sullie with a double gin and tonic, lemon, and a lot of ice.

"There you go, Sullie. I fixed it just the way you like it."

Molly set the drink upon a plain, white, cardboard coaster.

"Is there anything else I can do for you?"

"No, no thanks, pet. I'll sit here awhile and wait for Gerrad to return. Don't bother about me, love. It looks like you're going to have your hands full."

And indeed, as Molly McNamara, with hands resting on her pleasantly rounded hips, glanced to the front door, she saw the menfolk starting to dribble in. She scurried to the bar, leaving Mary Margaret to her drink.

After taking a swig of gin, Sullie reached into her handbag for a fresh pack of Rothmans. She played with the beads around her neck, twirling them tighter and tighter. But no matter what she did, she grew more anxious. How long would she have to sit here? Just when would the boys come bursting through the door, and how in the hell would she divert them?

Nearly jumping out of her skin, she looked for something to do. In the center of the table she saw a pencil. Perhaps it was Molly's or one Kerry in his haste had left behind.

With an eye still on the door, she sipped her gin, smoked her Rothmans, and absently began doodling on the coaster. When her drink was almost empty and the ashtray filled with an endless chain of smoked Rothmans, Mary Margaret couldn't stand the suspense of waiting a minute longer.

She wondered how much time had passed. Without a watch, she could only guess. An hour perhaps, maybe more. Where was Kerry? Had Gerrad guided them out of the channel safely, or had they been discovered by Maloney and his thugs along the way? Why had the IRA not come to search this pub? Could it be that Kerry lay dead?

Not knowing the answer, she had to see for herself. She knew where McNamara docked his boat. If she could make her way to the marina, she would have her answer. Gazing about the pub, she searched for Molly McNamara.

"Mind me drink and Rothmans, pet. I've got to get a breath of fresh air. I'll be back in a few minutes."

Despite the small crowd that was gathering in the pub, the harried barmaid assured Mary Margaret that her seat and her things would be safe. Shaking her head, she wondered what caused Sullie to leave in such a hurry, for not only had she left her drink and cigarettes behind, but her rather large, black handbag as well. Leaving her place as she found it—with drink, cigarettes and the coaster upon which she had doodled—Molly picked up Sullie's purse and brought it with her, tucking it safely behind the bar. A drink or some smokes, she reasoned, were of little consequence, but a woman's handbag was another matter.

Just then, a group of men entered the pub, none of whom she recognized. Pausing in the doorway, they glanced about . . . carefully . . . as if searching for someone. Not knowing them, pretty young Molly was hesitant to step forward.

"Seat yourself, gentlemen," she called from behind the bar. "Or come up here and I'll pour you a pint."

"Could we have a word with you, ma'am?" the leader of the group demanded.

"All right," she agreed, leaning forward. "What is it you want?"

"We're looking for a tall Irishman with a limp and an American woman with red hair. Have you seen them?"

Staring blankly, Molly McNamara at first did not reply.

"The man's name is Kerry Donavan. Do you know him?"

"No," the barmaid replied. "I do not."

But there was a flicker of fear in her eyes that seemed to betray her, and so Eddy Maloney changed tack.

"We wish them no harm, ma'am. I'm a friend of his, that's all. And I have a message to deliver of some importance. A member of his family has taken ill and he's needed. Has he been here?"

Since Gerrad McNamara had failed to warn her, the trusting, naive young woman believed Maloney's story and immediately replied, "Aye, he's been here. But he's gone now, been gone now for some time."

His cold, steely eyes narrowing, Maloney continued, "Would you have any notion where he's gone?"

"No, sir, I don't. He left in a flurry with my husband. But if you need to find him, you can ask Mary Margaret O'Sullivan. She was with him. She's stepped out for a moment, but she's coming right back. Her drink and her smokes are over there."

Pointing to the small table secluded in the far corner of the room, Molly asked, "Can I get you a drink while you wait?"

Tipping his cap rather graciously, Maloney replied, "No, ma'am. Me and the boys will wait for Miss O'Sullivan. Thanks just the same."

Eddy Maloney turned to the others, then in a low hush instructed them to wait outside, spread out and hidden so as not to alarm O'Sullivan. Slowly he meandered over to her table, pondering the information the barmaid had given him. Kerry Donavan was gone and so was the woman. How, and where? He'd seen the van and the rental car parked around back on the blind side of the building. Could they have left by road, perhaps in another vehicle? More than likely, he decided, someone had tipped them off. If that were true, no telling where they had gone or how.

Slowly, Eddy Maloney approached Sullie's table. What would he say when she returned? The antique jewelry dealer knew Eddy Maloney and his brothers, at least by sight, as she did most everyone in Limerick. Mary Margaret O'Sullivan would not buy the story the barmaid had swallowed. Eddy Maloney was no friend of Kerry Donavan's. Could he force her to talk? He wondered. Of course, he reasoned, a man had his ways. Balling his fist, he frowned. Messy business with a woman—always has been, always would be.

His gaze roaming the table, he noticed the filled ashtray first. She must be upset, he thought, for it looked as if she'd smoked nearly a full pack of cigarettes. Her drink, too, was nearly empty. Just alongside her tall glass was the coaster upon which she had doodled. Fascinated, Eddy Maloney picked it up.

She must have been very nervous, he decided, to have doodled in such a frenzied manner. Peering closer, Maloney thought he detected a word hidden among the many abstract circular motions of an anxious woman. Confused, the IRA man tried to make sense of her scribbling. Poor Mary Margaret . . . doodling was such an innocent and natural thing to do . . . particularly when one feels helpless and alone. It was only a word . . . a single word . . . that she probably didn't even consciously write. But it was the one word, if she knew that Kerry's enemy had discovered it, she would regret with all her heart that she had divulged.

Almost tasting the word on his lips, Eddy Maloney sounded out the letters.

"D-U-B-A-I."

Frowning, the IRA man pondered the situation carefully. Kerry Donavan was gone. It was pointless waiting here any longer. There was no need to meet with Mary Margaret O'Sullivan. There was nothing she could tell him he didn't have right here. Glancing at the coaster a final time, Eddy Maloney smiled and decided to take his leave.

"DUBAI."

Repeating the word interwoven in the pattern of senseless doodlings on a discarded coaster, suddenly everything seemed to make a bit of sense. Eddy Maloney had heard of a *place* called Dubai in the not-too-distant past. Where it was, he didn't know. There was a man, a very learned, well-traveled man, who would know. And that man had an interest in finding Kerry Donavan as well. Eddy Maloney left Mad Molly's and instructed his buddies to go home as well.

But it was not home that he would go . . . not just yet anyway. He had a stop to make first—a very important stop—at the estate just up the road from his meager abode, to the home of the learned man, to the home of Liam Thompson.

The hum of the engines was enough to put most passengers
to sleep, but not Kerry Donavan, nor even Sydney Lawrence.
Though both were exhausted beyond endurance, there were still
too many questions unanswered and too many issues unresolved.

The plane was crowded, so they had to settle for two seats in
the rear of the coach section. Finding it difficult to get comfortable
in the cramped, narrow space by the window, Kerry leaned back
against the cushion of his seat. His head was throbbing from sheer
weariness, and his eyes were so bleary it was difficult to focus.
His sharply defined, angular features looked haggard, and, rubbing his chin, he noticed the stubble of a beard. Then he remembered that he hadn't shaved in at least a day, or was it now two?

It was 2:00 p.m. London time, and Emirates Airline Flight 2
had been under way for nearly an hour. During that time, neither
Sydney nor Kerry found it necessary to speak. Each lost in their
own thoughts, they struggled to cope in their own fashion.

For Kerry, it was a recall of the events of the past day—a day
that now seemed more like a month. After docking at Portumna,
they had located a phone, just as Gerrad McNamara had promised,
and summoned a taxi. But the wait, a half-hour, seemed interminable. Then, when the taxi arrived, they were disappointed,
for the driver, an older man rather set in his ways, refused to take
them to Dublin. His shift would end within the hour, and he had
no intention of extending his time, despite the money Kerry

offered. It seemed as if he sensed, in his wise old heart, that this couple, no matter how attractive or wealthy they might be, were on the run. And to that end he wanted no part.

He would take them to catch a train, but that was as far as the cabby would go. The nearest station was Limerick Junction, but Kerry feared that was too risky. If the IRA was still watching the roads, the taxi would be spotted. It was at this moment of despair that a rather intriguing idea dawned.

"Hey, buddy," he had said, "let me take another look at the schedule." The driver handed Donavan the train schedule he always carried with him.

"Yes," Kerry nearly shouted, "that's it! Take us to Port Laoise." Despite throwing them a quizzical glance, the cabby shrugged and headed northwest. Port Laoise was a town of little distinction, except for the fact that the train made one of its last stops for the night there, and it was home to the foreboding prison dedicated to the internment of the IRA.

The prison at Port Laoise was one of the most dreaded institutions in all of Ireland, for once the iron gate clanged shut, rarely was a man seen again. No sane, free IRA member would dare cross the line into Port Laoise. It was not worth the risk.

The taxi ride to Port Laoise took eighty minutes, leaving them plenty of leeway to catch the eleven o'clock train to Dublin. By the time they arrived at the Dublin station and caught a taxi to the airport, it was well past one in the morning. They spent the remaining hours pacing the terminal until their nine o'clock departure on Aer Lingus to London. Like fugitives on the run, they didn't feel safe in one place, so they kept moving about the airport, always looking over their shoulders.

The flight to Heathrow Airport was a short one, but then they had to catch a train to Gatwick to make their one o'clock connection to Dubai. Now, finding themselves settled on board, they had only an endless, tiring flight to look forward to. With the time change, they would not touch down in Dubai until 11:59 p.m.

No matter how much he yearned for rest, sleep refused to come. Images of Donavan's past kept racing through his mind. Having seen his homeland for the first time in nearly a decade,

Kerry struggled to impress every detail of the countryside into the recesses of his memory.

Closing his eyes, Kerry tried to erase the haunting faces that mocked him, but the terror in his sister's eyes as she confronted her husband would not let him be. He tried to console himself with the fact that they had escaped Ireland safely, that finally, once and for all, his past was behind him. He had no way of knowing that two devils had struck a bargain and that his encounter with a treacherous past had only just begun.

■

True to his plan, Eddy Maloney left Ballina and drove to Lisnagry. At first, no one responded when he knocked at the estate of Liam Thompson. Finally, when he could stand the incessant pounding not a minute longer, Liam opened the door a crack, annoyed to find the intruder on his porch. His hair was askew, his cheeks flushed and puffy, even his speech was slurred. "Just what in the hell are you doing here, Maloney?"

"I must speak with you," Eddy responded. "The hour is late, but we have business that can't wait."

Being a man who rarely drank, Liam's tolerance for alcohol was limited. His mind was foggy and his reflexes dull. He was powerless to stop Maloney when he barged through the front door, sneering, "Aren't you going to invite me in?"

Swallowing hard, Thompson had no choice but to permit the repugnant terrorist to enter the drawing room. Seeing the bloodied, battered remains of Barbara, Maloney gasped.

"Oh my God, man! What have you done?"

"This doesn't concern you," Thompson retorted. "What are you doing here? Have you come to tell me my wife's brother is dead?"

Without invitation, Eddy Maloney walked to Liam's bar and poured himself a double shot. Steadying his nerves, he turned back around to the Brit, trying like hell not to stare at what once had been the face of a beautiful woman. Swallowing hard, he blurted out, "Kerry Donavan got away! We lost him in the town of Ballina."

"Jesus Christ," Thompson swore. "You imbecile! You had him in the palm of your hand! How in the hell could you let him get away?"

"Take it easy, Mr. Thompson. I think I know where he's gone. Look at this."

Eddy Maloney retrieved the coaster from his hip pocket.

"There, right there. Do you see the word 'Dubai'? Mary Margaret O'Sullivan scribbled the word after Donavan escaped."

Liam Thompson sought a pair of glasses from the mantel and studied the absent doodlings carefully. Sobering quickly, he glanced up and set the coaster aside.

"O'Sullivan told me the woman's child had been abducted and that they had come here to discover where she might have gone. I must say it looks as if you're right, Maloney. The bastard has gone to Dubai."

"What do we do now?" the IRA man queried.

"Be quiet and let me think."

Thompson slumped into one of the satin love seats. Before him his wife lay dead, but not so her brother. His dreams, his plans for the Donavan fortune, had suddenly, in the passage of the last few hours, slipped away.

No, it couldn't be. He had worked and struggled too hard. He'd put up with his insipid wife for years. He deserved now to reap the harvest of her death. No man, not even Kerry Donavan, could be permitted to stand in his way.

"Dubai is one of the seven states that make up the United Arab Emirates. If recollection serves me, there's a power base of IRA in the Middle East. Am I not correct, Maloney? Isn't that where you people go to train?"

"Aye, sir, it is," the terrorist replied. "The Council of Four buys its arms from dealers in the Arab world, and the elite special forces of the IRA do indeed train with Qaddafi's army."

"Well then," said Thompson, "we must contact them at once. Tell me who to call and how to do it."

Even small men of little consequence get drunk on the fumes of power. And so it was that Eddy Maloney drew himself to full stature and dared to confront Liam Thompson on equal footing.

"No, sir, your plan is no good. The boys don't know you from Adam. Yes, there's a bounty on Donavan's head, but in the grand scheme of things, he's insignificant. If you want him killed, you'll have to go through me. Don't you see? I can make the arrangements. I know what he looks like and I understand the inner workings of the organization. I'll track him down. But it will cost you, sir."

Poignantly, Eddy Maloney's eyes came to rest upon the gruesome remains of Barbara Thompson. "It seems to me that you have the most to gain from Donavan's death . . . and the most to lose if he lives."

His eyes narrowing, Liam Thompson knew he'd been caught in a fool's game. Eddy Maloney had him hands down. He was being blackmailed. Well, so be it, he reasoned, but he'd make damn sure the stakes were doubled from one body to two.

"All right, Maloney, we'll do as you say. I'll pay your expenses to Dubai and ten thousand pounds to boot if you're successful. But there's one more thing that you must do."

Liam Thompson hoisted himself to his feet, albeit shakily. Weaving to the sight of the murder, he paused and glanced down at the gray corpse.

"Take my beloved wife, Barbara, and dump her in the Shannon River near the power dam at Annacoty. She'll be swallowed up by the intake valves and cut to shreds. The remains will never be found."

Turning back to Maloney, Thompson smiled, but it was the sick grin of a pathetic mind. "Poor, poor Barbara," he intoned. "She was so distraught over seeing her brother again and reliving his shame that her mind snapped. She was a delicate soul, and when the burden became too much to bear, she simply took her life, drowning herself in the treacherous waters of the Shannon River."

■

"What now, Kerry? Where do we go from here?"

Sydney was tired, and it showed. Her makeup had long since worn off, and she had no desire, no energy, to repair it.

"We're traveling as man and wife," Kerry replied. "Meat exporters from the city of Limerick. We'll be staying at the Hyatt Regency Hotel and we'll arrange our visas once we arrive. We'll need clothes. It's hot in Dubai, but everything we need can be purchased right there, at one of the hotel shops. We'll make a final plan once we're settled."

Sydney frowned as she struggled to comprehend. "Why the Hyatt Regency?" she asked.

Kerry paled slightly, not knowing how much of the truth Sydney could handle. He reached out and took her hand in his own.

"Sydney, we're checking into the Hyatt Regency because that's where we've located Lydia."

High atop the Hyatt Hotel, in the most elaborate suite of the exclusive Regency Club, a young girl sat at her bedroom window, gazing past the clear waters of the Arabian Gulf to the beckoning horizon beyond.

The scene was a tranquil one, but the early morning sea failed to soothe her. In fact, her mind was focused on a very different scene, in a country far away.

Then, she had been a shy, lovely girl of fourteen, caught in that precarious abyss between childhood and adulthood. She had been an exquisite girl with luminous indigo hair and bright ebony eyes that lit a room with brightness while searching a curious world for new adventures. Then, it had been her glorious face of porcelain skin and ruby red cheeks that caught a stranger's notice. With heart-shaped, chiseled lips that parted in a smile before erupting in unabashed gleeful giggles, it was her trusting, vulnerable innocence that lingered long after her mere presence had departed.

She had been a happy child then, blossoming under the protective nurturing of a woman who adored her, in the inviting green spaces of a land that enriched her. But that was then and this was now.

Slowly, she removed her gaze from the sea and turned away from the window. Catching a glimpse of herself in the mirror just above the dresser, Lydia shuddered. Her once lustrous hair hung limp and unattended, strewn carelessly about her rounded shoulders. Her eyes were muddy and dull, and the rosy hue had long since departed from her hollowed cheeks and cracked lips.

Shutting out the image confronting her in the mirror, the child tried to make believe all this was merely a terrifying nightmare, and that soon her misery would end. Squeezing her eyes tightly shut, she prayed with all her might that she would wake up in her own bed to the sound of horses whinnying in the pasture, with Mack and Sydney by her side, and Billy Ray in the barn just beyond. Then she could return to being an innocent girl living in a place where people were still good and life held nothing but promise.

But as the young woman slowly opened her eyes and confronted the reality of herself once again, she knew that she could never return to the life she had known, to the innocence she had taken for granted. The image reflecting from the mirror was a haunting one. The child known as Lydia Hassan Ellis was no more. Only the heart remained of a once lovely, trusting girl and the memories that sustained her.

How long had it been since the terrible reunion with her father had occurred? To Lydia, time no longer seemed relevant. It had been a glorious spring day in April, that much she remembered. School had gone well, and like always she was anxious to see her mother when she returned home. As was her custom, she had peered through the window, expecting to see her mother as the bus crested its final hill before reaching Mack's place, but Sydney had not been there.

At first Lydia had not been alarmed. Sydney had been delayed, that's all. Lydia had jumped down from the bus and waved good-bye to her friends, knowing she would see her mother at any moment. Instead she heard the roar of a car's engine, the squealing of tires, and the abrupt swish of a car door opening. From the rear of the vehicle a man had emerged. He had the features she recognized as those of her father, but deep in his eyes Lydia saw something that she suddenly feared.

Instinctively she turned away, searching frantically for her mother. She had seen her then, hurrying down the path. Lydia bolted, but the man's powerful grasp had been too strong. She remembered being dragged to the car screaming. Her cries for help echoed mockingly down the country lane until the brutal slap of the man she once revered silenced her.

The rest of the day and the night had been a blur. To quiet her hysteria, Hassan had given her something to make her drowsy. They had flown to New York, that much she remembered, where they remained but a single night. Traveling under assumed identities, no one at Kennedy Airport had challenged the wanted felon, or his abducted daughter.

They settled in Dubai, where Hassan resumed his lucrative business dealings, and Lydia, confined to the penthouse suite, learned more about her father than she ever wanted to know. Many years ago, Ali Hassan had been a trusted minister of the Shah of Iran. Heading the secret police, the Savak, his ingenious methods of torture were feared throughout the country. Ali Hassan had taken great pleasure in inflicting unspeakable pain upon anyone who dared to question the policies or dictates of the shah.

During the Khomeini revolution, Hassan fled Iran. His wealth intact, he sought refuge with his daughter in the United States. Under the guise of a rug dealer, he had lived with Lydia in Kansas City, seemingly adapting to Western ways. But Ali Hassan was and always had been more than a mere dealer of rugs. With a secret society of the shah's elite, he had masterminded a plot to broker human organs in order to buy arms and train terrorists.

Ali Hassan, with his tall, stocky body and rugged features, was becoming a power broker in the Middle East. He was learning how to play one country against another, dealing arms to terrorists and revolutionaries alike. Once obsessed by his own causes, little mattered to Hassan now but a terrorist's ability to pay.

Ali Hassan had maintained a low profile while living in Kansas City. Lydia had been sheltered, and their privacy at all costs guarded. But he had permitted her to attend school and adapt to the culture. Now, back in the Middle East where Islam was revered, he had reverted back to the old ways. He was a hard man, but he loved his daughter. However, Lydia was not the same child he was forced to abandon. Lydia had changed under Sydney's care. She had become like her, a part of her. And that he could not tolerate.

So to him, her father, fell the responsibility of purging her of Western ways. At first he tried to reason with his daughter, but words would not sway her. He was forced to resort to the dictates his culture demanded. Under Islamic law, a woman is a man's property, with ownership resting first with the father, then later with the husband of the father's choosing. And when a woman fails to obey the male's command, she has to be punished. And so, Ali Hassan resorted to his fist. Her spirit and fight, once thought to be so fragile, amazed him. Soon her iron will would crack, and she, like all good Islamic women, would submit without question to her father's rule.

Sickened by the sight of herself in the mirror, Lydia returned to the window. Once again, she struggled to see beyond the horizon, daring to recall a distant land, another time, and a woman who adored her. Where was her mother? Had she forgotten her by now? How in God's name would Sydney find her?

Tormenting questions, questions with no answers, vied for space in the child's troubled mind. Yet no matter what her father said or did, something inside of her begged her to hold on . . . if only for a little longer.

Lydia reached inside the deep pocket of her traditional Muslim dress where she hid her most precious possession. It was the mustard seed locket Sydney had given her. A slow tear worked its way down her cheek. Fingering the locket, she called up the image of the tall, svelte woman with the flaming hair and hazel eyes.

"Mommy," she cried in a choked, husky whisper, "where are you?"

It was Kerry who arose first that morning. He just couldn't sleep, despite the fact he was so weary even the cushions between his bones ached. And so, easing himself out the left side of the king-sized bed, he limped to the bathroom to shower, shave and dress.

It had been well past midnight by the time they landed at Dubai International Airport, cleared customs, and caught a taxi for the ten-minute ride to the Hyatt Regency.

Traveling as husband and wife but without a reservation, Sydney and Kerry found themselves at the mercy of the hotel clerk who informed them the Hyatt was full . . . except for a standard room on the second floor with a single king-sized bed, a dresser, two chairs and a small table.

Walking from the bathroom back to the bedroom, towel-drying his hair with one hand while balancing a cup of brewed coffee in the other, Kerry smiled. Never would he forget the look on Sydney's face as she realized she had no choice but to share a bed with the man she so desperately needed yet so irrationally feared. She had succumbed to sleep, finally, after much consternation, fully clothed, atop the sheets where she lay slumbering still.

Setting the towel aside, Kerry glanced out the window, then fumbled with the collar of his red-plaid Pendleton shirt. Even though the hotel was air-conditioned, the searing heat of the morning sun reflected off the windows of the nearby glass and steel buildings, making him hot and edgy. It was not yet midmorning and yet the temperature was already climbing toward 90°.

Donavan yearned for a cigarette, realizing, of course, that he had none. Smoking, such a customary habit in Ireland, was one he had long ago abandoned; yet this morning the pleasurable memory of the nicotine rush bit him hard. Perspiring now from the morning sun and the rub of his irritating wool collar, he turned away from the window and sipped his coffee.

As his eyes slowly scanned the tastefully decorated bedroom, Kerry was reminded of any number of hotel rooms in any number of cities. The rooms all looked the same, usually painted in various shades of mauve and turquoise. The mattress was too soft, the pillows a bit too firm. And the amenities . . . always the same in every fine hotel all over the world, from the shampoo to the mouthwash in tiny plastic bottles. Bringing the insipid brew to his lips once again, Kerry grimaced. Just the latest in the familiar stream of hotel niceties . . . tasteless coffee brewed in the room.

Yet this room wasn't the same as others in a free world. Nothing was the same for Kerry Donavan, a despised stranger in a hostile, foreign world.

It was Kerry who understood what Sydney didn't. Should they fail, should they be caught, there was *nothing* anyone, anywhere in the world, could do to help them.

They were in Dubai, after all—a Muslim city in the United Arab Emirates. It looked modern, westernized even, but it was a city that loathed them and all they stood for.

Kerry was determined to formulate a plan. There were four things he had to do straight away. First, secure their visas. Second, change Irish pounds into Arab dirhams. Third, locate Paddy McDowell's Irish contacts, and last, buy each of them some lightweight cotton clothing.

Kerry leaned over the bed and studied Sydney's sweet sleeping face. With her fiery mane of coppery tangles spread carelessly over the pillow, Sydney was a ludicrous sight, and one that Kerry, despite himself, found totally alluring. Kneeling down beside her, he softly stroked her hair until her eyes fluttered open.

"Go back to sleep," he whispered. "It's early yet. I have to leave you for a while. I have business to attend to."

"I'll go with you," she said in a groggy voice.

Kerry's response was firm. "No, you must stay here. Remember, Hassan knows you. You could be recognized. Then everything we've gone through would be for nothing. I'll be back in an hour, at the most two. Order breakfast if you're hungry. Just remember to sign the ticket *Margaret Flynn.*"

Kerry shut the door behind him and waited for the automatic click of the lock before proceeding to the elevator. Since it was still early, he hoped he would find the hotel quiet, where a stranger could meander about relatively unnoticed. But when the elevator door opened, he encountered a lobby teeming with businessmen in lightweight summer suits speaking languages he failed to comprehend. There was no way he could remain inconspicuous. He was, after all, a man with a distinct limp, a disability that set him apart. His handsome, angular features were decidedly Gaelic, and he was dressed not for the searing heat of the Middle East, but for the cold, wet winds of Ireland.

Worse, there was no one at the concierge desk. Late last night, when they checked in, he had been forced to leave his traveling papers with the desk clerk. He was told it was a routine matter of policy. Visas were required in the United Arab Emirates, yet only the concierge could take care of the matter and he, unfortunately, had left for the night. Their passports would be locked in the vault. Their visas would be waiting in the morning.

Suddenly a thin Arab man appeared behind the desk. The man's features were small and pinched, with dark, unfriendly eyes and thin lips that refused to smile. His name tag read "AZIMA."

Despite a bad case of the nerves, Kerry Donavan flashed a broad, toothy grin. Feeling and looking like a dumb Irish Paddy, he decided to act like one. When he spoke, it was with a thick, embellished brogue.

"Top of the morning to you, me man. Could you ever tell me where the concierge is? Me name is Sean Flynn and I'm in need of me passport and visa."

In the precise clipped speech of one who has been educated

in England, Azima replied, "The concierge has gone to break, but let me have a look."

He shuffled through a pile of papers stacked behind the desk.

"Here we go. Sean and Margaret Flynn?"

Azima frowned, as for what seemed an eternity he compared the information contained in the passport and visa with the photograph of the man standing before him.

"It says here, Mr. Flynn, that you are traveling with your wife and that you are a meat exporter from Ireland."

"Aye," Kerry replied calmly, "that's right."

"What kind of . . . meat . . . do you export?"

"Cattle," Kerry replied, "fine, fat Irish cattle."

The acting manager of the hotel started to question Mr. Flynn further, but a queue had begun to form and Azima was short-handed.

He handed the paperwork to Kerry. "Well, all right then, here are your passports and your visas. Have a pleasant stay."

Donavan nodded his thanks and started to walk away.

"How long will you be staying in Dubai, Mr. Flynn?" Azima called after him.

"A few days," Kerry replied, "a week at most."

"Well then, perhaps you had better purchase some light-weight clothing." The thin man with tightly pinched lips stared at the Irishman. "Either you were ill-advised as to our climate or you made your travel arrangements in too much haste. In any event, you'll find some nice shops to the right of the lobby in the arcade."

Donavan paused to wipe the perspiration from his brow as he made his way to the area just off the lobby called the arcade. He felt exposed like a piece of raw beef and he swore under his breath. Thanks to the bastard Azima, the item that had been last on his list had now become a top priority.

Exhaling sharply, he entered an exclusive boutique on his left. He wondered where to begin. Start with the obvious, he reasoned, shop for what you're most familiar with. Then, realizing the absurdity of his thoughts, he nearly laughed aloud. For Kerry Donavan, as rich and sophisticated as he might be, couldn't recall the last time he had indulged himself in new clothes. It was not a matter of money, but rather a lack of necessity. By the very nature of the reclusive life he had chosen, he required very little.

He began rummaging through racks of designer clothes, locating what he thought were his sizes and best colors. He came up with two pairs of pants—one tan, another dark blue—and two polo shirts. Then he looked for a pair of comfortable loafers. He failed to notice the petite, dark-haired woman studying him with bright, inquisitive eyes. She was an incredibly beautiful woman, in her late forties. She had eyes the color of light mocha, and a delicate, heart-shaped mouth etched in pink. Her long titian hair, which had not yet begun to gray, was worn loose and straight, falling just below her waist.

"May I help you, sir?" she said finally. Kerry wheeled around. "Would you like me to hold your things?" she continued.

"Yes . . . please," he stammered as he handed her the pants and shirts. He noticed a gleaming pair of Italian loafers. "In an American shoe, I would wear a size eleven. Do you think you have a pair to fit?"

"Yes, I believe so. Just one moment, please."

Soon she was back. "Size eleven, you said? Here you go."

Kerry removed his dirty boots and slipped on the soft brown loafers. "Very good. I'll take the shoes and the clothes as well."

Kerry then meandered to the opposite side of the room and began browsing for Sydney. The smile faded from his lips. He felt lost. What size skirt did she wear? What were her favorite colors? Did she like silk blouses or would she prefer cotton?

If it had been years since he had shopped for himself, it had been a lifetime since he had shopped for a woman. The last time . . . when was the last time? The last time he had been with Patricia.

Without warning, images of his wife's face appeared, flooding his mind with thoughts of her glistening blond hair, porcelain skin and soulful blue eyes. Blinking hard, he forced his gaze about the shop, finally coming to rest on a black, sequined gown.

He remembered another time, another place. A party they had attended when she had worn a dress very much like this one. He could still remember the smile upon Patricia's lips when he encountered her in the bedroom later, the tight black garment clinging seductively to her body.

He forced the picture of his dead wife from his mind. Patricia was gone. He had killed her. It was Sydney he had to worry about now.

He glanced around the exclusive shop again. But it was not this boutique that he saw, but Harrods, the wonderful store in London. Patricia's favorite—and baby Kate's. In his mind he heard their laughter and then . . . the terrible explosion.

Closing his eyes, he started to tremble.

Alarmed, the boutique clerk hurried up to him.

"Sir, you look ill. Should I summon help?"

The sound of her lilting accent drew him back to the present.

"I'm sorry, it's nothing. My wife and I had a spat, that's all. Would you help me select something pretty for her? I'm afraid I'm so rattled I can't think. My wife . . . Margaret . . . is tall and thin." He gave a helpless gesture. "She has wavy auburn hair and hazel eyes. I have no idea what size she wears."

"Nevermind," said the woman, "I think I know. With her hair and coloring, perhaps we should select something in pink or a rich shade of emerald green."

"Yes," said Kerry, "that would do nicely."

Donavan realized that he did not even know the gentle woman's name.

"I appreciate your kindness. What is your name, please?"

"Madeline," she answered quietly.

"Well, Madeline, I'd like to find a nice dress for my wife and perhaps a pair of slacks and a silk blouse. Could you find a scarf as well and something lightweight to sleep in?"

Embarrassed, he glanced down to his own heavy wool clothing. "I'm afraid we are ill-prepared for the heat of Dubai."

There was a twinkle in Madeline's eyes as she studied the stranger. He must love his wife dearly to be so upset. Well, she'd go through her inventory carefully. She'd select the perfect things.

"If you like, monsieur, I will choose the outfits you require and have them sent up to your room this afternoon. Would that suit you?"

"Oh, yes," Kerry sighed, greatly relieved. The last thing he was equipped to do was choose clothes for Sydney.

"My name is Flynn . . . Sean Flynn. We're staying in room 218."

The Frenchwoman nodded.

"You've been most kind," he said. Then on impulse he asked, "Have you worked in the hotel long?"

"Three years, monsieur," she replied.

"I'm trying to locate two of my countrymen. Brothers named Seamus and Michal O'Daugherty. Would you know them?"

Madeline lowered her eyes. "I'm afraid I know very few people here."

Kerry waited, hoping she would continue.

"I'm not from Dubai, sir. I'm from Avignon. I'm here only because of my daughter."

Kerry's sympathetic look encouraged her to go on.

"My husband is a citizen of the United Arab Emirates. We married in France, but he brought our daughter here when she was ten. We are divorced now, but if I wish to have any contact with my daughter I must remain here. It is the custom of the country. I am permitted to work, but I am not permitted to socialize. I'm afraid I can't help you."

Busying herself, Madeline sought to turn away, but Kerry remained fixed. "I'm sorry to hear this," he said. "Perhaps then you'd be kind enough to call the personnel department. I really must locate the brothers."

With obvious distress, Madeline shook her head no. "Sir, we are not permitted to give out any information on hotel employees. You'll have to ask at the front desk."

Another confrontation with Azima was the last thing Kerry wanted. He tried one last desperate ploy.

"Please, Madeline, it would mean so much to my wife. You see, these brothers are friends of her family. Locating them would please her so . . ."

Feigning helplessness, he shrugged. Resignedly, Madeline walked to the back room to use the phone. Returning in a few minutes, she handed Kerry a piece of paper with the information that he sought.

"The older brother is in the hotel now. He works the day shift. The younger one won't come in until later."

Kerry took the piece of paper then bent down and gallantly kissed the woman's hand.

"Thank you, Madeline." At the entrance of the shop, he paused. "Don't worry, Madeline," he promised. "This will remain our secret."

Despite his cheerful words, Kerry was troubled. The woman had been so kind, but in the end he had caused her distress. She had lived a life of sorrow—that much he knew. But her choices had been relatively simple. To be near her only daughter, she lived this drab existence. For her it was worth the price. Choices had never been that simple for Kerry nor, he suspected, for Sydney.

Kerry fetched the piece of paper he had crammed into his pocket. In a beautiful hand, she had scrolled the two names he sought and the departments in which each of them worked. The older brother, Seamus, was the one he had to encounter first. He was here now, in the hotel, working the day shift in maintenance. Casting his gaze across the lobby, he saw the elevator and, just to the right, a staircase.

Maintenance, he reasoned, would be on the lower level, the area of the hotel off-limits to guests. Averting his gaze, he hurried across the lobby, hoping not to attract attention, despite his limp and the clothes he still wore. At the door to the stairs he paused, then turned the knob. Luckily, the door was unlocked.

The sound of his feet echoed on the bare metal as he descended the stairs. At the bottom, he encountered yet another steel door. Mercifully, this door, too, remained open.

It was stifling on the lower level. It was noisy as well, with the exposed pipes rattling just above his head. To the right was the laundry, just beyond the hotel kitchen, and to the left a huge storage area for banquet tables and chairs.

He was not alone as he slowly made his way down the narrow passageway. Scattered about were a number of hotel employees sneaking a smoke with their ties loosened and their curious eyes fixed upon the tall man with a limp. Passing the electronic time clock, Kerry's thoughts were focused upon the man he sought. Paddy had told him little, only that his name was Seamus O'Daugherty and that he was from Cork. His father had been sympathetic to the cause, but he had died when Seamus was sixteen, leaving his widowed mother alone to raise a brood of eight.

Without a father's firm hand to guide them, the two eldest O'Daugherty boys had grown up on the wharf with a knack for getting into trouble. But they had been likable lads who were loyal to their mum, and so, through the years, Paddy McDowell had endeavored to help them in any way he could.

Five years ago, Seamus and Michal got into the last of a long line of scrapes. This time it was a fatal fight. It didn't matter that they were outnumbered or jumped from behind in a dispute over cards. It didn't matter that someone pulled a gun, forcing Michal to defend himself with a knife and forcing Seamus to grab a broken beer bottle. All that mattered was that, at the end of it all, one man lay dead and another critically wounded.

The dead man was the son of the chief of police, the other man, the son of a well-known politician. Therefore, it was to the O'Daugherty brothers alone that the bloody hands of justice looked. Knowing the O'Daughertys would never get a fair trial, Paddy McDowell hid the brothers until, using his IRA connections, he slipped them out of the country and relocated them in Dubai, where they quickly found work. The money was good, even if the conditions were deplorable. Freedom had been worth the price. And so, here in the obscurity of the Middle East, they would remain until it was safe to return to Ireland. But nobody believed that day would come.

Because of Paddy McDowell, the O'Daugherty brothers had been spared a lifetime behind prison bars. They owed the IRA man and they owed him big.

At the far end of the hallway, Donavan saw the door marked "Maintenance." Approaching slowly, he encountered a small Pakistani. He beckoned the wary man closer.

"Do you speak English?" he inquired.

The worker nodded almost imperceptibly.

"I'm looking for someone, and I wondered if you might know him. His name is Seamus O'Daugherty."

A spark of recognition lit up the man's eyes. "Yes, I know him."

"Is he here now?" Kerry queried.

The man threw his head in the direction of the maintenance department.

"Would you be so kind as to fetch him for me?" Reaching into his pocket, Kerry retrieved the handful of dirhams he had secured at the airport. After placing them in the Pakistani's hands, the smaller man nodded and disappeared through the door.

Within a minute, a man in his late twenties appeared. He was short and squat with hard features, thin hair and acne-pitted skin.

He didn't smile, and his murky eyes were guarded. In short, he was not at all what Kerry expected.

In a mean, thick brogue, he growled, "You wanted to see me?"

"Are you Seamus O'Daugherty?" Donavan asked.

"Who wants to know?" the other retorted.

"I do," Kerry replied, keeping both his voice and his eyes steady. "I bring greetings from a friend in Cork."

Kerry waited for some trace of recognition or emotion, but the man named Seamus O'Daugherty denied him both.

"Is there somewhere private we can talk?"

Grunting, O'Daugherty turned and motioned Kerry to follow him through an unmarked door, opening onto the alley.

Stepping out into the blistering hot sun of Dubai, Kerry waited. Seamus O'Daugherty waited as well, saying nothing. His jagged face reminded Kerry of a junkyard dog, but his huge triceps commanded respect.

Fetching a pack of cigarettes from the sleeve of his rolled shirt, Seamus O'Daugherty lit a cigarette, inhaled deeply, and offered a smoke to Donavan. Surprising himself, Kerry accepted. He inhaled the cigarette lightly. Even so, the first rush of nicotine made him dizzy.

"Paddy McDowell sends his regards," said Kerry at last.

O'Daugherty stared down at his dirty, nicotine-stained nails. Somehow he knew this day would come, but Lord, how he hoped it never would. "And how is my friend, Paddy McDowell?"

"He's well, as is your mother. Your sister is expecting her third baby."

Seamus grunted, seemingly grateful for the bit of news.

"And you, who might you be?"

"My name is Kerry Donavan. I know Paddy well."

"What do you want with me?"

His voice had grown less harsh, but he kept his eyes on his calloused hands as he waited for Kerry's answer.

"I need your help," Donavan stated, "and the help of your brother as well."

O'Daugherty's jaw tightened and the muscle just above his cheek twitched.

Kerry studied the man carefully. Could he trust him? Only time would tell. Laying his hand atop Seamus O'Daugherty's rippled shoulder, he said calmly, "Paddy says the time has come to pay your dues."

Mesmerized, Kerry sat silently on the edge of the bed, his eyes fixed upon the lovely woman who seemed transformed by a few hours of sleep and a pretty, new ensemble. Her freshly washed, gleaming hair was caught in a bow at the nape of her neck, matching the wispy pink silk blouse and pants that Madeline had chosen.

Her eyes were shining like bright new copper pennies as she strained to hear the knock they expected any minute at the door. Kerry, too, had showered and changed, and although his new clothes provided him relief from the heat, they didn't bring him any peace of mind. With every minute that passed he wondered if the O'Daugherty boys would keep their appointment. If they didn't . . . there was nothing he could do. He and Sydney would be helplessly, hopelessly, on their own.

A soft rap at the door jarred them both. Sydney stood. So did Kerry.

"Remember what I told you, Sydney. Stay calm and focused. Give them the facts, that's all. The decision to help must be theirs alone. Anything else . . . would be unfair."

Opening the door a crack, Donavan let the two men quickly into the room. Seamus, the older one, had not taken the time to wash or change, and so, reeking of sweat, he kept his hand to himself. The younger man, Michal, immediately thrust out his hand for a shake.

Unlike his older brother, Michal O'Daugherty, at twenty-five, was a tall, broad-shouldered fellow. He was a grand-looking lad, with a thick, full head of red hair and a typically Irish, rosy complexion. He had lively, cornflower blue eyes, and a big smile. He had a pleasant, open face and a gentle demeanor. Perhaps this was why Michal worked room service in the evenings where a handsome face and an outgoing personality were prerequisites, while his brother was relegated to the solitary confinement of the basement with his machinery and a pouch filled with tools.

Kerry and Sydney sat on the edge of the bed, leaving the two chairs for the brothers.

"Thank you for coming, gentlemen," said Kerry. "Seamus, Michal, I would like you to meet Sydney. We asked you here because we need your help, but first we'd like you to hear Sydney's story."

Instinctively, Sydney leaned toward the two men. "About three years ago, my late husband and I moved to Kansas City, Missouri. We bought a house next-door to an Iranian businessman and his eleven-year-old daughter. Lydia's mother had died when she was a baby, and since Sam and I had no children, it was natural that we would become quite close. But Lydia's father was not at all what he appeared. In fact, he was a terrorist arms dealer who masterminded a plot to broker human organs. He abandoned Lydia to our care and signed away his paternal rights when he had to flee the country as a wanted felon."

Kerry had urged her to remain unruffled and rational, detached even, as she shared her story. That's why her words came out in a rush and her sentences merged one into the other. But, in speaking of the child she loved so dearly and the loathsome man who had wrenched her away, Sydney faltered.

"Sydney's husband, Sam, was killed in February. She and Lydia left Kansas City and returned to her father's home in Kentucky. That's where we became . . . friends."

Stumbling over the word "friends," Kerry turned to Sydney and sheepishly smiled. Thrown together by passion, their relationship was a tumultuous one at best. No, Kerry reasoned, glancing at the woman who stirred him in a way he cared not to admit, by now, with their lives hopelessly entangled, the word *friends* paid them a terrible injustice.

Taking a deep breath, Sydney continued, but her voice was raspy.

"We were just starting to get back on our feet when . . . he . . . came back . . . out of nowhere. The school bus dropped Lydia off on the road just down from our house. She was waiting for me, you see. I used to meet her every day at the same time. I was delayed. I was running down the lane when I saw the car. Two men got out. Then I heard Lydia scream. One man had a gun. He aimed it at me. I froze. Lydia tried to run, but her father grabbed her. She fought him. He hit her. He dragged her to the car and sped away. I will never forget the sound of her voice as she cried out for help."

Sydney's eyes glistened and her voice caught in her throat.

Kerry studied the brothers carefully, but neither Seamus nor Michal said or did anything. Neither one betrayed a single emotion. Perhaps Sydney's plight meant nothing to these two men, so calloused by life.

"Don't you see?" said Kerry. "In every way, Sydney is Lydia's mother. The adoption in the States is final. The father gave up his rights to the child when he abandoned her. He allowed a bond, an irrevocable bond, to develop between this woman and this child. And then, without warning, he came back to claim her like a forgotten piece of property. It's not right! Her mother wants her back."

It was Seamus who spoke up in a grave voice that was firm, but not unkind.

"What does this have to do with us?"

Kerry and Sydney exchanged glances.

"We've traced the man and the girl to Dubai. They're here in the hotel. They're residing in the penthouse suite of the Regency Club. The man's name is Ali Hassan."

Now it was the O'Daugherty boys who stared at one another.

"Have you seen them?" Sydney asked.

Clearing his throat, Michal asked, "The girl . . . what does she look like?"

"She's quite pretty," Kerry responded quickly. "She's fourteen but she's a delicate little thing. I doubt she stands much over five feet tall. She has coal black hair that curls right here around her face." Clumsily, Donavan gestured, trying to show the men just what he meant.

Sydney quickly interjected, "Lydia is very shy and sweet. Smart, too. She's everything you could ask for in a daughter . . ." Abruptly, Sydney halted. Her eyes searched those of the brothers, demanding no less than the truth. "My daughter . . . you've seen her, haven't you?"

Yet again Michal threw a glance to his older brother. Seamus nodded. "Tell them," he directed.

Clearing his throat again, Michal struggled to find the right words. "I've delivered dinner to their suite a number of times. The man, is he big and muscular? Kind of mean looking, ugly even?"

"Yes," Kerry whispered, "go on."

"I've seen the girl, but only briefly. She was dressed all in black. You know, like any other Muslim female. Her head was covered, but I saw her face . . ." He looked down.

Michal turned away. He couldn't bear to look at Sydney any longer.

"What is it?" she pleaded. "What's wrong?"

With all defenses worn away, Sydney forgot Kerry's instructions for behaving. Grabbing Michal by the arm, she jerked him harshly until he was forced to confront her.

"Tell me what you've seen!" she cried.

"The child's face was bruised and swollen. It was obvious that she had been beaten. Then another time, I saw them walking through the lobby. The girl was muzzled like a dog. I came home and told my brother all about her. It bothered me so bad I couldn't sleep. You see, we have little sisters at home. I couldn't bear to see anyone hurt them. It's not right what he's doing to her! It's just not right!"

Kerry watched her across the table for two, but her eyes were averted and she didn't know he was staring. It was dark now in the city of Dubai, just past nine o'clock, as they dined alone in their hotel room on a scrumptious meal of sole amandine. A single candle set in the center of the table softly illuminated the room. Outside, the city lights beckoned, yet the sea was still, the mood quiet.

It was a time not for talking but for reflecting. It was a time of waiting. It was a time to be left alone.

Michal, as promised, had delivered dinner. He had little more to report since leaving their room at six. He and his brother were committed, no questions asked, to aiding in Lydia's rescue. For now, he would gather information as unobtrusively as possible. Who was in the hotel? What was going on? Was it safe for Kerry and Sydney to wander about, or should they remain in their room until it was time to act?

The brothers' other tasks were to observe Hassan—his comings and his goings—to determine if there was a time, a scheduled time, that Lydia might find herself alone, and quietly to question trusted members of the staff. Who had access to the room? For what purpose? For how long? At what time of day?

Meanwhile, Kerry and Sydney were left to wait until tomorrow evening in between the brothers' shifts. Then, pooling their information, they would know if a rescue mission was indeed possible.

Feeling his inquisitive gaze upon her, Sydney lifted her eyes to his.

"What is it?" she gently asked.

Embarrassed, he merely shrugged. "It's nothing. I was watching the candlelight dancing across your face. You look lovely tonight, Sydney."

Without thinking, she reached across the table, laying her hand ever so gently atop his. He didn't flinch and she didn't falter.

"It was sweet of you to be so thoughtful, Kerry."

And he knew exactly what she meant. The peignoir set Madeline had chosen was exquisite. The gown looked like something a bride might choose for her wedding night. The top of the gown, made of delicate ivory lace, was low-cut, revealing the plummeting cleavage of Sydney's breasts. Beaded with pearls, the bodice clung to her body, falling into a satin skirt cut in jagged, uneven lacy edges just above the knees. A simple, satin bed jacket graced her shoulders, giving her a sense of modesty the gown, by itself, immediately took away.

Kerry was with Sydney when the clothes were delivered. And when she unwrapped the box containing the lovely gown and jacket, he had been horrified.

"What must she think?" he had wondered.

But rather than being upset, Sydney had been pleased. Because of her heartbreak with Sam and then the crisis with Lydia, a part of her, the feminine side, had been secreted away. There was something about the sheer beauty of the gown and jacket that opened the door, if ever so slightly. Thinking it was he who had chosen the lovely ensemble somehow made her feel attractive, pretty even—a feeling she'd not known in months.

Disturbed after the meeting with the brothers, Sydney had indulged in a hot, relaxing bath. Then, just before dinner she had changed into the gown and jacket, perhaps thinking it would make her feel better; perhaps deluding herself that for a few hours, anyway, she could forget where she was and why.

Was it that she felt safe with Kerry, or did she think he would fail to notice how truly lovely . . . and desirable . . . she looked?

With her hair brushed loose and free and her skin glowing in the candlelight, perhaps she did know all too well.

Sydney brought the chilled glass of chardonnay to her lips. While savoring the wine, it was Kerry she found herself enjoying. He was wearing only a hotel robe fastened loosely about the waist, but what attracted Sydney most just then was the blueness of his eyes. And his hair—such a strange mixture of chestnut flecked with gray.

Her mind flashed to their first encounter in the barn. She thought him to be a stable hand! He thought her to be a snob! In those first few moments of their meeting, she had found him to be primitive, exciting and virile. And if the truth be known, she had desired him even then.

Slowly she let her eyes fall. His robe was askew, held tentatively in place by a mere loose knot at the waist, revealing a full chest, covered in the same mixture of chestnut, flecked with gray.

Gulping the wine, she tried focusing her attention upon her plate. But her hunger at this moment was not for food. And so it was that her eyes slowly traveled from her plate to his chest and then finally to his eyes, where they remained fixed and filled with raw, honest desire.

"Oh my God," she whispered, "what's happening?"

Kerry knew. All too well. He recognized the look in her eyes as a reflection of his own desire. He stood and, without a word, pushed away the table that separated them. Then he went to her and enveloped her in his arms.

"Say nothing," he ordered. For he knew every argument her mind would utter. Now was not the time to reason. Now was the moment to surrender.

His lips found hers and sought to taste every crevice, every inch of her sweet mouth. This woman was unlike any woman he had ever desired. She needed love and she deserved a man who desired nothing more than to make her feel like a woman.

"Sydney," he whispered huskily, "dear Sydney."

Their lips clinging together, Kerry guided Sydney to the bed and threw back the sheets. Sydney loosened the tie about his waist. She pushed back the robe from his arms and, with his help, allowed it to fall. Standing naked, he closed his eyes and relished her touch as she ran her fingers through his thick maze of hair from the top of his chest to the bottom then slowly back again. Gently he lowered her onto the bed.

"Are you sure this is what you want?" he asked.

This time she answered with no hesitation, no doubt. The time had come for each of them to put the past behind. Sam was gone. So was Patricia. For Sydney and Kerry, there might not be a tomorrow. Now was the time. Here was the place.

Carefully, so as not to rip the precious garments, Kerry helped Sydney with the jacket and then the gown, lifting it above her head.

"Oh God, Sydney, you're more beautiful than I had imagined. Please, for tonight, allow me just to love you."

Starting with the top of her head and moving downward, Kerry began his slow, sensual journey to discover and ignite every crevice of her being. Like a soft, whispering wind, his tongue fell upon her, tasting the saltiness of her pores and the sweetness of her flesh. Cupping her breasts in his calloused hands, he flicked his tongue across her nipples until they stood firm and ready.

Sydney closed her eyes and savored every flick of his tongue upon her body. At last he found his way through her triangle of auburn hair to the area of her greatest sensitivity. There his tongue remained until her first spasms of orgasms began.

"Wait," she pleaded, "come with me."

"No," he whispered, "not yet." And so she let go to experience her first great gasp of pleasure. But far from over, this was merely the beginning of the greatest hours of pleasure Sydney had ever known.

Caressing her inner thighs with his lips, Kerry's mouth traveled down her smoothly shaven legs to her delicate feet. One by one, he sucked her toes, teasingly at first, and then with great abandon. Clawing his back, she yearned to scream and to rip apart his flesh with every spasm.

Suddenly, without warning, Kerry rose. Grasping her roughly he flipped her over, only to begin the process once again.

Beginning with the soles of her feet, he journeyed upward, his tongue playing games with her skin. Feeling sensations she had denied for a lifetime, Sydney knew not whether she was in exquisite pleasure or exquisite pain. A part of her wanted Kerry to consummate their union and be done with it. A part of her wanted him to play his song upon her body all night long.

Finally, when he could stand his own want not a minute longer, he lay down gently atop her. Tasting her name with his lips, he maneuvered himself into her vagina from the rear. As she arched her back, he cupped her breasts firmly, and they moved together as one, in a slow, gentle rhythm. It didn't remain gentle for long. Massaging her clitoris, he thrust again and again until the swell of raw, wet desire erupted.

It was then, finally, together as one, that they experienced the deep climax that only a man and a woman destined to be together know. Later, lying in the safety of each other's arms, the pain they had brought to this union, this bed, for now no longer mattered. Nothing in life can compare to the joy a man and a woman feel when, having suffered so long, two broken hearts mend as one.

Sunlight was streaming through the window when Kerry first awoke. Glancing about his surroundings, the Irishman felt confused and disoriented. Blinking his eyes, Donavan realized at once that he was not at home. He was in a hotel room. He was in Dubai. It was the Hyatt, of course.

The room looked exactly as it had before. Nothing had changed. The sun rising above the horizon was the same sun that had graced the planet for centuries. Yet, this morning, everything looked different, smelled different, and seemed different. Nothing, no one, was the same.

Then his gaze drifted to the lady cradled in his arms, sound asleep. For hours she lay unmoving, tranquil in his embrace, with her wild mass of coppery hair spilled carelessly all over the pillow. It was then, gazing at her face, that he understood why everything had changed in the course of a few hours.

Very softly, so as not to wake her, Kerry reached out to stroke her hair. Pausing just above her head, he hesitated as if he dared not, as if he had no right. Then, tentatively laying his hand atop her head, he felt the silky hair.

Then he closed his eyes, remembering every detail of their encounter, from the feel of her sumptuously rounded breasts to the sound of her husky moaning as they climaxed together. Thinking about it only made him want her that much more again.

Suddenly Kerry opened his eyes. For there, seemingly standing before him, was not Sydney but the image of his dead wife, Patricia. He shuddered, then shut his eyes tightly, trying to force the ghost to disappear. Yet the apparition stood firm, because the vision of Patricia came not from without but from within the hidden recesses of his mind.

Cradling Sydney in his arms, Kerry realized just how different the two women were. Where Patricia was flawlessly beautiful, Sydney, with all her imperfections, was incredibly real. Where Patricia was cool and aloof, Sydney was hot-tempered, outspoken and passionate. Where Patricia had been someone to revere, Sydney was a woman who touched his soul. Patricia had seemed ethereal—not of this world. Sydney was very much here, very much now.

And so, weary of the guilt he'd harbored for years, Kerry bade a silent good-bye to the haunting memories of his dead wife.

Turning to the woman beside him, Kerry first let his eyes and then his hands play over her naked body. His touch was teasingly restrained, yet his loins were hungry as he stirred his lady love from slumber.

Slow to awake, Sydney turned to face the man who had changed the course of her life in a single night. Alive, desirable, attractive—these were the adjectives she used to describe herself in his presence. This was the way he made her feel.

"Good morning," she whispered, lifting her eyes to his. At first glance, his eyes seemed much too cool and remote. Yet just below the surface there lurked a passion for life and love, for the mysterious and the forbidden.

But then she thought about another pair of eyes . . . eyes that had captured her heart and held her dear . . . the eyes of the man she had loved and married.

Sam's eyes had been gentle and kind, and like his heart, open and full of wonder. He had been a man who was easy to love. Like floating a raft in a calm, steady stream, her life with Sam had been secure and predictable, with definite boundaries and a positive direction.

Sydney tried to imagine what her life would be like entwined with this passionate, hot-tempered Irishman. Like a treacherous sea in a raging storm, Kerry Donavan would be anything but easy to love. And in that realization, she missed Sam and missed him dreadfully. A slow sad tear graced her cheek. Kerry saw it but said nothing, for a part of him already knew. Stroking Sydney's hair softly, he allowed her the space to say her own good-byes.

■

Limerick, Ireland

The ashtray was full of crushed Rothmans, and a thick cloud of smoke choked the air. The lonely remains of a gin and tonic sat on the table next to the phone. It was dark outside, still the middle of the night in Ireland. Mary Margaret O'Sullivan stared absently out of the window, looking for some hint of dawn.

She reached for the phone for the fifth time in less than a half-hour. But she could not bring the receiver to her ear, not yet anyway. She still hadn't found the words to tell her dear Kerry that his younger sister was dead.

In front of her lay a copy of the *Irish Times* with the tragic story about Barbara Donavan Thompson. A probable suicide, the police thought—her battered body was discovered on the rocks near the power dam at Annacoty. Her husband, Liam, was distraught. The only motive he could discern for his wife's suicide was the unexpected visit by her renegade brother, which had dredged up painful memories of the shame he had brought upon her family.

Poor Barbara, the tongues of Limerick wagged. A girl born with everything ending up as fish bait in the Shannon River. Poor, poor, unhappy Barbara. And such a sweet, devoted husband she'd left behind.

Sullie knew Liam Thompson was responsible. But to prove it might be a most difficult matter. To tell Kerry now might jeopardize everything for Sydney. To deny him the truth about his sister might jeopardize everything else Kerry Donavan held dear.

In her hand was a tattered piece of paper with the name Sean Flynn and the phone number for the Hyatt Hotel in Dubai.

"Oh, dear Lord!" she cried, clutching the paper to her bosom. How she begged Paddy McDowell to tell her where Kerry had gone, and under what identity! Believing in his heart that Kerry had the right to know, Paddy finally acquiesced, betraying his oath of silence.

Yet again, Mary Margaret reached for the phone. Yet again, the phone line remained silent. Not until she found the right words would she place the call to tell Kerry that his sister lay dead, and that the remainder of her fortune now rested in the hands of her sole beneficiary—Liam Thompson.

"We have to get up, Sydney," said Kerry, bringing her fingers to his lips a final time. "We've lingered too long." But neither of them stirred, neither of them had any desire to see their precious hours together come to an end. Drenched in sweat from an afternoon of ardent lovemaking, Kerry stroked Sydney's glistening hair.

"Let's shower," he suggested, and he did not mean alone. Aside from a late breakfast delivered at noon by room service, Kerry and Sydney had done nothing with their day but experience one another . . . from the hidden crevices of each other's body to the hopes and dreams buried deep within their hearts.

Having no idea what news Seamus and Michal would deliver, and being totally ignorant of the tragedy that had befallen Barbara in Ireland, they showered and dressed. Exiting the bathroom, Kerry walked to the phone to order coffee. But hearing a light knock, he turned around and saw something being passed underneath the door.

Bending down, he picked up the brochure entitled *The Mystique of Dubai*. He opened the brochure. There was a note with a crudely drawn map tucked inside.

"It's not safe to meet here. Follow my map to the market. It's only a few blocks from the hotel. Look for the gold stall. We'll meet you there at 5:15."

Kerry checked the time. It was almost 5:00 p.m.

Sydney and Kerry left their room quickly. Kerry was dressed

in his new lightweight clothing. Sydney wore rose-colored slacks with a pink and yellow flower-patterned shirt. She covered her red hair with a matching silk scarf.

They moved smartly through the lobby and out the main door. No one paid them any notice. They paused for a moment. The afternoon heat was oppressive. Kerry studied Seamus's map, trying to get his bearings. Smelling the salty air, Sydney glanced left to the sea and then right to the city streets. What she saw surprised her. Known as the city of merchants, Dubai had large skyscrapers and crowded streets.

Traffic was heavy on the main street in front of the hotel. They crossed carefully, then headed down a side street for their five-minute walk to the open-air market called a *souk.* They tried to get a feel for the city. There was a pulse, an electricity here not unlike New York City, but the streets were clean and the architecture pristine. Like most metropolitan cities, there was a variety of shops and restaurants. The mix of people on the street—Arab and European—reminded them of London.

After walking several blocks, they came to the square. It was then that they saw the market. But it was not what they expected. Kerry had thought the souk would be filled with vegetable and fruit vendors, while Sydney envisioned a flea market. The souk was filled with merchants, but their wares were not edible or cheap. There were booths of silk as well as electronics—television, stereos, and even computers. There were fine dresses and precious gems. Just to the right of the main entrance was the gold booth where the brothers were to meet them. It was not a *gold* booth as Kerry surmised, but a stall filled with gold coins and jewelry. Sydney wondered how much the gold on display was worth.

Seamus suddenly appeared. Saying nothing, he led them through the market, which was teeming with people. It was noisy and hot. Seamus made a sudden right turn out of the souk and across the street to a small, narrow alley. There in the shadows, Michal was waiting.

Lighting a cigarette, Seamus stood watch while Kerry, Sydney and Michal crowded behind him.

"What have you discovered?" Kerry began.

Seamus responded, "The penthouse floor is called the Regency Club. Security is pretty tight, but the suite is cleaned every day."

"When does this usually happen?" Donavan asked.

"They clean first thing in the morning around eight o'clock."

Sydney edged closer to the brothers. "Who's there at that time?"

"I have a lady friend who works in housekeeping. She told me there is always a woman in the suite tending to the child. Sometimes there's a bodyguard, too, but most of the time the woman and the child are alone."

Kerry seemed pleased with the information. "Okay, what do we know about Hassan? What is he up to? What is his daily routine?"

Michal glanced quickly to his brother before displaying a somewhat smug grin.

"Me friends tell me that the hotel is full and that there's a bit of a convention going on here. But it's not like anything they've seen before. Ali Hassan has become a powerful man in the Middle East. He has the resources to get the finest arms that money can buy. He's called a meeting of terrorists from around the world. It seems that the demand for arms is great, but the supply is limited. For the next few days, he's reserved the conference room to meet with the leaders of each of the groups to broker deals. So if we're going to strike, the time couldn't be better."

Sydney broke out into a smile. With hopeful eyes, she turned to Kerry, but his expression was guarded.

"We still have a number of questions to answer," he said. "How do we get Lydia out of the suite, out of the hotel, and finally out of the country? Do we go by land, sea or air?"

Seamus cleared his throat. "I've been giving this a lot of thought and I think I've got a plan."

Kerry urged the man from Cork to proceed.

"It's simple really. I go into work early. I put me hands on the keys to one of the laundry trucks outside. If Michal can sweet-talk his lady friend out of her uniform, Sydney can dress up as the maid. She goes into the room and grabs the girl. Then we sneak her out in the laundry truck. Nobody thinks nothing about it."

Seamus waited expectantly. His plan was promising, but in

Kerry's mind there were too many holes. The thought of Sydney going into Hassan's suite alone was more than he could bear.

"It's no good. We have to find someone else. Sydney could be recognized."

Seeing the look in Kerry's eyes, Seamus immediately understood.

"Aye, me friend, but who else can we trust? You could pay someone to do the job, but the boys here are loose cannons. If something goes wrong they might panic, then somebody could get hurt. You don't want to put Lydia in that kind of danger."

In a soft, quiet voice, Sydney agreed. Reaching out, she gently stroked Kerry's hand.

"He's right, you know, Kerry. It has to be me. I'm the only one who has a legal right to Lydia. I'm the only one who can physically remove her."

"Your rights mean nothing here," Donavan countered sharply, yet he knew his argument was futile. It was indeed the only way . . . if they had any chance of succeeding.

"All right," he acquiesced, "I'm not saying I agree, but let's suppose we get Sydney into the room. How in the hell can we sneak a fourteen-year-old girl out of the hotel? She's too big to be carried and too small to dress like a maid."

"I've got an idea," Michal said, an easy smile creasing his features. "Seamus, how does the laundry come downstairs? It can't be carried by hand, and I haven't seen any chutes."

"Aye, the maids pile the bedclothes in big baskets on wheels. Then someone brings them down the service elevator to the laundry room. The linens are sorted there. Some are done here in the hotel, but most are sent out."

"So we could smuggle Lydia out in a basket," Michal said. "Load her on the truck, and away we go."

"That might work," Kerry agreed, "but only if one of us goes in with Sydney. It's too risky for her alone. We'll decide which one of us later. Now we come to the second dilemma. How do we get out of the country?"

To this question, the O'Daugherty boys at first remained mute, but, taking a deep breath, Seamus finally plunged ahead.

"To go by car or taxi is too dangerous. Me brother and I have lived in this hellhole for five years now. If nothing else, we've learned that you can't trust nobody but one of our own. The taxis are owned by nationals. Them or their Pakistani drivers will cut your fucking throat for a fistful of bloody dirhams.

"If you hire a car it'll take too damn long to get out of the Emirates. By the time you make it, Hassan will have the borders closed. You got to remember who you're dealing with, Kerry. In this part of the world, Hassan has become almost as powerful as Allah."

"So where does that leave us?" Donavan asked.

"The fastest way out of the country is by air. From here, you're only ten minutes away from the airport. You could book a commercial flight or you could hire a private plane to fly you out of the Emirates." Seamus hesitated, then in a lowered voice went on. "We keep to ourselves here, Kerry. We live in shacks not fit for rats, but we got each other. You're one of us. Either way you want to go, I know people who can help. It's up to you."

Kerry nodded. He needed to give the plan some thought.

"I've got to go," Michal said. "I can't be late for work."

Seamus departed quickly along with his brother. Sydney and Kerry took their time wandering around the souk. It was nearly nine o'clock before, back in their room, they ordered supper from room service.

Sydney called home. She was relieved to hear that Mack was feeling okay.

Amusing herself until dinner arrived, Sydney reread the brochure Seamus had slipped under their door. She was surprised to learn that English was spoken fluently throughout the city.

"Kerry, it says here that Dubai has something for everyone and that travelers are sure to be charmed by the city's warmth and friendliness. I wonder if that's true."

Kerry answered the door when Michal delivered their order.

"Seamus is making inquiries as to the best way for you to leave the city. He'll get back to us later."

Michal was neatly arranging the plates of food when the phone rang, startling them all.

"Who knows we're here?" Sydney asked.

"Only one man," Kerry answered. Quickly he moved to the desk across the room. Perhaps it was a wrong number or a desk clerk concerning their stay. In any case, Kerry tried to remain calm. He answered the phone on the fourth ring.

"Hello, pet. How have you been keeping?"

Hearing the familiar voice of Mary Margaret O'Sullivan, Kerry became visibly shaken. "How did you find me here?" he asked softly.

"I have me ways," Sullie answered cautiously. "You know what they are."

Without a doubt, Kerry understood. And with this realization, he felt a sudden dread. There was no way Paddy McDowell would have revealed his whereabouts and false identity without a damned good reason. Something had to be wrong.

"You don't sound good, Sullie. What is it?"

"I'm not good, pet," his friend responded. She had agonized for hours, trying to find the right words to cushion the blow she had to deliver. In the end, there were none. "It's Barbara, love. She's dead."

Clutching the desk, Kerry struggled to remain on his feet.

"How?" he stammered. "When?"

"They found her body yesterday, floating in the Shannon. She washed up on the rocks near the power dam at Annacoty."

"Who did it, Sullie?" he demanded, a dangerous edge in his voice.

O'Sullivan opened her mouth to answer, but the words refused to come. For a moment there was only static on the line between Ireland and the Emirates.

"Tell me who did it, Sullie!"

"The police think it was suicide. Gerrad McNamara thinks something different."

"I *know* Barbara didn't kill herself! Tell me what McNamara said!"

"Gerrad was there when they pulled her from the river. Her face looked like raw pulp. Her skull was crushed and some of her organs had ruptured."

"Oh, dear God," Kerry moaned.

"Gerrad told me that Barbara might have been cut by some jagged rocks, but she wouldn't have been lashed about to that extent. He thinks she was murdered first and dumped in the river later. Whoever did it thought she would be swallowed up and mutilated by the intake valves at the power dam. Then nobody would have recognized the body."

"What about her car?" Donavan asked.

"It was found near the river, off the main road. The police are checking it now."

His words were thick with grief, but his mind was rational. "It wasn't suicide, Sullie, that much I know! Barbara was terrified of the water . . . had been ever since she was a little girl when our boat capsized and she nearly drowned. She wouldn't go near the water after that. No matter how bad things were, there was no way she could have thrown herself into the water to drown. Besides, she had access to pills. If she had wanted to die she would have taken an overdose. God knows Liam kept the medicine chest full."

"I couldn't agree more, Kerry. Barbara and I talked a lot in recent years. Even when things got bad with you, she never considered taking her own life. She was more Catholic than you or I could ever hope to be. She wouldn't risk damning her soul to hell."

"So what are you saying, Sullie? Barbara was murdered, and we both know who did it!"

Mary Margaret hesitated. "There's something else weighing on me mind. Liam is Barbara's primary beneficiary. If he goes free, he inherits everything . . . the house . . . the land . . . everything! I thought you had a right to know."

Kerry wiped his brow. He now faced a dilemma, and a decision he wasn't equipped to make.

"How much time do we have, Sullie?"

"I don't know, pet. I took the liberty of calling your solicitor. You can have all the family assets frozen until the police investigation is complete. But if they rule her death a suicide . . . there's nothing you can do to stop him. Liam will inherit everything."

"Can you stall?" Kerry asked.

"I have me friends in the guarda, but unless they find hard evidence that Barbara was murdered . . . well . . . I can't put them off forever."

"Okay, Sullie, I'll be in touch."

"Are you coming home, love?"

Mary Margaret strained to hear the answer, but the line from Limerick to Dubai had gone dead.

Seeing how distraught Kerry was, Sydney rose from the chair and approached him slowly. She tried to embrace him, but he waved her away. His face looked ashen when he turned to Michal.

"I want to be alone now. My sister was found murdered, and I'm needed back in Ireland. I don't know what to do. Come back when your shift ends, Michal. I'll tell you then whether we go . . . or whether we scrap."

Kerry spent the next few hours alone by the balcony window. Gazing out into darkness, he tried to imagine the last few hours of his sister's life. There was no way she had committed suicide, that much he knew. She'd been murdered savagely by the man who claimed to love her. Now the bloody bastard stood to inherit everything.

The choice was simple, but one that tore Kerry apart. His was the age-old struggle of man. How easy it would be to forsake Sydney and this insane mission to rescue Lydia for the pleasure of crushing Liam's throat with his bare hands. How easy and how justifiable. To do less would require surrendering to the reckless abandon of love. It came down to simply this—hate versus love, vengeance versus justice.

The tormented Irishman was not the only one who went without sleep that night. It was sometime after midnight when Sydney finally dared to approach Kerry. God, how she yearned to reach out and console him, for it was obvious he was in terrible pain, but she had stayed away. She felt she had no right to interfere, even though his decision ultimately could destroy her.

She bent down and softly kissed his cheek.

"Whatever you decide, Kerry, I understand."

He nodded, but his reddened eyes refused to meet hers. Releasing him, she turned to walk away. His silence could only mean that he had decided. The mission was now over before it had even begun. They would leave Dubai without Lydia. Never would she see her precious daughter again.

As expected, there came a knock on the door in the wee hours of the morning. Wearily, Kerry rose to answer. Quickly, so as not to draw attention to himself, Michal stepped inside.

Sydney waited for Kerry to utter the words she knew he must. But in the end, the man she thought she had come to know so well surprised her.

"We must act quickly, Michal. Tell Seamus we have to finalize our plans tomorrow if we're to strike the day after."

Friday, May 1
7:30 a.m.

Her body was disguised in the shapeless brown uniform, and her unruly red hair was pulled back in a knot at the nape of her neck and covered with a sheer netting, a requirement of every maid in the hotel. Her face, devoid of makeup, was pale and drawn. Her eyes were bleary from lack of sleep, and her hands trembled slightly as she brought yet another cup of coffee to her quivering lips.

Beside her on the sofa, Kerry studied Sydney carefully. He was disturbed. To pull off the rescue scheduled to begin in less than thirty minutes, he needed Sydney at her best, with her mind clear and her wits sharp. And this was not the image she now presented. Something was eating at her, something—despite the past twenty-four hours of endless planning—they had not discussed.

He asked directly. "Tell me what's bothering you."

"The plan . . . it's all wrong."

Biting his lower lip, Kerry merely responded, "But we've been over it time and time again."

"I can't go through with it," Sydney stammered, "not without speaking to Lydia first."

"I don't understand," Kerry countered.

"I know we don't have much time. We don't even know who

will be in the suite when Michal and I go in. But no matter what, we can't just grab her. It's not fair. I have to speak with her alone first. I have to give her the choice to come with me . . . or to stay with him."

"You can't risk it, Sydney. We only have one shot at the child. If you're discovered, it's all over."

Sydney put the half-empty cup on the table.

"Don't you see? If we go in and just take her, I'm no better than Hassan. I *have* to speak to her alone. For my own peace of mind, I need to know that this is what she wants."

His voice was firm, harsh even, when he countered, "And what will you do if the answer is no? Can you walk away, Sydney? After all of this, can you leave Lydia behind?"

Sydney stood. The time was drawing near.

"Hold me," she pleaded.

Her fate rested solely in the hands of someone else, and he, Kerry Donavan, was powerless to protect her.

"Remember what I told you, Sydney. Get in and get out. Talk to Lydia if you must, but make it fast."

Kerry checked the time. It was exactly 7:45 a.m.

Sydney nodded, "I understand, Kerry," and started to walk toward the door.

"Sydney, wait!" Kerry called out. Pivoting, she slowly turned to face him.

The words he felt in his heart rested on his lips, yet somehow he couldn't say that which she yearned so desperately to hear. Instead he merely mouthed, "Be careful."

Kerry couldn't describe the unbelievably empty feeling he felt in his heart the minute she passed from his view. The half-hour that lay ahead seemed endless. Turning his back on the closed door, he marched to the phone and dialed the front desk. Impatiently, he waited for someone to answer. Hearing a dreaded familiar voice, he grimaced.

"Good morning, Mr. Azima. This is Sean Flynn. Would you prepare my final bill? I'll be checking out immediately."

He faltered over the answer to the acting manager's question.

"No, that won't be necessary. We'll need no help with our luggage."

Slamming down the phone, he picked up their two carry-on bags and slung them over his shoulder. Grabbing the hotel key, he fled the room. The sooner they were out of the Hyatt Regency the better he'd feel. The time was 7:50 a.m.

■

When the elevator door opened onto the lobby, Donavan swore. A queue had formed and checkout would take longer than he had anticipated. For a fleeting moment he thought about leaving the hotel and forgetting the bill. They were traveling under assumed names. So what difference did it really make?

Ah well, he mused, he did have a bit of time to spare. He'd give the line ten minutes at most to clear, and then he'd leave. Unfortunately, he was an Irish Paddy whose heart was oftentimes bigger than his brain. That's what had gotten him into this mess. He'd feel guilty for stiffing the hotel, especially since he could afford to pay. Besides, he had the gentle shopwoman named Madeline to consider. He had charged several hundred dollars' worth of clothes to his room. To fail to pay might put her job in jeopardy, and this, if at all possible, he could not do.

Trying to steady his nerves, he reminded himself of the advice he had given Sydney. Get in. Get out. He'd pay his bill, leaving no tracks or spotty footprints behind. Give no one reason for suspicion.

As the line inched forward, Kerry glanced up, meeting the eyes of Azima, the suspicious acting manager of the hotel.

■

8:00 a.m.

Michal was sweating profusely, staining the uniform that was too small and short for his muscular frame. Fumbling with the

large ring of keys he held in his sweaty palm, he unlocked the service elevator leading to the exclusive Regency Club.

As the elevator made its slow progress toward the penthouse
floor, Sydney reached over and tenderly patted Michal's freckled
hand.

"No matter what happens, I want you to know how much I
appreciate what you're doing for Lydia and for me."

He gave her a quick smile and nodded as the elevator door
opened. The top floor of the hotel in the Regency Club consisted
of a single huge suite, two smaller adjoining rooms, a television
lounge and a security desk. Taking a deep breath, they nodded
and together moved forward, pushing the rickety old linen basket found in a lost corner of the basement toward the reception
area of the Regency Club. No one was monitoring the security
desk. No one was in the TV lounge, or drinking the pot of free
coffee. For now, Michal O'Daugherty and Sydney Lawrence
found themselves alone.

Michal put his ear to the door of the penthouse suite. It was
quiet inside. He knocked lightly three times. When no one
answered, he tried the key. Throwing open the door, he glanced
about the magnificent suite until his eyes came to rest upon the
Muslim woman, garbed in black, sitting alone in the corner.

Masking his shock, he set the laundry basket aside and bowed
politely to the older woman. "Top of the morning to you, madam.
We've come to clean."

With her arms folded about her massive bosom, the Arab
woman said nothing, but her steady eyes never wavered, and
Michal wondered if she understood English.

Sydney briefly met the woman's eyes, then averted her gaze.
Michal continued. "We're new to this floor, madam. May we
proceed?"

Her quizzical glance fell first to one and then to the other.
Finally she nodded. Picking up an Arabic newspaper, she seemingly paid them no heed.

Michal began tidying the living room near the woman, while
Sydney slipped down the hall.

The door to the master suite was ajar, revealing a huge, king-sized bed that was empty and unmade. Ali Hassan was nowhere in view. Across the hall was a small bathroom, and just beyond what Sydney guessed to be the second bedroom. The door was shut.

Approaching cautiously, Sydney glanced over her shoulder. No one was watching. Michal busied himself in the living room, yet the Muslim woman paid him no notice. With trembling hand, Sydney turned the knob and slipped inside, carefully shutting the door behind her.

Her eyes came to rest upon the slender form by the window. Attired only in a nightdress, the child was perched on the window ledge with her back to the door, her knees tucked neatly under her chin, and her right hand tightly clenched. She heard nothing because her thoughts were focused elsewhere, somewhere far beyond the window, the sea, even the distant horizon.

Finding herself alone in Lydia's presence, every conceivable emotion—from anger to intense joy—rose to the surface, and for a few precious seconds Sydney was powerless to react. But a higher force within prevailed, and, forcing her steps to glide silently across the carpet, she came to rest just behind the child. Placing her hands atop Lydia's shoulders she whispered, "Lydia, it's Sydney."

Hearing the voice she had merely dreamed about for days, Lydia spun around, half expecting to be greeted by yet another mirage, another ghost, but the gentle loving eyes of her mother seemed so real that the child nearly screamed.

Cupping Lydia's mouth quickly, she warned, "Hush, darling, hush."

Lydia's left hand flew to her mother's face, pawing the flesh she yearned to touch.

Lydia opened her right hand. There was the mustard seed locket Sydney had given her, the necklace she'd hidden from her father.

"I knew you would come," said Lydia.

"Oh God," Sydney whispered, pulling Lydia to her. Silent tears ran down her cheeks as she held the child close once again. Backing away, she saw . . . really saw . . . Lydia for the first time.

Her eyes were hollow. Her lips, once so red, were pale. There were yellowed bruises underneath one eye and on her cheeks.

"What has he done to you?" she whispered.

Holding Lydia at arm's length, Sydney forced the child to confront her. Peering deep into her eyes, Sydney spoke as slowly as her racing heart would allow and as firmly as her shaky voice would permit.

"I've come to take you home, but only if you want to go. It's up to you, Lydia. Do you want to come with me?" Sydney's eyes searched the frightened eyes of her daughter. "Or do you want to stay with him?"

For Lydia there was neither a choice nor a decision. The man she had once revered as her father was gone. The woman she had come to love as her mother was here.

"Take me home. Take me home now!"

In a relieved rush, Sydney blurted, "Okay, listen to me carefully. Do you remember Kerry Donavan?"

"Yes," Lydia nodded.

"He's downstairs with a truck. There's a plane waiting to fly the three of us out of here. But first we have to get you safely out of the hotel. Where's your father?"

"I don't know," Lydia answered. "He's gone most mornings when I wake up and he doesn't return until dark."

"Good," Sydney answered. "I saw the woman in the living room. Is she the only one who is here to watch you?"

Lydia shrugged. "I think so. I'm not permitted outside my room alone so I never know who's here for sure."

Taking a deep breath, Sydney hurried on.

"We have to sneak you out in the laundry basket with the bed linen. You'll have to be very still and very quiet. Are you game?"

Lydia smiled and nodded her head vigorously.

Glancing about the room, Sydney had to ask, "What clothes do you have to wear?"

"Papa took away my things. I have this nightdress and my milaya, that's all."

"Your what?"

"The black dress and veil of the Muslim woman. I have nothing else."

"Nevermind, it doesn't matter. You can change into something of mine once we're out of the hotel. Lydia, I have to leave you for a minute, but I'll be right back."

Lydia moaned like a wounded animal as Sydney started to pull away. "Please, honey, we have to hurry. You must be very quiet and very brave." Lydia's eyes were terrified, but Lydia finally released her. Putting two fingers to her lips to indicate silence, Sydney hurried toward the door. Her feet yearned to run, but she forced her legs to move slowly, stealthily down the hall and into the living room. Pausing, she waited until Michal turned around. Then she simply nodded, as was their signal.

Setting down his furniture polish and his cloth, Michal stood erect. Feigning a yawn he stretched, glanced to the Muslim woman and smiled. Seemingly once again paying him no mind, her eyes returned to the paper. Slowly, Michal stepped backward. Turning, he fetched the linen basket and carefully maneuvered it down the hall.

Quickly, without a word, Michal shut the door to Lydia's bedroom, then he and Sydney stripped her bed.

"Come here, darling," Sydney whispered. "Climb in."

Michal helped the girl inside the linen basket, then stuffed the sheets all about her, leaving plenty of room for her to breathe. The basket was full now, and much more awkward to push as they made their way out of the bedroom and down the hall.

Sydney felt the Muslim woman's eyes upon her as she helped Michal push the cart through the living room. Saying nothing, she kept her glance averted until the door to the penthouse suite had closed and they had taken their first steps down the hall toward the service elevator. Halfway there, she dared to lean forward and whisper, "Are you all right, Lydia?"

"Yes," the girl replied, and there was a measure of both fear and relief in her thin voice. Trying to appear relaxed, Michal and Sydney made their way down the hall, just in front of the reception area. Michal's eyes scanned the area. Still no one was at the security desk.

There were two elevators opposite the reception area. One was for the guests, the other for employees. Michal summoned the service elevator. Sydney, with her eyes cast to the floor, waited for the door to open, but it seemed to take forever to arrive. Michal kept pushing the button, to no avail. Then he glanced at the other elevator. But that was risky. He'd have no excuse for being seen on a public elevator, not as a member of the housekeeping staff disposing of dirty bed linen. Despite the danger, he thought about taking it anyway, but he delayed his decision too long.

Just then the door to the service elevator opened. Sydney did what anyone would . . . she glanced up and she was startled. Exiting the elevator, just in front of them, was a large, muscular man of Persian descent. Michal did what one might expect. He smiled politely at the stranger, but then quickly lowered his glance and focused on the task of loading the cart. Sydney did just the opposite. Freezing for a split second, her eyes locked with those of the man before her. The guard remained mute, but he coldly studied Sydney. He had not seen her on this floor before, of that he was certain. But she looked familiar.

Thrusting his arm forward, he held the door open, allowing Sydney to pass first, followed by Michal pushing the linen cart. On the surface he seemed unconcerned, but he watched them closely, finding their movements strangely puzzling. Waiting for the elevator door to close, his eyes remained fixed first upon Michal, then the cart, and finally Sydney. It was she whom he found most interesting. Where had he seen the woman and when?

When the elevator finally closed, Sydney sagged against the wall. For the steely eyes of the Iranian were all too familiar. Her mind flashed to another time, another place. She was running down the lane screaming for her daughter. A man got out of the front seat of the car and, without missing a beat, thrust his arm forward just as this man had, leveling a gun at her head. He was some distance away but his aim was sure, his nerves steady. He seemed devoid of all human emotion—a devil, Hassan's personal devil, the bodyguard she had just now confronted.

Ali Hassan demanded certain things of his employees, particularly those he trusted with his life. First was loyalty. Second was the ability to follow orders without question, no matter the consequences. But last and perhaps most important were a sharp mind and keen powers of observation.

There was something about the scene he just witnessed that disturbed Raoul Sabid. In the days following Lydia's abduction, the thirty-eight-year-old guard had been assigned to protect Hassan's most precious property. He had remained with the child at all times. But with the arms negotiations taking place, Hassan needed him. The watch on Lydia had been relaxed. And so, Raoul Sabid was assigned to guard Hassan during his negotiations and to monitor the penthouse suite from time to time when Hassan demanded.

He was on the floor at this time of the morning, as always, simply making rounds. He made it a point to observe every member of the hotel staff who had access to the exclusive Regency Club. Never had he seen the team he had just encountered. And never had he witnessed housekeeping personnel carting bed linens out in a basket.

The woman's face continued to haunt him. She was not Arabic, nor were her features particularly European. So where had he encountered her pretty face before? It was then he remembered the lovely woman with flaming red hair crumpled on her knees in the road. It was then he remembered his own rush of adrenaline as he captured her face in the sights of his gun and felt his finger tentatively squeezing the trigger. How easy it would have been to shoot and to feel the thrill of finding his target. In those seconds while he waited for his master's command, he remembered thinking what a waste it would be to splatter her beautiful face on the pavement. Mercifully, Hassan had ordered a retreat.

Putting an identity with the face, Raoul Sabid picked up his feet and ran down the corridor, bursting through the door of the penthouse suite.

■

Their footsteps echoed noisily on the concrete floor of the basement as they ran, frantically pushing the rickety cart. Bursting through a side door that Seamus had left open, they were blinded by the bright intense heat of Dubai's fearsome sun.

Suddenly a man jumped out of the shadows. "What's wrong?" Seamus O'Daugherty demanded.

Breathlessly, Michal answered. "Sydney thinks she was recognized by Hassan's bodyguard. Where's Kerry?"

"I don't know," Seamus answered, wrenching open the rear door of the laundry truck. "He's been delayed."

Michal helped Sydney in, then they loaded the cart. Slamming the door shut, Michal turned to his older brother. Michal's handsome face was ashen. "What should we do?" he said.

Seamus hesitated only a second. "Take the back roads to the airstrip. I'll borrow a car and bring Kerry. But don't wait too long. If we don't show up soon, have the pilot fly out with Sydney and the child. Kerry can meet them in Cairo later."

Seamus O'Daugherty did something he had not done in many years. He reached out and embraced his younger brother. There was fear in his eyes when he finally released him.

"Now go, Michal . . . and Godspeed!"

■

Standing in the middle of a deserted airfield on the outskirts of the city, a small, wiry man checked the time. It was just past nine o'clock, and his people were running late. After finishing a final inspection of his Beechcraft Baron, Eric Blond lit a cigarette and waited in the scorching heat.

Born forty-five years ago in Dublin, Eric was the unique combination of an Irish mother and English father, a combination not particularly embraced in either land. Educated in London, Eric grew up with a keen sense of adventure, but never knew where he belonged. A brief tour with the Royal Air Force taught the young man the skill of flying, but a stint in the Middle East left him with a sweet taste for forbidden fruit and an unquenchable desire to live life dangerously close to the edge. So after completing his tour with the Air Corps, he had made his home in Dubai, where he used his skills as a private pilot to squire about those people who dared not fly commercially.

Brushing his thinning brown hair from his eyes, he thought about the passengers he had flown over the years . . . the rich, the spoiled and the ruthless. If nothing else, he had learned to ask no questions, do the job and collect the fees. Eric Blond patted his bulging pocket. Just to fly three people out of the country, he'd done an Irish Paddy a favor, and he had already collected a double fee with more expected upon their arrival.

Blond smiled. Today promised to be a very lucrative day. For a moment he permitted himself to wonder about the passengers he would soon encounter. All he knew for sure was that the man was an Irishman, the lady an American and the child . . . well, he really didn't ask questions about the child.

Suddenly a wind came up, blowing stinging dust in his eyes. Retrieving his sunglasses, he glanced yet again to the road leading to the airstrip. In the distance, he spied a swirling thick cloud of dust and he knew his passengers were approaching. Jumping on board his aircraft, he fired up the engines. His flight plan was already filed. Their destination was Cairo, Egypt.

Takeoff would be immediate. And unless there was a problem, a fueling stop would not be necessary. Cairo was only fifteen
hundred miles away. His Beechcraft Baron could do two thousand without fluttering an engine.

■

Swearing under his breath, Kerry raced down the steps as
quickly as his maimed leg would permit, cursing his Paddy heart
all the way. What a goddamn twisted sense of morality he had. To
jeopardize the entire mission over a lousy hotel bill! He'd never
forgive himself if anything went wrong.

The line had moved at a snail's pace, the staff incredibly
incompetent and slow. And by the time he arrived at the desk, it
was too late to turn back, and much too late to flee. Making the
best of things, he tried to hurry Azima along, but the Arab
seemed to take delight in making the Irishman squirm.

"I see you purchased more appropriate clothing," Azima said,
after studying the bill. "Good for you, Mr. Flynn."

"I trust your wife enjoyed her stay. It's a pity we never saw
her . . .

"You're paying in cash, sir? We're far more accustomed to
credit cards here . . ."

Having had enough of Azima's drivel, Kerry's voice was tinged
with anger. "Would you hurry please? Our flight leaves shortly."

It was then Faul Azima broke out in a grin. He picked up the
international flight schedule he kept behind the desk. "Are you
quite sure, Mr. Flynn? We don't have a flight to Ireland until much
later this afternoon . . ."

Their banter ended on Azima's sour note, and with his final
coup de grâce, Kerry was forced to wait patiently while the acting manager of the hotel dawdled. He forced himself to appear
relaxed, yet out of the corner of his eye he watched for any sudden, unexpected movements. To his relief he detected none.

Finally settling his account, Kerry fled the lobby through
the door leading to the basement. The only sounds louder than

his footsteps echoing on concrete were the "if onlys" shouting in his mind.

If only he had left the bill unpaid!

If only he had not given Azima one more chance to intimidate him!

If only he weren't running late!

"Oh dear God!" he cried. "Don't let anything go wrong!"

Throwing open the side door Seamus had left unlocked, he was horrified to find no truck, no linen cart, no Sydney.

Where in God's name had they gone?

A firm hand suddenly gripped his shoulder.

"Come with me, Kerry. I have a car. I had to send Michal and Sydney on to the plane. They've got the child."

Jumping into an ancient, battered, red car, Seamus and Kerry sped away, never knowing that the squeal of their tires, which seemed deafening, was in truth nothing compared to the alarm now being sounded throughout the city of Dubai.

Susan M. Hoskins

The truck barreled down the dirt road in a swirl of dust. Squinting, Eric Blond watched his passengers approach, but slowly his amusement turned to fret as the truck came sharply into focus.

"What the hell?" he muttered as he read the lettering on the side panel. He had seen limousines of every shape and description delivering his passengers, but never had a laundry truck been the primary means of transportation to this, his own private airstrip.

The confused pilot removed his sunglasses, leaning forward for a closer look, as Michal O'Daugherty, still garbed in the housekeeping uniform, hurried to open the rear door. To his amazement, a woman emerged first, dressed in the same uniform as the man. But it was when the two of them turned to assist the child—clad only in a nightdress—that Eric Blond knew something was dreadfully wrong.

"Oh Christ!" he swore. Switching off the engine of the Beechcraft, he jumped immediately from the seat of the plane and hit the airfield running.

Sydney, Michal and Lydia froze as the slender man came toward them, shouting and flailing his arms.

"What the hell is going on here?" he shouted, jerking Michal O'Daugherty aside. "You're Seamus's brother, aren't you? What have you gotten mixed up in, man?"

"Please, Eric, let me explain."

"Good God, Michal! What the hell am I supposed to think? You come tearing down the road in a laundry truck with an American woman dressed like a maid!"

Eric Blond's eyes sought the child's. Lydia kept her glance averted, but it was clear by her coal black hair and olive skin that she was neither Irish nor American.

"Your brother told me I'd be flying an Irishman, an American and a child to Cairo. Nobody said anything about a goddamn kidnapping!"

Eric Blond backed away from Michal O'Daugherty with a look of disgust on his tanned face. Withdrawing a bulging packet of cash, he glared at the envelope as if it were soiling his hands, then abruptly he threw it to the ground. "Tell your brother he's a fucking liar. There's no amount of money that could make me get involved in this. Now get off my airstrip or I'll turn you into the police myself!"

Eric Blond wheeled about and headed back toward the plane. His morals might be shaky, but he had certain scruples. Getting involved in something like this . . . well, it would ruin him in the Muslim community!

"Wait!" Sydney roared, running after him, but Eric Blond merely waved her away. Not to be deterred, Sydney grabbed him by the arm. Instinctively, he balled his fist, ready to strike as he pivoted to face her. Much to his amazement, Sydney Lawrence neither cowered nor retreated.

"Now you listen to me!" she cried. "This child is my daughter!" Still holding Blond by his arm, she beckoned Lydia to her. "Lydia's father is Iranian. His name is Ali Hassan."

Hearing the name of the man he knew only by dreaded reputation, Eric Blond paled.

"He's an arms dealer, but I can see you already know him. He lived in the United States for several years with Lydia. He committed a terrible crime in Kansas City. To escape arrest he fled the country, leaving Lydia with me. Her adoption in the States is final. She's mine, but he came back last week and abducted her at gunpoint."

"Look, lady," Blond pleaded, "I'm sorry for your trouble, but I can't get involved. The rules are different here . . ."

Sydney released Eric Blond long enough to grab her daughter. Clutching the child's shoulders she demanded, "Show him your face, Lydia."

Lydia Hassan Ellis slowly lifted her saddened eyes to Blond's. Standing immobile, she watched his expression change from anger to something much different.

Reaching out, he touched her battered cheek. "Oh God," he muttered.

"Now do you understand?" Sydney questioned softly. "Hassan muzzled her like a dog and paraded her through the lobby of the Hyatt simply because she talked back. No child deserves this. Ask her, Mr. Blond, ask her if I've taken her against her will."

Michal O'Daugherty cautiously approached the others. Sighing, Blond pushed strands of stray brown hair from his forehead. "Do you have papers to get her out of the country?"

"Yes," Sydney hastily answered. "We have passports for ourselves and for Lydia. They're with my friend, Kerry Donavan."

Michal explained, "We got nervous and left the hotel early. Seamus is bringing Mr. Donavan. He's got their papers and their clothing."

"Look, folks, you're asking me to jeopardize everything if we get caught. My business . . . my reputation . . . perhaps even my life! How can I pretend I don't know what you're up to? The way you're dressed and all! Besides, your adoption means nothing here, lady. We're in a Muslim country. Hassan has the right to do whatever he pleases to the child. I'm sorry, but—"

Lydia Hassan broke free of Sydney's embrace. "You haven't asked me what I want!" she said, confronting the pilot directly. "I want to go home! I want to be with my mother! Please, sir, will you help us?"

For a moment nothing stirred on the airstrip as Eric Blond stared helplessly at the child. No matter how much his rational brain begged him to turn away, his Irish heart melted in the anguish of the child's eyes.

He sighed. "Go ahead and take your seats. I'll fire up the

engines, but we have to wait for your friend. There's no way I can enter another country without your passports."

Michal ushered Sydney and Lydia toward the plane, not wanting to give the pilot a chance to reconsider. Eric gazed toward the back road leading to the city, but at the moment all was quiet.

"God help me," he muttered. Stooping, he retrieved the packet of fallen money. He stuffed it back in his pocket, then returned to the plane in order to prepare for takeoff, knowing deep in his heart that despite his good intentions, his actions were hopelessly, haplessly wrong.

■

The streets were congested. But what did Kerry expect? Dubai in the United Arab Emirates was more than a desert paradise with only cactus and white sand. It was a city as cosmopolitan as any in the United States or in western Europe. It had traffic jams, imposing glass and steel buildings, and exclusive shops. It had all the modern conveniences and every amenity one might expect. Like fire protection and hospitals. Like police squad cars . . . and alarm systems . . . even all-points bulletins.

The old car Seamus had borrowed had no muffler. The car was noisy, but not noisy enough to drown out the sound of approaching sirens. Kerry and Seamus froze as three truckloads of armed militia weaved through the thick throng of paralyzed traffic. With their lights and sirens blaring, they sped past the two men in the direction from which they had just come . . . in the direction of the Hyatt Regency Hotel.

Seamus turned to Kerry. He glanced at his passenger only a moment, but his features were creased with concern.

"What will we do?" Kerry shouted.

"We've got to hurry!" Seamus cried. "And we have to get out of this traffic! Hang on!"

Veering the car sharply to the right, Seamus sped away from the heart of the city toward the back roads leading to the airstrip.

The time was 9:30 a.m.

■

As the minutes ticked endlessly by, Eric Blond continued to stare at the control panels of his plane. Checking and rechecking his instruments, he sought to pass the time with as little thought as possible.

Strapped into their seats, Sydney and Lydia waited . . . saying nothing . . . while Michal nervously scanned the horizon for a glimpse of Kerry Donavan, the man who in all of this held the key.

Time—which they had planned to have plenty of—was a precious commodity they now had too little of.

Then suddenly Michal saw the mirage he had prayed for. Shouting loudly, he drew the others' attention to a cloud of dust in the distance. Both Sydney and Lydia broke out in a smile. Even the cool, reserved pilot nodded his relief. Smiling, they focused on the dustball, in only one direction. There was no way they could see the other trucks . . . until it was much too late.

■

Seemingly on its last gasp, the sputtering old car crested the final hill leading to the strip. As the deserted airfield came into focus, Seamus and Kerry both saw the airplane standing alone and unprotected in the center of the isolated piece of land.

"Oh my God!" Kerry cried, slamming his fist, nearly shattering the windshield. Squealing the brakes of the battered old vehicle, Seamus swerved the car, hiding it from view behind a sand dune. Turning off the engine, the two men sat in shock and utter silence as they watched the militia converge upon the tiny airfield from all directions. A dozen soldiers with guns drawn jumped out of the trucks and surrounded the plane. Sydney and Lydia were forced out first, crying quietly and huddling together. Michal was dragged out next, followed lastly by the pilot.

One of the soldiers laughed and, without provocation, struck Michal in the head with the butt of his gun, driving him to his knees. Without thinking, Eric Blond stepped forward, demanding that the soldiers back off. It was then that the soldiers surrounded the pilot . . . the brash rogue of an English-Irishman who lived life too close to the edge.

"Oh, dear God!" Seamus cried as he watched his friend, Eric Blond—with a blow of the butt of a gun mercilessly following another—viciously beaten to a senseless, bloody death.

Ali Hassan paced the floor while the Muslim woman, cowering in the corner, shed silent tears. Standing at attention near the window, Raoul Sabid waited respectfully for his master's command. Also present in the suite was the acting manager of the hotel, Faul Azima.

Hassan grabbed the phone the instant it sounded. Saying nothing, he waited while the message that Lydia had been found and her abductors captured was delivered from a remote phone in the commander's truck. His cheeks were red with rage, but his eyes were strangely cold and uncommunicative. Everyone in the room tensed, waiting for the news and his reaction.

When he spoke, his intent was clear. "Bring them to me *alive.* I want to see them face to face."

■

Obscured from view by the sand dune, Kerry and Seamus watched helplessly from the car as Michal was taunted, Sydney and Lydia terrorized, and Eric Blond beaten to death. Kerry lunged for the door, but Seamus quickly restrained him.

"There's nothing we can do," Seamus cried. "We're outnumbered six to one!"

"But Sydney . . ." Kerry whispered, tears welling in his eyes.

Seamus released his grip on Kerry, but his voice was husky. "I know, me friend, I know. That's me brother lying bleeding on the ground."

With hopeless resignation, the two men watched as the commander of the soldiers returned from his truck and ordered the others to disperse. With guns drawn, the soldiers shoved Sydney and Lydia into the lead vehicle. Dragging Michal to his feet, they forced him into a second truck. It was only those few left behind who turned their attention to the fallen pilot. Laughing, three of them picked up his lifeless body and tossed it unceremoniously into the rear of the last vehicle.

Seamus knew they had to leave . . . and leave quickly. Restarting the car, O'Daugherty backed away from the sand dune and sped away as quickly as the battered, old car would allow. For now they had to seek refuge and gather information. Only then could they formulate a plan.

■

At fifty, Ali Hassan was tall and rugged looking, with swarthy, pitted skin and eyes so dark as to be unreadable. His mere presence in a room was frightening. Never more so than when the door to the penthouse suite was thrown open and the prisoners were displayed before him.

Dazed and bleeding, Michal O'Daugherty was thrown to his knees, ten feet away from the arms dealer.

"Who is this man?" Hassan cried.

The acting manager of the Hyatt Regency Hotel shuddered as he recognized his own employee.

"He's an Irishman by the name of O'Daugherty," replied Azima. "He and his brother have been with us for years. He's a good boy. I have no idea how he got mixed up in this."

Ali Hassan walked slowly toward the hurt, bleeding man. With no pity and little emotion, he drew back and kicked Michal in the face with his heavy black boot.

"Why?" he demanded. "Why did you do it?"

Michal refused to answer. Hassan started toward him again, but the sound of Lydia's crying stopped him.

Turning his back on the fallen man, Hassan's eyes sought those of his daughter. He dropped to his knees, then threw open his arms and beckoned, "Come to Daddy."

But turning away from her father, Lydia buried her head in Sydney's arms and clung to her mother with all her might.

"Come to your father!" Hassan roared, slowly rising from his knees.

Sydney eyed Hassan with pure contempt as she held fast to the child. Refusing to abandon Lydia, she cried, "Leave her alone!"

Hassan grabbed his daughter by the arm, brutally wrenching her from Sydney's weaker grasp. Lydia fought him until, drawing back his massive hand, he slapped her hard, sending her reeling across the room.

Ominously, he promised, "I'll deal with you later, Lydia."

"You have no right to touch her!" Sydney cried.

"I have every right!" he bellowed. "I am her father!"

"You are no father," Sydney spat. "You're an animal."

Enraged, Ali Hassan balled his fist and hit Sydney Lawrence full force in the nose, shattering the bone to pieces. "It is you who have no rights, not here anyway! You should have remained in America where you belong and left well enough alone."

With blood gushing down her face, Sydney fell to her knees in agony, and yet she still defied him. "You bastard!"

In a voice that was not quite human, Ali Hassan bellowed as his face contorted with rage. No woman had ever dared to speak to him thus. With full force he kicked her. This time it was the bone just below her eye that found his mark. "I love you, Lydia!" Sydney cried as she struggled to remain conscious. "Be strong!" Hassan prepared to finish her with a crushing blow to the head. Only the sound of his daughter's anguished screams caused him to stop.

"Take them away," he told the commander. "Charge them with kidnapping. I want them stoned!"

In desperation, Lydia ran to her fallen mother. Throwing her own body over Sydney, she tried to shield her from the three soldiers who approached to carry her away. Ali Hassan moved toward her. It was Raoul Sabid, the trusted bodyguard, who interceded. He was fond of the girl. He had no desire to see her hurt further. And so, restraining Lydia in his own strong embrace, he waved the soldiers forward.

"Lock Lydia in her bedroom," Hassan demanded. Obediently, Raoul Sabid did what he was told, then returned to the others.

Faul Azima sat in stunned silence as the soldiers surrounded the lifeless form of the American woman and started to drag her away. Her face was covered in blood, and he wondered if she was alive or dead. She was dressed in the uniform of a hotel maid, and yet he knew that he'd never seen her before. Still, when she first entered the room, the image of her face looked vaguely familiar. Where had he seen her face before?

Hassan bade the commander of the militia to tarry a moment after the others had departed. Pausing in the doorway, he said, "You have done well, my friend. Your loyalty will not be forgotten. There is one more thing you can do. Find out who else was involved in this plot to steal my daughter. I demand that everyone be brought to justice."

Hassan returned to the living room. It was then he remembered the Muslim woman still cowering in the far corner of the room.

"Incompetent whore!" he cried. "How could you have let this happen?"

The poor woman shrank to her knees, pleading for mercy. But on this day of his greatest betrayal, Ali Hassan had none to spare.

Turning to his trusted bodyguard, the one who had in time discovered the plot, he said, "Dispose of the dog."

The woman's curdling screams filled the hallway. Faul Azima rose to his feet. Oh, how he wished that the real manager of the hotel were here to do his duty! This had been Azima's week to shine while his boss was away, vacationing somewhere in the Canary Islands. For eight glorious days, Azima was the man in charge.

"I'm so very sorry this has happened, sir," said Azima. "We will do whatever we can to right the wrong."

Ali Hassan took a menacing step toward the smaller man. "I

hold you personally responsible for this travesty, Azima. I was assured that my daughter would be safe here. You find out why your employee got involved in this and who else was involved." Deliberately pausing, Ali Hassan held the terrified man in the web of his hate-filled eyes. "Don't let me down again."

Susan M. Hoskins

Foreigners in Dubai live among their own kind. Hidden in a squalid shanty in the center of the Irish ghetto, two men waited to hear some word on the fate of their loved ones. Isolated for hours, they had heard nothing. Then, shortly after three o'clock, a young man entered the darkened room. Approaching Seamus solemnly, the boy knelt down and spoke to his elder in a low, respectful hush.

Seamus nodded then, patting the teenager on the shoulder, dismissed him. The freckle-faced lad rose, glanced curiously at Kerry, and then quickly fled the room.

"The news is not good, me friend," O'Daugherty reluctantly admitted. "Michal and Sydney have been carted off to city prison. They'll be tried in a few days . . . as soon as . . . they're able. The charge is kidnapping. That's a capital offense in Dubai. The punishment is death by stoning."

"Oh, dear Lord," Kerry moaned. "What can we do? Where can we find a lawyer?"

"That's a joke," Seamus answered grimly. "There is no defense. They were caught with Hassan's kid. Me and the boys, we kept our noses clean. We knew the score straight from the start. If you get in trouble here, there's nobody to protect you. To tell you the truth, Kerry, short of storming the prison, I don't know of a damn thing we can do."

Donavan rose from his crouched position. Running his fingers through his thick chestnut hair, he struggled to think.

"I'm afraid there's more," said O'Daugherty quietly.

Kerry's eyes returned to his friend, but he didn't like the look on Seamus's face. "More?" he repeated. "Has something else happened to Sydney?"

"Sydney's hurt, Kerry, she's hurt real bad. She was brought before Hassan, and he beat her. Michal, too. But Sydney's the worse of the two."

Kerry's voice was a lethal mixture of agony and anger. "What did he do to her?"

"The lad didn't know for sure. She was covered in blood when she was brought out of the hotel."

"Surely they'll take her to a hospital . . ."

Seamus shook his head sadly. "You don't know these people like I do, Kerry. As far as her jailers are concerned, she's already been tried and found guilty. It makes no difference if she's stoned or beaten to death. She's a woman. Here in Dubai, her value is less than a pig."

Kerry thought about Sydney alone and in pain. Why couldn't it have been he who was captured? He would have known how to survive. She . . . she knew nothing . . . not of this side of life. She had lived with wealth and she understood power. But unlike him, she still believed people to be good.

"We have to do something, Seamus! She could die without medical attention!"

Glancing around O'Daugherty's pitiful surroundings, Kerry did not need to ask what conditions would be like in city prison. He knew from his own IRA experience just how abominably prisoners could be treated. The rats and roaches in their holes would be better off than they were.

Seamus's voice was soft. "What are we to do, Kerry? They know that there were other people involved. The boy told me that the search is on, and I, as Michal's brother, am first on the list."

Pacing to the far corner of the small, square room, Kerry rested his head against the wooden mantel. How like another night, he remembered, when things seemed so bleak and dismal. Then he had been in Kentucky, in Mack's house, waiting with Sydney for some word on Lydia. Then he had heard the front door open and the firm, controlled voice of another man. Purposefully he had remained there with his back to the others until he was forced to finally turn around and confront the one who knew the truth about him, the FBI man by the name of Joe Morrison.

It was then the answer came.

"Get up, Seamus, and come with me. Hurry, man, we have to find a phone!"

◾

With a time difference of nine hours, it was ironic that as one afternoon in the Middle East was mercifully coming to an end, the same day was only just dawning in the nation's capital of Washington, D.C. Having returned late the previous night from a grueling two-week field trip in the Northwest, Joe Morrison was exhausted. He'd fallen asleep on the couch watching a baseball game, where he remained still at 6:30 a.m.

Even in deep slumber, the FBI agent recognized the sound of the phone ringing. No one called him at home . . . not at this hour . . . unless it was something important . . . something to do with work.

Joe's mind sharpened as he wiped the fog from his eyes and asked the FBI operator, "What's up?"

"Sorry to disturb you, Joe, but I've got a call for you from Dubai. The man says you know him. His name is Kerry Donavan."

Joe Morrison sat bolt upright on his old, brown sofa. Feeling a knot of dread in his gut, he hated to ask, "What's wrong?"

"The man wouldn't say," the operator responded, "except it's about Sydney Lawrence and that she's in trouble."

Thinking of the willowy woman with flaming hair, hot hazel eyes, and a tongue every bit as sharp as her wits, Morrison mumbled, "Oh shit. Patch him through!"

◾

Exiting FBI headquarters, Morrison squinted against the bright afternoon sun. It had been a magnificent spring day in

Washington, with temperatures hovering near 70°, but neither the smell of the flowers nor the warmth of the sun meant a thing to Joe Morrison this day. For the past ten hours since speaking with Kerry, nothing had mattered but Sydney's dilemma and finding a way to help.

Hurrying down the street, he checked his watch. It was nearly 4:15. If he hustled, he could gather his thoughts over a beer before his boss arrived at 4:30.

On a quiet side street a few blocks from the federal building was a Mediterranean cafe by the name of Nabil's. It was a small, unpretentious place that served food continuously throughout the day. Nabil's was rather unremarkable, except for one thing. More deals were struck there than on any single floor in FBI headquarters. Why? The restaurant was quiet and comfortable. It was off the beaten path, and it was safe.

Joe knew the owner, Nabil, quite well, as did his boss, John Taylor. After a hearty greeting, Morrison was ushered to a back booth, isolated from the main part of the dining room and well out of the way of other traffic. In the quiet interlude between lunch and dinner, the two FBI agents counted on finding themselves alone. Their conversation was too risky for the curious ears inside FBI headquarters.

"John will be here in a few minutes, Nabil. Bring me a cold draft of Harp now, and another when he arrives. Thanks, pal."

Nabil returned with a chilled mug, then left Joe alone with his own thoughts. Joe Morrison had the reputation of being an oddball, the guy who somehow never fit in. He was respected by most of his fellow agents—that much Nabil had gathered over the years—if not well liked or understood. He was a maverick and a loner. Never had he been one of the boys.

Morrison removed his sunglasses, then fumbled in his pocket for a smoke. Lighting the Marlboro, he inhaled deeply. With his cigarette in one hand and his mug in the other, he allowed his mind to roam yet again to a city far away and a woman in grave danger.

Joe Morrison was a complicated man. He'd been married once, but his wife and son were killed in an automobile accident. He'd never gotten over their deaths.

Two traits kept Morrison from getting close to people. He was a cynic and a confirmed pessimist. Outside of his job, there were only three things that mattered: good sex, a cold beer and a full pack of cigarettes. And as far as friends were concerned— well, he'd count his boss as one, and after that there were only two others. He'd buried one less than a year ago, and the other one needed him now. And no matter what he had to do, Joe Morrison was determined to save her.

Hearing footsteps, he glanced up, relieved to see the haggard face of the man who, despite Joe's rotten temperament, understood him better than anyone else.

"Hi, John. I'm glad you could make it."

Rising, Joe leaned across the table and grasped his boss's hand. Taking his seat across from Joe, Taylor laid an unmarked manila envelope on the table.

"I appreciate your meeting me here on such short notice, John."

"What choice did I have?" Taylor quipped. "Here or there, what difference does it make? I still have to put up with your ugly face. At least here I can get a beer."

Signaling Nabil, Taylor ordered himself a cold draft of Harp. John Taylor was a gaunt man in his late fifties, given to wearing rumpled white shirts with paisley ties. The two men sat in silence until their chilled mugs were delivered.

Taylor spoke first. "Any other word on Sydney?"

"The American Embassy in Dubai confirmed a few hours ago that she is in city prison and kidnapping charges have been filed. They couldn't confirm or deny her medical condition. It'll take a few days to cut through the red tape and get somebody in to see her."

John Taylor grimaced as he wiped the foamy froth from his mouth. From what Joe had reported this morning, he wasn't sure she had a few days to wait.

"So what do you have in mind?"

Taking a deep breath, Morrison gathered his thoughts as he lit another Marlboro.

"You won't like it," he muttered, "but I've got a plan." He

leaned forward. "Look, you made it clear this morning that our government will do nothing to help Sydney. She's an independent citizen functioning completely on her own. She knew that from the start and so did Donavan."

Sipping his beer, Taylor studied his protégé carefully. Morrison was upset, more upset than Taylor had ever seen him.

"I've been with the bureau for almost twenty years," said Joe, "and I've never asked a favor . . . not for myself anyway. All the guys do it. It's a perk of the job . . . a little surveillance here . . . a little protection there. It's done all the time."

Taylor said nothing, forcing Joe to continue.

"I don't have many friends, but I guess you know that by now. Just never could figure out how to let people in. Sam and Sydney, though . . . they were different. Down to earth. You know . . . real. And how they took that little girl into their hearts . . . well, they got to me in a way no one else had."

"I know that you want to help, Joe," Taylor said. "But truthfully, there's nothing you can do."

"Yeah, I know, I know. Our government won't get involved. Who the hell is Sydney Lawrence anyway? Shit, they let Terry Anderson rot in hell for eight years. Who gives a damn about one insignificant woman?"

"The system stinks, Joe, we all agree. That doesn't leave you with many options, my friend."

"No, it doesn't," Morrison retorted sadly.

"Okay, so what do you want to do?" Taylor queried.

"I want to take a leave of absence," replied Morrison. "Lord knows, I have plenty of time built up. Let me go over there and see what I can do to help."

Taylor nodded. He had expected the request. "Let's say we grant you leave, Joe. What then? The way I see it, there isn't much you can do to help this woman other than find her a damn good Arab lawyer who speaks English and likes Americans. Then you can fight the case in court. Given the extenuating circumstances, the court might be lenient."

"Lenient, my ass!" Morrison shot back. "Who are you kidding? She's in a Muslim country where women have no rights. As far as they're concerned, she's no better than a stranger trying to abduct Hassan's child."

"So what else do you have in mind?"

"I want to go to Hassan and strike a deal. Get him to drop the charges."

Taylor shot his subordinate a quizzical glance. "How? Ali Hassan is now one of the most powerful men in the Emirates. He's a god playing by his own rules. What could we possibly have that he wants? Have you forgotten the basic rule of negotiation, Joe? You have to trade something to get something."

It was then for the first time that Joe Morrison smiled. "We *do* have something that Hassan wants. Something he wants very badly. Think about it, John."

For a long, pregnant pause the FBI boss looked blank.

"Let me give you a hint. What he wants is sitting right in the middle of a Kansas wheat field."

"Holy shit!" Taylor swore, slamming his beer down on the table. "Are you fucking me?" His words were harsh, but his expression had softened as the truth of Joe's words sank in. "Farhad Rajid, his brother. Oh Christ, Joe, that's brilliant!"

"Can you arrange it?" Morrison pleaded. "A swap. The freedom of one Iranian, no-good son of a bitch for a well-known, respected American citizen. Who would balk at that? The taxpayers would be relieved of the burden of housing Rajid for the rest of his life. It's perfect and it's the only chance we got."

Taylor's eyes lit up, and for the first time in a long time his permanently etched frown turned into a grin. "If we can get a federal judge to release Farhad Rajid into your custody, we could deport him immediately. That way I could even justify sending you with him on a government jet, just to see that he makes it . . . safely."

Morrison couldn't help showing his excitement, but Taylor quickly cut him short.

"There's something you have to do before we can pull this off."

"I'll do anything, John, just name it."

"We need the permission of the ruling family of Dubai to enter their country and negotiate any deals. Knowing you'd come up with some half-assed plan, I did a little homework on the situation today."

Taylor reached across the table and grabbed the manila envelope. Handing it to Joe, he spoke in a low quiet voice. "The man you want to see is Sheik Mohammed al Maktoum, the youngest son of the ruling family. I ordered a profile on him this morning. As it happens, the sheik is here in the United States right now at his horse farm in Kentucky. Pay him a visit, Joe. If Sheik Mohammed gives you permission to negotiate the deal for Sydney's release, I'll pull every string I have."

Draining the last of his mug, John Taylor stood, as did a greatly relieved Joe Morrison.

"I know how much this means to you, Joe. Just do what I ask, and we'll be here to support you. Read the packet, book a flight, then get the hell out of my sight!"

Lexington, Kentucky
Sunday, May 3
4:45 p.m.

The flight had been miserable—every seat booked and the air conditioning not working. The plane, lurching in the sky like a kite in the wind, tore Joe Morrison's nervous gut apart. Eating Rolaids like he might a pack of Life Savers, Morrison cursed his ulcer, his job, and even Sydney Lawrence for putting him in this predicament.

On the ground at last, Morrison steered his rented Ford Taurus toward the main road leading to the Lexington-Frankfort Highway, but a huge 747 jet, abandoned on a quiet strip just inside the grounds, caught his eye. There was no mistaking the Arabic lettering on the side or the placement of the jet, which could be viewed from the road. The message was clear. Sheik Mohammed al Maktoum was in residence . . . with all his wealth and all his splendor.

Popping yet another antacid, Joe took his time meandering down the highway from Lexington to Versailles. It was not that he had time to kill. No, quite the contrary. His plane had landed a bit late. The sheik was a very busy man with little time to spare. It took some heavy arm-twisting from the United States government to convince the sheik to grant Joe a brief audience. After all, Joe mused cynically, Sheik Mohammed had a party to host tonight. It was the week of the Kentucky Derby and the sheik was entertaining the nobility of horse racing. How much time could he devote to the fate of a lowly, insignificant woman? Well, be that as it may, the sheik might have to wait, because Joe Morrison needed a few extra minutes to settle his stomach and steel his nerves before his scheduled 5:30 meeting. For as trivial as the encounter might seem to the sheik, to Joe the outcome meant everything.

Some fifteen minutes later, Morrison signaled his turn off the main Lexington-Frankfort Highway onto the smaller Midway Road. And suddenly his heart grew heavy as he remembered another night, a short time ago, when he was forced to make this same journey. Then it had been to deliver the bad news that Farhad Rajid knew nothing about Lydia's abduction. Then he had been forced to confront the devastated, despairing eyes of a mother who, in the mishap of a few minutes, had lost a child she had grown to love as her own.

Morrison slowed just before the turn into the sheik's estate. The lane just down the road caught his notice. It was at the bottom of that lane where Lydia had been abducted. Allowing his eyes to wander, he imagined the spot a few hundred yards farther where the road forks . . . the spot where Sydney first saw the car . . . the car that didn't belong. And Hassan with his men. And the gun leveled squarely at her head.

Joe Morrison felt sick. Not from the flight nor even his ulcer. His heart hurt; even his soul was in pain because of the sins and the selfishness of humanity. Soon he would have to pay a visit to the older gentleman who lived at the far end of the lane. He owed him that much. Mack Lawrence was still alive, that much he had determined from Billy Ray earlier this morning. Billy had promised to have Mack there, ready to receive the news that Joe would bring about his only daughter.

The speed bumps in the drive of Sheik Mohammed al Maktoum's estate caused Joe to slow down and drink in the sheer opulence of his surroundings. The lawn looked as if it had been manicured by hand, and flowers of every kind and color adorned the path. Halfway down the drive, he came to the renowned fountain and bridge, which had cost the sheik over a million dollars to build.

Crossing the bridge, Morrison's rented Taurus was waved to a halt by two men in dark suits. While one man waited in the distance, a second man approached Joe's car cautiously. He was an American with blond hair and blue eyes, somewhere in his early thirties. His demeanor was pleasant, but his eyes wary, as he leaned down to talk to Morrison.

"Good afternoon, sir. Would you state your business, please?"

Flashing his badge, the FBI agent replied, "My name is Morrison, Joe Morrison."

"Ah yes," the security guard responded. "We were told to expect you." Stepping away from the car, the first of the two men nodded to the other. "If you will follow Greg, I will notify the sheik that you are here."

Joe allowed the younger man to mount his scooter and lead him down the paved drive, away from the house and toward the stable.

As the mansion, shielded by a wall of shrubs, disappeared from view, Morrison felt a bit cheated. For as much as he tried to dismiss the sheik and his lifestyle, he harbored an intense curiosity about the man and his wealth.

At the end of the asphalt drive, Greg came to a halt, signaling Joe to park his Taurus near the first of three stables. The stables alone were worth well over six million dollars. That much Joe knew from the dossier John Taylor had prepared. And the horses grazing in the fields were each more magnificent than the next.

"If you will come with me, sir," said Greg. And Joe Morrison, used to giving orders, followed.

Unlocking the door to the rear office, the young security guard bade Joe to enter.

"Sheik Mohammed thought this office would give you more privacy to talk. Unfortunately, he's hosting quite a bash this evening, so the main house is in a bit of chaos. If you will make yourself comfortable, the sheik will be here shortly."

Closing the door behind him, the polite young man departed, leaving Joe to settle himself. The office was small, but impeccably decorated in sporty, masculine colors of hunter green and mahogany. The desk was a gleaming cherry, and the two chairs opposite, plush leather.

Joe was edgy and in desperate need of a cigarette, but he had no intention of offending the sheik. Setting his briefcase atop the desk, Joe walked to the bookcase at the far corner of the room. Smiling with great amusement, he picked up the gilded framed photograph of the sheik, a horse, and the queen of England.

"Ugly," he muttered, peering closer, "butt ugly!"

"I do hope you're not referring to my horse," a cultured, well-modulated voice despaired. "Mr. Morrison, I presume?"

The brash FBI agent in the rumpled polyester suit wheeled around to confront the dark, dancing eyes of a trim, impeccably dressed man in khaki slacks and a Ralph Lauren polo shirt.

"I hope I didn't startle you. I'm Sheik Mohammed al Maktoum and that's a picture of my horse you're holding."

"Lovely animal," Morrison stammered, carefully setting the photograph down.

"Are you a horseman?" the sheik queried.

"Not hardly," Joe replied a bit caustically.

"Would you care to sit?" Mohammed beckoned. "I understand that there is a matter of some importance you wish to discuss."

Morrison took the leather chair next to the sheik. Sheik Mohammed al Maktoum was a handsome, debonair man whom Joe guessed to be in his mid-forties. He had pleasant features, black hair, and a coarse beard flecked with gray. His onyx eyes seemed intelligent and curious, but guarded. He waited—neither smiling nor frowning—for Morrison to begin.

Joe wasn't entirely sure what he expected, but Sheik Mohammed definitely did not fit the bill. Was it the turban he missed, or the long flowing robes? Whatever it was, Mohammed looked like a well-heeled, regular guy—a neighbor from up the street . . . or down the road as they might say here . . . not one of the wealthiest men in the world from the enigmatic place known as the United Arab Emirates.

"Is there something wrong?" asked Sheik Mohammed, with a hint of amusement.

"I beg your pardon, sir," Morrison stammered. "But you're not what I expected."

"And what was that?" the sheik responded.

Morrison grinned. "Be damned if I know!"

Sheik Mohammed al Maktoum leaned conspiratorially toward Joe. His voice was softer and more intimate as he posed his next question.

"Tell me, Mr. Morrison, is it quite exciting being a G-man?"

And Morrison laughed aloud. He'd been called many things in his life, but never a G-man.

"I think you've been watching too many movies, your . . . what should I call you?"

"Please call me Mohammed. And I will call you Joe."

"Done," Morrison nodded, grinning. "You asked me if it's exciting being an FBI agent. Well, it has its moments. Tell me, Mohammed, what's it like being a sheik?"

Now it was Mohammed's turn to smile.

"It's quite nice, actually, although I wouldn't know any difference. I certainly live well, and I have everything a man could desire. I suppose that makes life a bit dull, however. You see, I'm the youngest of three brothers. There's not a great deal for me to do except play with my horses and minister to my country. Sometimes the passion is lacking . . . and people always want something from me."

Mohammed's expression turned suddenly more grave, as the light banter of their conversation ebbed to focus on the real reason for their encounter. "Now tell me, Joe, what can I do for you?"

The irony of the sheik's own words was not lost on the agent.

"How well do you know your neighbors, sir?" Morrison asked.

"Some I know quite well, like the group I'm hosting here tonight; others, not at all."

"Just down the road lives a man by the name of Donavan, Kerry Donavan. Have you met him?"

Sheik Mohammed al Maktoum grimaced, but his look was one of decided amusement. "If you mean the Irishman with the limp who owns Shadow Lane Farm—well, I know him better than I care to."

Morrison looked puzzled.

"He beat me at my own game, Joe. That's something most men never have a chance to do. I must say I respect him, though. He bought a lovely mare right out from under my nose at the Keeneland yearling sale. What I would give for one of her offspring! Is that the man you mean?"

"It is," Morrison replied, edging a bit closer. "Adjacent to Donavan's farm lives an older fellow, a veterinarian by the name of Mack Lawrence. Would you know him?"

"I'm afraid I don't," Mohammed replied. "But his name is mentioned with great reverence within my circle of friends. He's a famous man around here."

"Mack Lawrence has a daughter named Sydney. She was married to a doctor in Kansas City, but he was murdered earlier this year. Sydney moved back here, right after her husband's funeral, to be near her daddy. He's dying of cancer, you know."

"I didn't know," the sheik replied, frowning. "Nasty business, cancer. I'm sorry to hear that."

"Sydney and her husband, Sam, legally adopted a daughter by the name of Lydia. Her heritage is Iranian. Her father is a wanted felon here in the States. He abandoned the child to Sydney's care nearly two years ago when he fled the country. He's an arms dealer, and I think you might know him. His name is Ali Hassan."

Sheik Mohammed seemed to pale slightly, although with his swarthy features it was difficult to tell. But his jaw tightened and his features grew a bit more rigid when he spoke again.

"I make it my business to know important people residing within my city."

"Using a false identity, Hassan entered this country illegally, for the express purpose of abducting Lydia at gunpoint. He returned to Dubai immediately afterward and is residing with her there."

Sheik Mohammed said nothing. His cautious eyes had narrowed as he focused on every word that Morrison uttered. He played his hand close to the chest because, until he knew what the FBI agent wanted, he refused to betray the slightest emotion.

"Sydney, together with Kerry Donavan, located Lydia a few days ago. Sydney was captured in an attempt to reclaim the child who is now rightfully hers. Hassan beat her savagely and then had her thrown into prison without medical attention. That's where you come in. I need your help."

A man of superior intelligence, Sheik Mohammed al Maktoum pondered the situation carefully. When he finally spoke, his words were measured. "I must repeat the question I asked earlier. What do you want from me? Other than providing immediate medical attention for your friend and a personal introduction to the finest lawyer in Dubai, I'm not sure what else I can do. Unfortunately, if she tried to take the child away from Hassan, she is guilty in my country of kidnapping. Her adoption here in the States means nothing there. It may seem unjust, but that is Islamic law."

"Yes, it does seem unfair, damned unfair, if you'll pardon me, sir! But hear me out. You and I both know that Sydney Lawrence stands an ice cube's chance in hell of being acquitted in your court, no matter what attorney she has. Ali Hassan commands a great deal of power and respect in the Middle East. If he wants her stoned, she will be. Tell me Mohammed, am I wrong?"

The sheik merely shrugged. Truth, after all, was truth.

"Well, I have a plan, but I need your permission to carry it out. I want to arrange a deal. Do you know what the word 'swap' means?"

A quizzical look creased his handsome features. "No, I'm not familiar with that term."

"I wish to trade the life of Farhad Rajid, Hassan's brother, for the lives of Sydney, Kerry Donavan and two Irishmen who tried to help them. May I have your permission, sir, to negotiate a deal, swapping Farhad Rajid for the others, granting them safe passage out of your country?"

A shrewd businessman, the sheik weighed the considerations carefully.

"This man, Farhad Rajid. Who is he? Where is he?"

"Right now, sir, he's serving time in a federal penitentiary in Leavenworth, Kansas. He was convicted last year of human organ theft. He was sentenced to life in prison without parole."

"And you wish to bring such a man into my country? I think not, Joe. Despite your good intentions, I think not."

"I only wish to make the swap. What you do with him after that, sir, is your business. One lousy, worthless life traded for the lives of four decent people. Surely, sir, we could arrange the trade. After that, he could be exiled from your country. With Hassan's connections, finding his brother a home should be no problem. Any terrorist group in the Middle East would welcome him with open arms in exchange for a shipment of Hassan's wares. You and I both know that, sir."

"Suppose I consider your request favorably," said Mohammed after a pause, "what then?"

"I was hoping you would let me take the child as well."

Shaking his head vigorously, Sheik Mohammed was adamant in his reply.

"This I cannot do. By the dictates of Islamic law, the child is the sole property of her father. I cannot change the sacred law and I will not tamper with it. You must understand, Joe. I dwell with my feet planted precariously in both worlds . . . yours and mine. But first and foremost, I am the servant of my people. I must deny your request."

Joe Morrison leaned back in his chair and smiled, catching the sheik a bit off guard. He liked Mohammed. He rather wished they could be friends.

"I suspected that would be your reply. But in the event the deal we spoke about . . . falls through . . . I was wondering if you might sign these papers?"

Pushing his luck to the very outer limits, Morrison leaned across the gleaming desk and retrieved his briefcase. Taking out three separate documents, he reached for a pen, then handed the pen and the documents to the sheik.

"The first is exactly what we talked about. It gives me permission to enter your country with Farhad Rajid. If we can arrange the swap, I will obtain a federal order for Rajid's release into my custody for immediate deportation to the Emirates. The second part of this document gives your permission for Sydney, Kerry and the O'Daugherty brothers to leave Dubai and return to the United States. Would you sign this, please?"

Sheik Mohammed studied the two-page document carefully.

In a lovely flowing scroll, Sheik Mohammed signed his name.

"In order for this to be legal, my official seal must be affixed to the document. If you would be so kind as to get it from the desk, Joe."

Morrison leapt to his feet and walked to the front of the desk. There was the heavy ornate seal. He placed it in the hands of the sheik.

Gingerly tucking the first signed document back into his briefcase, Joe set the next set of papers before the sheik.

"What is this?" Mohammed inquired.

"In the event Ali Hassan reneges on our deal, I have an extradition order for his arrest. He is, after all, a wanted felon here in the States. Pardon me, sir, but if he screws with me, I want to nail his ass. Understand?"

While Mohammed found Joe's choice of words amusing, he was disturbed by their content.

"What you ask, Joe, is not desirable. Ali Hassan may be a criminal in your country, but he commands respect in mine. While I personally do not approve of his dealings, it is nonetheless a sticky situation. I'm afraid what you ask is impossible."

"Is it, Mohammed? Let's go back to your analogy. You say you dwell with one foot in this country and one foot in your own. From what I've read, your reputation is quite important to you here, as well as your acceptance into the inner circles of horse-racing society. Otherwise, why would you bother to host the party tonight?"

Warily, the sheik nodded, unsure where the conversation was going.

"You may not be aware, sir, but members of your staff harbored Hassan for days right here on these premises. Your own people helped him commit yet another crime in this country. Would you want the media to make that public? Hassan may be a well-respected man in your country, but in ours he's a common criminal. Would you want your name linked to his?"

Sheik Mohammed al Maktoum's expression turned stony cold. Any hint of friendship was quickly extinguished from his eyes.

"You know damn well I don't want any bad publicity! I'm not

well thought of here in the States except within my own circle of friends. My people in general are treated with suspicion in your country. I do not wish to do further damage. I will sign the paper. But listen carefully, Joe Morrison. In return for my signature, I must have your solemn oath that there will be no publicity about this incident . . . anything about this incident . . . from its inception to its conclusion . . . in your country or in mine. It must remain our secret. Is that clear?"

"I understand and I swear," Joe promised, relieved beyond measure that his ploy had worked. But there was still a hurdle he had to traverse, even though it was a desperate one, and one he did not expect to conquer. Trying to soothe the ruffled feathers of the man he had just offended, Morrison spoke calmly and quietly in as steady a voice as his racing heart could muster. It was paramount that he make the sheik understand.

"One final thing, sir. If something were to happen to Ali Hassan, who would be granted custody of the child?"

"Custody would pass to the closest male relative. I suppose that would be his brother, Farhad Rajid."

"Yes," Morrison agreed, "as far as we know, Farhad Rajid is the only living relative Hassan has. But you said yourself, sir, that the son of a bitch must be deported from your country immediately. Therefore, wouldn't he be unsuitable?"

All too familiar now with Morrison's shrewd tactics, Mohammed wisely and cautiously countered, "What are you driving at?"

"I have a personal favor to ask, sir. In the event of Hassan's death, I implore you to take personal custody of Lydia. She's a lovely child and she deserves to be happy. She lived here in the United States most of her life, and she has grown to love Sydney dearly. I would ask that, in the event of her father's death or imprisonment in the States, you return Lydia to her mother. If that is not possible, I would ask that you see she is raised properly. I know that I'm asking a lot, but I must, for Sydney's sake and for the child's."

Sheik Mohammed al Maktoum pondered Joe Morrison's request. There was pain in the FBI agent's eyes and a depth of sincerity that the sheik respected. Finally, after what seemed an interminable pause, he spoke the words Joe so desperately yearned to hear.

"I will do as you ask, but I need your promise that you will make no trouble in my country. You will proceed exactly as we have discussed. You will try to work a deal. Only if this fails will you implement the second plan. Is that agreed?"

"It is!" Joe said, with more relief and gratitude in his voice than he thought he was capable of. He waited then in respectful silence, with beads of perspiration dotting his brow, until the sheik affixed his signature and seal to the final documents.

When the sheik had finished, Joe carefully locked the papers away in his briefcase. Rising with Mohammed, Morrison thrust out his hand firmly, warmly.

"Would you like my office to arrange the meeting with Ali Hassan?"

"Yes, sir," Joe replied. "That would simplify matters greatly. He's currently residing at the Hyatt Regency in Dubai."

Trying out his newly acquired word, Mohammed asked, "Where would you like the . . . swap . . . to take place?"

Not familiar with his options, Joe merely replied, "On the grounds of the American Embassy."

"I will provide an honor guard of my militia just to ensure your safety . . . and privacy . . . with this matter. I will have my secretary call you when the arrangements have been completed. Where can I reach you?"

"I'll stay at the Ramada Inn near the airport tonight and proceed to Leavenworth tomorrow." Reaching in his pocket, Morrison retrieved his card and presented it to the sheik. "You could leave a message for me at the hotel tonight or at my office in Washington tomorrow."

Nodding, the sheik started toward the door, but a bizarre idea stopped him. Despite Joe's unorthodox tactics, which Mohammed found both intriguing and distasteful, he liked the FBI agent. Turning back to Joe, he said, "Would you care to stay for the evening? You'd be most welcome at my party."

Joe Morrison was genuinely flattered. He respected the sheik, and under different circumstances . . . but the circumstances were what they were.

Besides, he had a father to see about his only daughter. He had a message to deliver, and not a very pretty one; but thanks to Sheik Mohammed al Maktoum, at least now there was a thin, delicate ribbon of hope.

35

Dubai
Monday, May 4

The stocky Irishman entered the lobby of the Hyatt Regency Hotel shortly after 10:00 a.m. Standing in the middle of the opulent room, he stared agape, marveling at his lavish surroundings. Eddy Maloney had never before traveled beyond the shores of his motherland, never in all his born days.

He'd been in Dubai since yesterday, searching for the one he knew so well—his grade-school chum, his former IRA pal, the one so despised by Liam Thompson. This was the fifth hotel on his circuit. So far, he had turned up nothing. But with his pockets well padded, he could afford to take his time. Sooner or later, he'd find his mark.

Shoving his hands in his pockets, he slowly meandered toward the huge, oaken reception desk. It was quiet in the hotel, nothing much stirring. There was a lovely young lady behind the desk and a stuffy-looking Arab man standing a few feet behind her. The young woman glanced up and smiled. Eddy Maloney returned the favor, but then hastily avoided her glance. A chauvinist at heart, he sought the attention of the male to provide him with the information he needed . . . the short, dark-skinned man with the pinched lips, the man by the name of Azima.

"May I have a word with you, sir?"

Recognizing the distinct brogue of yet another Irishman, Faul Azima grimaced with more than a hint of disdain. "Yes? What can I do for you?"

Even though Eddy smiled his most engaging grin, his attempt at politeness was wasted on Azima, who found the Paddy standing before him—with rosy cheeks, a protruding belly, bad teeth and the manners of a commoner—quite repugnant. Dressed in a heavy woolen shirt, dark pants and a twill cap, Eddy Maloney reminded Azima briefly of another Irishman, equally poorly attired. The other man was certainly better looking, more affluent, and quite a bit more debonair, but still . . .

"Your business, sir?" Azima continued impatiently. "I'm afraid I'm rather busy . . ."

"I'm looking for a friend of mine, an old pal from Ireland. I have reason to think he might be staying here. Would you ever have a look at his picture and tell me if you might know him?"

Faul Azima rolled his eyes, but reluctantly accepted the photograph. Retrieving a pair of glasses from his pocket, he brought the photograph closer for a better look. It was an old picture, a bit frayed around the edges, but there was no mistaking the handsome features of the other Irishman Azima had encountered only recently.

Seeing the strange look on the acting manager's face, Eddy Maloney's voice rose. "You recognize this man?" he asked with obvious excitement.

"I might," the solemn one replied. "Who is he?"

Eddy Maloney leaned in toward Faul, resting his elbows on the oaken desk. Azima frowned, for the garlic on the man's breath was offensive.

"He's a pal of mine from Limerick. His name is Kerry Donavan. He's traveling with a good-looking redheaded woman, an American by the name of Sydney Lawrence."

Faul Azima's attitude changed. Removing his glasses, he smiled at the Irishman and spoke in a gentle tone. "And what did you say your name was?"

"Me name is Eddy Maloney."

"What is the nature of your business with this man?"

Now it was Eddy Maloney who changed. Growing cautious, his answer was guarded.

"Me business with him is personal. Nothing to concern yourself with. Tell me, good man, have you seen him?"

"Well now," Faul replied slowly, "if you would be so kind as to follow me, I believe that I can help you."

The acting manager of the Hyatt Regency Hotel beckoned the wary man to follow him around the desk and through the exit marked "Private." Ushering him down the hall of the executive wing, he unlocked the door to his boss's office and invited Maloney to sit.

"Bear with me a brief moment, sir," Azima implored. "There's a phone call I must make. I'll have my secretary bring you coffee."

Disarmed by Azima's sudden courtesy and his own feelings of importance, Eddy Maloney removed his twill cap and settled in to wait.

■

The ungodly hot, dry air clung to the city of Dubai like a woolen blanket. Kerry and Seamus could only mark time, waiting for the tortuous sun to wane and an important deal to be consummated. It would cost Kerry nearly all the money he'd brought with him, and their late-night venture would be a treacherous one, but he had to see Sydney before seeking sanctuary himself.

For the last few days since Sydney's capture, they had hidden with a family by the name of McCormack, refugees from Galway Bay on the shores of the Irish Atlantic. Kerry knew very little about the family, only that they had been most kind. Here in the settlement, a man was Irish, pure and simple. It made no difference whether he was Catholic or Protestant or whether he had a past. Everyone here had a past—something from which they were running. That's why they endured such deplorable conditions.

They were a community of lost souls—as strong as Kerry had ever seen—merely seeking to survive. Numbering more than two hundred, the families all worked together as one. They looked after each other, and heaven help the man who betrayed them.

That's why they risked their own lives to hide O'Daugherty and Donavan now. One of their own, Michal, was in grave danger, and they had sworn to help.

It was quiet in the Irish ghetto this afternoon. Most of the adults, including John and his wife, Molly, had gone to work, leaving their boy, Timothy, in charge. Tim was a fetching lad with carrot-colored hair, rosy cheeks, and a face that was more freckles than skin. He was a pleasant boy, but rather shy, who looked like he belonged in Ireland, roaming the sumptuous green fields in his wellies, not sweating in the squalor of a country that abhorred him.

The sound of an approaching car startled them. Here in the slums, hardly anyone had access to a car, relying instead on bicycles, feet and public transportation. Quickly the lad ran to the window to have a look.

"Big black Mercedes. Four men," he warned. "Better hide."

Leaping to their feet, the two men scrambled. Together with Tim, they moved the wooden table in the center of the room and threw back the tattered rug that covered the trapdoor to the cellar where the McCormacks hid their homemade brew, forbidden by Islamic law. Kerry eased himself down first, followed quickly by Seamus, leaving Tim to replace the rug and move back the table.

Crouched in the narrow, confined space of the cellar, Kerry and Seamus waited, leaving their fate in the hands of a boy. A heavy knock rattled the door of the three-room shack. Tim's voice was politely calm when he opened the door a few inches and queried, "Yes?"

A short man, seemingly of Irish descent, began. "Good day, lad. May we have a word with you?"

Warily opening the door a bit farther, the boy responded, "Aye."

The four men entered the clean but modest shack. While the Irishman focused upon the boy, the other three men had a brief look around. They were muscular men of Persian descent and they did not crack a smile. They seemed to be men with a mission.

"Your parents home?" the Irishman with the twill cap inquired.

"No, sir," Tim replied. "They're at work."

The stranger never took his eyes from the boy as he reached

in his pocket for a photograph. Throwing it under Tim's nose, he asked, "Have you seen this man?"

Young McCormack studied the yellowed photograph with the torn edges. It might be a dated picture, but the image of the man was clear.

"Who is he?" said the boy, all innocence.

"His name is Kerry Donavan. I asked you, boy, if you had seen him."

"'Fraid not."

Eddy Maloney studied the teenager carefully. The lad's eyes were curious, but his manner steady.

"Do you mind if we have a look around?" Maloney pressed.

"I'm not supposed to let strangers in, but if you promise to be quick . . ."

In the dark, narrow confines of the cellar, Kerry and Seamus held their breath. The footsteps were heavy above them. After a flutter of movement, there was a pause as the men gathered finally around the table.

"Mark me words, boy," said Maloney. "It would be foolish to hide this man. He's wanted for a serious crime. You tell the others, okay?"

Seamus O'Daugherty knew every Irishman within the city limits of Dubai. This man's voice was totally unfamiliar. Kerry Donavan knew no one in Dubai, but those he'd met in the ghetto. And yet the voice he heard upstairs was eerily familiar . . . like a ghost from his own tormented past.

Leaving the youngster with a final threat, Eddy Maloney gestured to the other men to follow. They had several more places to search. Stepping out into the bright afternoon sun, he squinted. It was hot here, so unbearably hot. What he would give for the cool, crisp air of Limerick and a chilled pint of Guinness.

Despite the lack of air and ale, life at the moment was not bad. He'd already met the powerful one by the name of Ali Hassan, the man who did business with the IRA Council of Four—the revered heroes Maloney had only dreamed of meeting. Here he was, a wretched boor from Limerick, befriended by the most renowned arms dealer in the Middle East. After only a few minutes, Eddy Maloney and Ali Hassan had discovered they shared something very important in common, and that was their desire to hunt down and kill Kerry Donavan.

■

It was just past midnight when the antiquated taxicab rolled to a stop at the main entrance of the prison. The ride from town had been dark and foreboding. As it happened, the horribly feared structure known as city prison wasn't in the city at all, but isolated on a barren strip of desert some twenty minutes away from the hubbub of Dubai.

Trapped in the back seat of the cab with no means of escape, Kerry waited anxiously as the first man approached the vehicle. Glancing through the windshield to the walkway and guard tower above them, Donavan counted seven men with their guns drawn and pointed. Thrusting his head through the window of the car, the guard fired questions at the driver in a language Kerry did not comprehend. The taxi driver merely smiled, glanced at his passenger in the rear seat, and made his reply. Grunting, the guard accepted a gift from the Pakistani driver, then grudgingly waved them through.

True to his word, Seamus had found the right man to get the job done . . . for a price. He was a Pakistani cab driver whom Seamus knew well, a man by the name of Ismael. His English was decent, his questions few, and his manner kind and gentle.

"We are here, my friend. Your instructions are simple. This is the main building. You are to enter and pause in the hallway. My brother will locate you there. You have been granted only a few minutes for your visit. To try anything foolish or to stay longer will put us all in dire jeopardy. I will wait here."

Climbing out, Kerry clasped the driver by the shoulder. "If anything happens to me, you have your orders. Locate Seamus and get him to safety at once. Understood?"

Ismael merely nodded.

It had been a fight, an agonizing fight, convincing Seamus O'Daugherty to stay behind, hidden and safe, but Kerry had no choice. One of them had to remain in touch with Joe Morrison at all times. Kerry had promised to see Michal himself and to deliver the cigarettes tucked safely in his pocket. Despite the fact that he had brought a great deal of money to arrange the visit, he couldn't be entirely sure he would not be betrayed. He was lucky that he was the one who had carried the money. Had it been Sydney, he would have had nothing with which to barter. He was unlucky in that he did not know the people . . . whom he could trust . . . and whom he could not.

Be that as it may, he had to see Sydney firsthand, before he could do anything to save himself. Time was running out, that he knew. The Irish ghetto was no longer safe.

With limping gait, he crunched along the gravel to the main building. He could feel the unseen eyes of men watching his every movement, their guns leveled. His heart pounded, but his mind was calm. He was prepared to die, if need be.

Kerry entered the building and waited, just as he had been told. A man appeared, seemingly out of nowhere. He was swarthy, a smaller version of Kerry's driver. And for some reason Donavan felt a bit safer.

"Good evening," the stranger replied. "I believe I am the one you seek. Have you brought the gift?"

"I have," Kerry replied. Not wanting to make a sudden movement, he asked quietly, "May I reach for it now?"

"Yes," the dark-skinned man replied.

Kerry produced the envelope filled with ten thousand dollars' worth of dirhams. Having never seen this much money at one time, the smaller man smiled.

"Your . . . gift . . . is most generous, sir, but then we must make a great many people happy. If you will follow me, please."

Kerry Donavan did as he was told. He knew from Ismael that his brother's name was Jamil. Yet he hesitated to call him by name for fear of causing the man alarm. He followed the shadow of the Pakistani down a narrow, dark corridor leading to a set of winding stairs. The steps had long ago decayed, and Kerry stumbled, barely managing to catch himself before tumbling to the concrete floor below.

It was unbearably hot in the catacomb of the prison, and Kerry broke out in a nauseating sweat. There was no light in the dungeon, and the stench was overpowering.

"Which one would you like to see first?" asked Jamil.

Donavan inhaled sharply. He knew what his answer should be, but he said what the truth had to be.

"Take me to the woman."

Kerry followed in silence as the jailer made his way down the treacherous, unlit corridor using a flashlight as his only guide, until he came to the back cells where only the most despised prisoners were kept. Rotted flesh, blood, excrement—these were the smells that filled the air.

Jamil halted. Thrusting his hand through the jagged metal bars, he shone the beam around the narrow enclosure. Blinded by the sudden light, the rats froze. There were no facilities in the ten-by-ten-foot cell, only a crude hole for bodily functions in one corner and a roach-infested straw mat in the other.

At first Sydney was nowhere to be found. Then the jailer's light located a mass curled in the corner of the cell, farthest away from the stinking sewer hole.

"Let me in," Kerry pleaded.

"Oh no, sir," Jamil protested. "That would never do."

Without thinking, Donavan grabbed the smaller man by the collar and jerked him hard.

"Let me in," he repeated. Jamil was frightened. Kerry realized this was a grave mistake. Frightened men do foolish things, such as yelling for other guards to help. Releasing the frailer man at once, he stammered, "I'm sorry. Please, I must see her."

Brushing himself off, Jamil's eyes were wary.

"You must understand that this is not my doing, sir."

"Please," Kerry implored, "let me in to see her."

Despite his better judgment, Sydney's jailer glanced furtively around in all directions.

"You must hurry, my friend. And I warn you, do nothing rash. You will never get out of here alive."

Fumbling with the ring of keys, Jamil unlocked the door to the cell.

"Five minutes," he declared. "No more."

Kerry hurried to the figure lying unmoving in the corner. Dropping to his knees, he gently turned her over. Her face was black and swollen. Her nose was shattered and there was blood caked in her hair. Her jaw hung limp, her mouth open and her eyes—glassy from too much pain—did not at first focus.

Fearing she was dead, Kerry shook her hard. "Sydney!"

Slowly her eyes sought the voice she thought she heard. It was nearly impossible for her to talk, but her lips tried to mouth the word "Kerry."

"Yes, darling, yes," he soothed, "it's me, Kerry. I had to see you."

Slowly Sydney's hand crept up, searching for the face she yearned to touch. She tried so hard to focus, but the cell was dark and her left eye was swollen shut. Her hand touched his lips, then his cheeks, which were wet from tears.

"Oh God, Sydney, why you? Why not me?"

She tried to speak. He couldn't hear. He leaned closer.

"Lydia?" she gasped.

"She's fine," he lied, for in truth he had no knowledge of the child who rested in the monster's hands.

"I had to try," she whispered.

"I know, Sydney. I know."

"I'm sorry . . ."

The jailer rapped hard on the bars of the cell.

"I beg you, only a minute more," Kerry pleaded.

Scooping Sydney up in his arms, he drew her close as he soothed her gently, "Listen, darling, we don't have much time. I've come to tell you the news. I've located Joe Morrison. He'll be here soon. He's taking care of everything. You'll be out of here in just a few days. Hang on, sweetheart. Just hang on!"

Sydney tried in vain to speak, but with every movement of her lips a searing pain ripped through her body.

"Don't talk!" Kerry cried. "Say nothing!"

But with every breath she took, she became that much more desperate to speak. Kerry leaned closer, straining to hear.

"You," she gasped. "Safe?"

Finally understanding, his words rushed forth, "Yes, Seamus

and I are both safe. We'll be seeking sanctuary at the American Embassy tonight. Joe's made all the arrangements. But I had to see you first."

Sydney, in her heart, smiled.

Cradling her in his arms, Kerry pulled Sydney as close as he dared. "Hang on, baby," he pleaded. "I need you."

Tears flowed down the cheeks of the man who had once built walls around his heart to keep himself from feeling. Piece by piece, though, during these past few weeks, a woman by the name of Sydney Lawrence had torn them down. Holding her in his arms, the final piece cracked.

"Oh, dear God, Sydney," he sobbed, "how I love you."

Dubai
Friday, May 8

Joe stepped out onto the front steps of the American Embassy, which was located halfway down the block known as Embassy Row. Nestled snugly among several other foreign embassies, Morrison wondered how these people took a piss in private, squeezed so tightly together. Joe lit a cigarette, then checked the time. It was precisely 2:00 p.m.

Sweltering in the 98° heat, Morrison glanced up the street. Nary a breeze was blowing, and it was still, deathly still. The American flag hung limply from its pole; the birds didn't chirp, not even the dust stirred. The sudden movement of a cat darting across the street startled Joe. Nervously his eyes shot up and down the block, where two jeeps filled with the sheik's honor guard had sealed off both entrances to Embassy Row. For the next few minutes, the street was closed. The only vehicles that would be allowed to pass through the roadblock would be Hassan's Mercedes and the van from city prison.

Per directive of the sheik, the honor guard was present to maintain order and to provide protection in case anything went wrong.

"Jesus Christ," Morrison muttered, "let's get the show on the road!" Thinking about his stay in Dubai, Morrison dredged up a few choice adjectives that applied. Hot . . . damned hot . . . fucking hot . . . unbearably hot!

Crushing out his first cigarette, Morrison immediately lit another. Slowly his eyes found their way across the street, where three of the elite guards waited, their guns at ease but their minds alert. Nodding to the commander of the guard, Joe pointed to his watch. Hassan's vehicle was running late.

Just as he predicted, Ali Hassan had agreed to the deal that would free his only brother, but he was sharp and every bit as cunning as Joe suspected. Ali Hassan would not be present to participate in the exchange of prisoners. He was sending a car with a driver and only one bodyguard to retrieve Rajid. He was still a wanted criminal in the United States. He wouldn't risk setting foot on soil belonging to the American Embassy for fear that Joe's jurisdiction would apply. Rightfully, he suspected that the FBI agent would use any ruse he could to get Hassan right where he wanted.

Pulling his lightweight Panama shirt from his sticky body, he glanced yet again up and down the street. People were watching from the doorways and from the windows. The soldiers could keep crowds from gathering outside, but there was nothing they could do about workers inside the other embassies.

Morrison had a funny feeling. It was a queasy, churning sensation, right in the middle of his gut. He had been bothered by queasiness all day, but particularly since he stepped outside. Morrison had learned early in his career to pay attention to his gut. His mind might deceive him, but his instincts never lied. Despite their careful planning, something didn't feel right. There were eyes somewhere watching—eyes that didn't belong.

The eyes that were watching—the eyes that Joe didn't see—belonged to Eddy Maloney.

During the past few days, everything had changed for the Irishman. Eddy Maloney had served a purpose for Hassan while they searched for Kerry Donavan. Now locating Kerry Donavan no longer mattered to Ali Hassan, only the safe return of his brother. Eddy was dismissed with instructions to do whatever he would with Kerry Donavan—even assassinate Sydney Lawrence if he could—but only after the exchange had taken place and Farhad Rajid was back with his brother.

The sound of an approaching vehicle caught Joe's notice. A shiny, black Mercedes came to a halt at the roadblock. Two men in dark suits were asked to exit the vehicle. They and the Mercedes were briefly searched. Finding no weapons, the commander confiscated their cellular phone and then let them pass. The Mercedes cruised slowly down the narrow street, then parked precisely where instructed—just left, to the north of the American Embassy so as not to obstruct Joe's view.

Then a dark blue, windowless van approached. The van was stopped and the driver searched as well. Joe tensed as the rear door of the van was opened. Satisfied that Michal and Sydney were present, the door was shut. The driver of the prison van parked exactly where he had been told—and that was to the right, south of the American Embassy, likewise not obstructing Joe's vision.

The sheik's honor guard trained their eyes on Morrison, waiting for his signal. But Joe remained fixed on the front steps of the American Embassy as the sun beat down upon him. Puffing his cigarette, he let one minute and then two tick by. Rubbing his free hand over his gut, he tried to calm his nerves. Something was wrong. He knew it.

"Come on, come on," an agitated voice inside the open door of the embassy beckoned, "let's get them out of there. It must be 120° in the van. What's taking so long, Joe?"

"Keep your shirt on, Donavan," Morrison mumbled.

One last time, Joe glanced up and down the block, trying to see in every corner, behind every shrub, and on top of every roof line. Then crushing out his cigarette, he gave the command. "Okay, it's going down."

Morrison retreated inside the American Embassy. Kerry Donavan handed Joe the 9mm Beretta, which Joe shoved just inside the top of his pants. Then Morrison cuffed himself to Farhad Rajid. "Time to go, asshole."

"I told you my brother would triumph," Rajid sneered, "and he has!"

Morrison jerked the bound man hard. "The sooner I get rid of you, the cleaner I'll feel."

Once again, Morrison stepped out into the bright light of the desert sun. Once again, his eyes darted up and down the street, scanning every direction. Yet again, he failed to see the man hidden in the shadows of the French Embassy less than thirty feet away.

Signaling the prison guards to open the rear of the van, Joe waited, not knowing what to expect. Michal O'Daugherty was assisted from the van first. His head was bandaged, his face swollen, and his legs a bit wobbly, but to Seamus O'Daugherty, peering from inside the front door, his brother looked damned good.

It took both the driver and Michal to offload Sydney. Seeing her terribly battered face—the face he found so lovely—Joe whispered under his breath, "Oh God, Sydney, what has Hassan done to you?"

With his prisoner cuffed to his left wrist and his right hand poised on the Beretta, Morrison proceeded slowly toward the Mercedes. It was then that Michal O'Daugherty and Sydney Lawrence were set free.

Putting his arm protectively around Sydney's waist, Michal started toward the American Embassy. But, dizzy from the sudden shock of the bright sunlight, Sydney stumbled and fell.

Bounding through the front door, Kerry Donavan ran for her, disobeying Joe Morrison's order to remain put.

Crying out her name, Kerry ran to help Sydney. He failed to notice Eddy Maloney. But Maloney saw him. And in that moment, all that mattered was revenge.

No, Kerry didn't see Maloney. Joe Morrison, with his attention riveted upon the Mercedes, didn't see him either. Only one man did.

"Watch out, Kerry!" Seamus O'Daugherty yelled, bounding out the door and down the steps of the embassy.

Kerry dove for the ground just as Maloney fired. Hearing the shot, Morrison drew his Beretta and wheeled around, flinging his cuffed prisoner to the ground. Instinctively, Maloney turned toward Joe and hastily fired. He missed, but Joe found his mark square in the chest of Eddy Maloney.

Grabbing a weapon concealed undetected underneath the front seat, Ali Hassan's bodyguard leapt from the Mercedes with his gun drawn, in a thoughtless attempt to protect Hassan's brother.

Sydney was safe and so was Michal. Seamus was uninjured, and Kerry Donavan's life had been spared. Only one man lay bleeding and moaning in pain. A man nobody recognized.

Morrison jerked Farhad Rajid to his feet. Then he turned and trained his gun on the bodyguard. The sheik's honor guard surrounded the man and disarmed him. Hassan's men had been instructed to come unarmed. Morrison unsnapped the cuffs that bound Rajid to his wrist, then quickly cuffed him to the car door. Short of dragging Rajid to his death, there was no way Hassan's driver could make an escape now.

Sydney was quickly carried inside the embassy. Kerry remained behind with Joe. A member of the guard retrieved Maloney's gun. Then Seamus O'Daugherty leaned over the bleeding man.

"Help me!" Eddy pleaded. "For the love of Mother Mary, help me!"

"He's Irish," Seamus said, "but I don't know him."

With sad eyes, Kerry met the glazed eyes of the man who had tried to kill him. "I do," he said.

There was blood oozing from a gaping hole in Maloney's shirt. Kerry knelt down beside his childhood chum, while Joe stood behind him. Both men knew that their moments with Maloney were few.

"Why did you do it, Eddy?" Kerry asked.

"You betrayed the boys," he answered. "You had to die." Then he shuddered. "Now I'm dying instead. God help me . . ." Eddy's words trailed to a whisper.

Kerry leaned in closer. "How did you find me here?"

"Hassan," he whispered, "Ali Hassan."

Suddenly Eddy reached out for Kerry's arm. His last words were, "Liam killed your sister." Then gasping for air, he expired.

Kerry slowly rose to his feet. His thoughts were scattered. He started for the embassy to see Sydney. Morrison stopped him.

"Did he say that Hassan was responsible for this?"

Kerry nodded.

"This changes everything."

At first Kerry didn't comprehend.

"The sheik gave me permission to arrest Hassan if he fucked up this exchange," Morrison explained. "That means we've got a shot at rescuing Lydia. But it's risky, Kerry. She could get hurt. What do you want me to do?"

Kerry thought for a moment then said, "I can't make that decision, Joe. It's up to Sydney."

■

Joe asked everyone but Kerry to leave the room where Sydney was resting on a couch.

When they were alone, he said, "Hi, lady. How you doing?"

Glancing first at Joe and then at Kerry, Sydney managed a smile. "A hell of a lot better now," she said.

Joe knelt down beside her. "I have to ask you something, Sydney. I'll do whatever you say. But you have to know the facts."

Sydney looked bewildered.

"I have a reason now to go after Hassan. That means we've got a chance of getting Lydia."

"Oh please, Joe!" Sydney implored.

"Listen to me, Sydney. It's dangerous. As far as I know, Hassan is still at the Hyatt Hotel. That's a lousy setup. If we had a big open space to take Hassan down, it would be no big deal. But we'll be entering his suite, and his bodyguards will be armed. Lydia could get hurt . . . or worse. It's up to you. Do you want me to go after Lydia, or not?"

Searching Joe's eyes and then Kerry's, Sydney struggled to answer. Images flooded her mind. Images of Lydia smiling . . . images of her beaten like a dog. She'd made a decision once that cost them dearly. Did she have the right to put Lydia in danger again? Perhaps it was better to let her go. At least she'd be alive. But then . . . what kind of a life would she have?

Tears glistened in her eyes as she started to answer. Then another image came to mind. It was Lydia clutching the mustard seed locket that Sydney had given her, saying, "I knew you would come."

Blinking back tears, she answered, "Bring my daughter home, Joe."

■

A few minutes later, Hassan's elegant Mercedes circled the drive of the Hyatt Regency Hotel. Kerry brought the car to a halt a few feet from the front door of the hotel. The sheik's honor guard followed. The commander exited the first of two jeeps and entered the hotel alone.

Back at the embassy, while Joe instructed Kerry on the use of a Beretta, the commander of the guard detained Hassan's men, then placed two phone calls. The first call was to his superior, getting permission to proceed. The second call, at Joe's request, was to Hassan, telling him that the prisoner exchange had been accomplished and that Rajid would be delivered soon. But there was paperwork that needed to be completed first.

Kerry glanced in his rearview mirror and locked eyes with those of Joe Morrison.

Brandishing his Beretta, Morrison leaned close to Hassan's brother and said, "You do anything out of line . . . a movement . . . a word . . . even a gesture . . . and I'll blow your head off. Understand?"

Focusing his attention then on Kerry, he said, "Keep your head down and your eyes averted, at least until we're inside the front door of the hotel. Then leave everything to me. Now, let's exit the car nice and easy. You first, Kerry."

Kerry slowly exited the front seat of the Mercedes. Morrison climbed out the rear door, then turned to assist Rajid. With his eyes averted, Kerry led the way with Rajid positioned directly behind him. The only thing separating Rajid from Joe was Morrison's Beretta. The rest of the honor guard followed.

The honor guard would not accompany them into Hassan's suite. Their function was to seal the hotel and protect other guests. They did not have the authority to assist Joe with the arrest. This was a matter strictly between the United States government and Hassan.

The commander met them at the elevator with the acting manager of the hotel.

"What is the meaning of this?" asked Faul Azima.

Kerry remained silent until everyone but the commander was situated in the elevator and the door closed. Then pushing the button to the penthouse floor, Donavan said, "Top of the day to you, Mr. Azima. How have you been keeping?"

Azima sagged. "What are you doing here?"

"Let me explain," said Morrison. "I'm an agent with the United States Federal Bureau of Investigation. In my breast pocket, I carry a warrant for the arrest of Ali Hassan and a signed extradition order by Sheik Mohammed al Maktoum. I presume you know the sheik?"

Azima's lower lip began to quiver.

"Now here's the plan. The hotel is being sealed. No one is getting in or out until we're finished. We're going to exit the elevator nice and slow. You're going to act as if everything is normal. Just do as you're told and you won't get hurt. Understand?"

Both Kerry and Joe readied their Berettas.

When the elevator door opened, Joe said, "Proceed down the hallway calmly. Knock on the door and announce Farhad Rajid's arrival. Then get the hell out of the way."

Trembling, Azima knocked on the door to the suite. "I have your brother, sir."

Hassan opened the door and, seeing only his brother at first, threw open his arms in greeting. "Brother!"

Shoving Rajid into the suite, Morrison quickly stepped inside and to the right, quickly surveying the room. There were three men in the room—Hassan and two bodyguards. Training his gun on Hassan, he roared, "Hands up! Don't move! I have a warrant for your arrest!"

Kerry quickly pinned Rajid's arm and placed his gun at the man's right temple. The bodyguard closest to Morrison—to the left of Hassan—drew his gun. Lydia, at the rear of the room and blocked from view by Hassan's second guard, screamed. Instinctively, Hassan's trusted bodyguard, Raoul, turned and threw Lydia to the floor. Joe aimed his Beretta and fired at the first bodyguard, but only after the man fired his round, striking Joe on the left side, just below his ribs. Clutching his side, Morrison fired across the room as Raoul turned back to fire, and killed the second bodyguard with a bullet to the heart.

Morrison tried gamely to hang onto consciousness, but his legs gave way, taking his senses with him. The exchange of gunfire happened so rapidly that Kerry Donavan had no time to react until the moment that Ali Hassan grabbed Lydia and lunged for Raoul's fallen gun. Kerry couldn't shoot Hassan for fear of hitting Lydia. So he pivoted slightly, using Rajid as a human shield as Ali Hassan fired . . . killing his own brother instantly.

Ali Hassan held Lydia tightly. "Drop the gun," he ordered Kerry.

"Let her go," Donavan pleaded.

Crouching behind his daughter, Hassan recklessly brandished his gun. "Move out of my way," he demanded.

Kerry held fast, but his gun hand began to quiver. To let Hassan pass ensured his freedom. The sheik's honor guard would not intercede. But Kerry could not guarantee his shot . . . not with Lydia in the way.

Hassan moved forward. Kerry's finger tightened on the trigger.

Lydia cast her eyes to her father. And for a moment, he looked at her. "Please, Daddy," she whispered.

Blinking hard, Ali Hassan pushed his daughter out of the way, then started to fire. But Kerry's aim was deadly.

It was a magnificent summer morning at the Donavan farm in Bluegrass Country. It was Sunday, June 28, shortly after eight o'clock. The sun was shining brilliantly, blanketing the Donavan farm in an array of golds and greens. The windows of the house were open and a gentle breeze wafted through the spacious kitchen. The horses could be heard whinnying in the pasture.

The chatter around the large, wooden table had been lively, but now a hush descended as four people finished their breakfast in contented silence.

"More eggs, anyone?" Sydney asked.

Joe Morrison groaned. "Good Lord in heaven, I couldn't eat another bite. I can't remember when I've eaten this much!"

"Well, at least let me pour you some coffee," Kerry insisted.

Passing his mug over to Kerry, Morrison said, "I don't know what I enjoyed more, the sausage and gravy, or the country ham and scrambled eggs. Sydney, when did you learn to cook?"

"I've learned a lot of things during the past few weeks." Throwing a knowing glance to Kerry, Sydney smiled. "I guess you could say I've changed."

"Well, the change from a camera lens to a frying pan has been a good one!"

Donavan glanced across the table and smiled at Sydney with pride. They planned to be married in the fall. In the meantime, Sydney was making his mansion a *home*.

"You outdid yourself, honey."

Stealing a moment when no one was watching, Joe studied Sydney carefully. No longer was she the celebrity journalist he had secretly admired for years. In her place was a far more compelling woman.

Her injuries at the hand of Hassan had been severe. Her ongoing recovery was slow and painful. The bones in her face were mending, but never would she be the same woman she had been before. Her face had taken on a depth of character only those who have suffered and survived recognize.

She wore her coppery hair shorter these days, tousled and carefree. Having been gently kissed by the sun, her freckled face required no makeup. Her cheeks had taken on a rosy glow. Absent were the designer clothes of the city girl. She wore only jeans and an oversized work shirt today. And to Joe, she had never seemed lovelier.

Growing rather solemn, Sydney's gaze roamed the table as she silently gave thanks for Kerry, her daughter, and Joe Morrison . . . the best friend she could ever have. She was delighted that Joe was spending a few days with them before returning to work at the bureau. His recovery had been more difficult than hers, because he had no one to nurture him as Kerry had nurtured her.

"If only Mack were here," she mused silently. She'd buried her father two weeks before. She missed her daddy dreadfully, but at least she'd been with him at the end.

Seeing her look of sadness, Kerry grew concerned. "Are you all right, sweetheart? Do you need to rest?"

Sydney met Kerry's eyes with a mist of tears, but a contented smile. "I'm fine, honey. It's just so good to have us all here."

The voice that had remained silent throughout most of the meal startled them now.

"Mother, we have to go!"

"Oh Lord," Sydney cried. "I nearly forgot."

Sydney rose from her chair. All eyes turned to face Lydia, as she said, "Mohammed is expecting us. I don't want to be late."

Sydney explained. "Lydia has a very special gift for the sheik. It's a surprise for his birthday. He's never forgiven Kerry for purchasing Dare to Dream at the Keeneland auction, and so we're making him a gift of her firstborn colt. It's the least we could do for giving us back our lives."

During the weeks that had passed since the nightmare in Dubai, Sheik Mohammed al Maktoum had taken his obligation to Lydia most seriously. With the death of Hassan and his brother, Farhad Rajid, custody of Lydia had passed to the sheik, thus fulfilling Islamic law, precisely as Joe had arranged. Mohammed had, of course, returned Lydia to Sydney's care, but that was by no means the end of his involvement. When he was in residence in Kentucky, he insisted that Lydia spend time with him at his estate. He was becoming a surrogate father, teaching her to make peace with both of her cultures—that which was hers by right, as well as that which was hers by birth. The two of them were growing close.

Sydney came around the table, throwing her arms around the passionate Irishman she had come to love. Sullie's words still echoed in her head as she remembered their talk in Ireland.

"Like it or not, Kerry Donavan makes you . . . feel . . . things, way down deep inside. If you allowed yourself to be swept away . . . just where would his love take you?"

With her arms fastened tightly about his neck, Sydney kissed Kerry's cheek lustily. Just as Mary Margaret had predicted, Sydney had finally succumbed to real love. At times, their life together seemed like a raft racing through uncharted waters, but the depth of their love was worth every bump along the ride.

"I'll be back in about an hour, Kerry. Why don't you take Joe to see the horses?"

Morrison was slow to rise from the table. Instinctively, his hand braced his side. Kerry waited for him at the door. A man who thought he was invincible had been struck down. And he wasn't bouncing back as quickly as he'd hoped.

"So, what do the doctors say?"

Joe tried to shrug it off. "Oh, you know the routine, Kerry. It'll just take time. I'm going back to work next week, but I'll have to settle for a desk job, at least for the next few months."

Kerry glanced at his friend as they slowly made their way from the house to the stable.

"There's more, isn't there?"

"This . . . thing . . . has changed me, Kerry. Coming so close to death like we did makes me realize I'm letting life pass me by. I've given everything I have to the bureau, but it's not enough. Frankly, I need to find a good woman and settle down."

Seeing the pain in his friend's eyes caused Kerry to get in touch with his own.

A commotion across the path caught their notice as Billy Ray and the O'Daugherty brothers struggled with the tethered colt, urging it toward the trailer. It was a comical scene. Both Seamus and Michal were adapting well to country life. They'd found a happy, permanent home here at Donavan's Place, but their skill with horses was still developing. And while Kerry seemed to be engrossed in the scene, the sadness in his eyes did not escape Joe's notice.

"What in the hell could be wrong?" he wondered silently. Here was a man who had everything. A beautiful woman and her lovely daughter. A magnificent horse farm. More money than he could possibly need. What else in life could a man want?

"What is it?" Morrison demanded. "What's eating you, Kerry?"

"I was thinking about my sister and the son of a bitch who killed her." Donavan's eyes hardened. "It doesn't matter how good life seems, Joe. I'll never rest until I see justice done."

■

As the Irish would say, "'Twas a lovely day in the land of the green." As one day was beginning in Kentucky, it was already late afternoon across the sea. Summer was pleasant in Ireland this year. Warm days but cool nights, causing the fires in the hearths to remain lit. It was the kind of day that made one feel vital and alive, the kind of day to do things one had put off for much too long. It was time to reflect upon life and death, upon friends past and present. So it was for Mary Margaret O'Sullivan as she slowly made her way toward Lisnagry and the former home of Kerry Donavan.

Heaving a deep sigh, Mary Margaret turned onto the Dublin

Highway leading to the estate. Glancing in the mirror, she brushed a stray lock of silver-streaked, black hair from her forehead. Mary Margaret was certainly not a vain woman, but to present herself this afternoon, everything had to be in order, from the new navy dress she wore to her matching silk stockings. Even her white gloves were starched and pressed. Indeed, Miss Mary Margaret O'Sullivan was at her finest today.

She had it on good authority that she would find Liam Thompson at home. The investigation into Barbara's death was over, the cause of death officially ruled a suicide. The door was now open for Liam to proceed and claim what was now his. It was only a matter of time until Liam possessed all that he desired.

Kerry was devastated. But safely back on American soil, Kerry had no choice but to remain where he was. To return to Ireland was unthinkable.

Sullie had spoken with Kerry a number of times during recent weeks, and he had never seemed happier. It seemed that he had finally overcome his past and put the haunting shadows behind him. Except for one thing . . . one thing that weighed heavily on his mind. Barbara's death remained unavenged, her murderer still free.

Their phone discussions in recent weeks had been heated.

"No, Kerry, hush! To take matters into your own hands would be disastrous! You have Sydney and Lydia to consider. Yes, dear, I know, there is no punishment horrible enough for Liam. Thinking about what he did to Barbara keeps me awake at night." Then, with a bit of a queer tinge to her voice, Sullie reminded him, "The law may be the law, but the Irish have their ways."

Driving the last bit of road between the highway and his home, Mary Margaret kept reminding herself of her reasons for making the journey. Deliberately she forced the image of Kerry's smiling face to remain embedded in the forefront of her brain and within her heart. Without that picture she couldn't do what she'd come to do. Signaling a turn into the drive, she spotted Liam right away. There he was, sitting on the front porch as if he owned the manor. And what rankled Mary Margaret O'Sullivan was that, in fact, he now did.

Coming to a stop, Mary Margaret eased her ample body out

of the van. Hesitating, she tentatively waved, then pretended a
hearty greeting. "Top of the day to you, Liam. I've come to call,
if you don't mind."

Rising to his feet, befitting his British upbringing, Liam
Thompson responded in kind. "It's always good to see you, Sullie,
though I must say this is a bit of a surprise."

Hesitating momentarily, Mary Margaret retrieved the plate of
cookies resting on the seat beside her. Then she proceeded
toward the porch.

"'Tis a lovely day, Liam. I thought you might like a bit of company. I made your favorite cookies, and if I must say . . . they're
me finest batch ever!"

Pausing at the steps to the porch, she ventured to query,
"Would you mind if I sit with you awhile?"

"Not at all, Sullie, not at all."

A bit winded, Mary Margaret took a seat on the wicker rock-
ing chair next to Liam. There she sat, with the plate of cookies
resting comfortably on her lap as she closed her eyes, seeking the
comforting warmth of the afternoon sun.

"I haven't seen you since Barbara's funeral, Liam. How in the
world have you been keeping?"

Mary Margaret O'Sullivan eyed Liam Thompson boldly as she
waited for his reply. He had not changed much since their last
encounter. He still had the same manicured hands, finger-waved
platinum hair, and delicate, almost pretty features.

"I miss her, Sullie. I miss her dreadfully. But somehow one
must muster the courage to go on."

Mary Margaret nodded sympathetically, but all the while her
insides were churning. God, how she yearned for a Rothman, but
Liam detested cigarette smoke, and today of all days she had no
desire to offend him. Besides, she wouldn't think of littering the
grounds of his estate with one of her telltale butts. No indeed . . .
on this particular day . . . that would never do. So instead she
smiled her most engaging grin as she offered him her plate of
goodies.

"Do have a cookie, dear. I baked them especially for you.
They're oatmeal and raisin, your favorite."

Liam eyed the cookies briefly but, hesitating, lifted his gaze to Mary Margaret instead. His eyes were cold and wary when he asked, "Why all the fuss, Sullie? You haven't spoken to me in weeks. It was no secret you blamed me for Barbara's death. Now today you show up on my doorstep with cookies? Why, Sullie?"

Mary Margaret lowered her gaze. Still plagued by the rebellious strands of hair clinging to her forehead, she shook her head and glanced away as a chilly wind stirred. With every fiber of her being quaking, Sullie struggled to find her voice in order to reply.

"I've given this a great deal of thought, Liam. I've behaved dreadfully. You and I have our differences, that's no secret. But right or wrong, Barbara loved you. She would never forgive me for treating you so shamefully."

Mary Margaret looked Liam in the eyes. "For Barbara's sake, let's put the past behind us. Accept my humble peace offering and let's go on."

Hearing the urgency in O'Sullivan's voice, Liam smiled. He loved watching people squirm, particularly self-righteous saints like this one.

"You are a mystery, Mary Margaret O'Sullivan, and I'll be damned if I can figure you out. But I accept your apology. I admit that I felt betrayed by your rejection, but I believe you were unduly influenced by Barbara's despicable brother. In any event, we shall indeed put the past behind us and get on with things."

Thompson inhaled the first of several cookies he'd taken. He permitted himself little overindulgence in matters of food and drink, but he harbored a secret passion for oatmeal and raisin cookies, as Mary Margaret well knew. She had delivered the one peace offering she knew Liam Thompson would accept.

"God almighty, these are good, Sullie! Much better than Barbara ever made. They're not nearly as sweet. How ever did you get them so chewy?"

"It's Mum's secret recipe, pet. Been in the family for generations. Don't be bashful, dear. Have another."

Sullie went on, "What are your plans, Liam, now that Barbara's case has been closed? Will you remain in Ireland?"

"You know how I loathe Irish winters, Sullie. And life on the continent is certainly more desirable. I'll probably spend most of my time abroad. Pass the cookies, Mary Margaret. They're absolutely delicious. I'm going to allow myself just one more."

It was after biting into the fourth cookie that Liam Thompson experienced the first twinge of pain. Thinking he had just overindulged, he started chewing the last remaining bites a bit slower. Seeing the strange look on his face, Mary Margaret looked concerned. She started to inquire, but just as quickly she glanced away. She realized there was no turning back. There was now nothing she could do for Liam Thompson, or for her own damned soul. An almost vengeful glee clouded her eyes. Gazing over the magnificent grounds that had once been the pride of the Donavan family, Mary Margaret claimed her final revenge.

"Life has a funny way of turning out. Don't you think so, Liam?"

But Liam Thompson couldn't answer as a searing pain ripped through his guts. Falling to the ground, he lay moaning, his eyes filled with terror. "Help me, Sullie! For the love of God, help me!"

"Did Barbara beg for mercy, Liam? Did she plead to God for help?"

As if a powerful machine were shredding his insides, Liam Thompson screamed from the sheer torture of the pain. It was then he began convulsing.

"Arsenic, lots of arsenic, that's the secret ingredient that made the cookies so different. A fitting ending, don't you think?"

Mary Margaret stood. Gazing down at the twisting, sobbing dandy, she wished she were the type of savage human being who could torture him further, just as he had his wife the night he killed her. But Mary Margaret O'Sullivan was not that kind of woman. Neither was she the saint everyone crowned her. She was a human being filled with rage, and consumed by a need to protect the one she loved most dearly.

It was simple really, black and white, clear as glass. Kerry Donavan was the son Mary Margaret had been denied, and she would do anything to save him. She knew Kerry well, perhaps better than anyone else. He was a man's man, and sooner or later guilt and grief would consume him to the point that he would risk everything to avenge his sister's death. He had escaped Ireland twice already, but his luck was unlikely to hold out a third time. The bounty on his head was much too high, and the hand of the IRA too far-reaching. Mary Margaret O'Sullivan felt she had no choice but to take matters into her own hands.

Blood slowly started seeping from his mouth, and Mary Margaret realized that Liam's stomach was hemorrhaging. Knowing that his life was ending, Sullie confronted the dying man with pity, perhaps even a measure of regret.

"Barbara was my best friend and you killed her. Horribly. Brutally. But I was more merciful, Liam. Your suffering will end shortly. May God forgive us both."

One last time, Mary Margaret pushed the stray lock of hair from her dampened forehead as she gathered up all traces of the remaining cookies. No telling how long it would take for someone to discover the body. Liam had fired the aging servants. Even after discovering the body, the Irish would be lazy with their investigation, particularly since they loathed Liam Thompson. Besides, no one in his right mind would suspect the pillar of Limerick society, Miss Mary Margaret O'Sullivan.

Bowing her head, she crossed herself and offered up a meager prayer for the dead. Then slowly, deliberately, she returned to her van and started the engine. Removing the primly starched, white gloves that left no prints, she searched her purse for a much needed Rothman. Lighting her cigarette, she turned the van around and headed out the drive toward Limerick.

She wondered what time it was in Kentucky. She had a most important phone call to make, and news to deliver . . . important news that just couldn't wait.

Susan M. Hoskins

To order copies of

Twisted Secrets
Twisted Lights

or

Dancing with Angels

And to arrange speaking engagements with Susan M. Hoskins

contact:

Integrity Press, Ltd.
P.O. Box 8277
Prairie Village, KS 66208
Phone: (913) 642-4100
Toll Free: (888) 860-2535

e-mail: integritypress@sprintmail.com

Susan M. Hoskins